TANGLED SERIES

SOPHIE ANDREWS

Digital ISBN 978-1-957580-17-3

Paperback ISBN 978-1-957580-24-1

*Previously published as Hating Mr. Perfect by Suzanne Baltsar

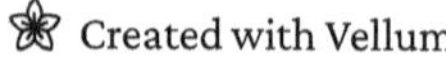 Created with Vellum

Content Note

Tangled Up is an open door romance between a perfectionist engineer and a foul-mouthed vegan yogi with lots of laughs and plenty of spice. There are also discussions about death/grief over loss of parents and abortion.

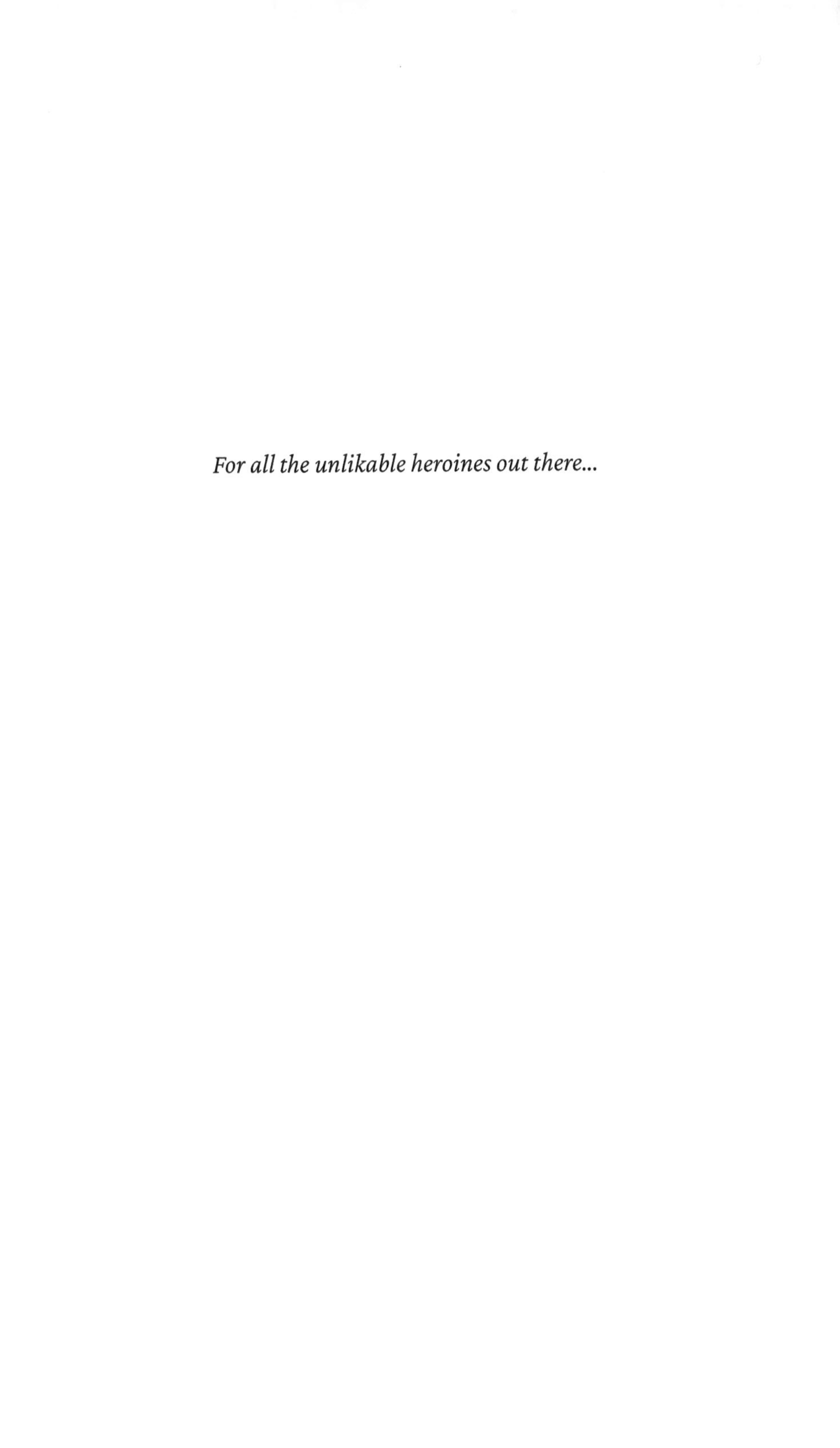

For all the unlikable heroines out there...

CHAPTER ONE

The lighting was terrible, the floor sticky, and the whole place smelled of stale beer and fried food, but we wouldn't have it any other way. All jammed together in an L-shaped corner booth. Between Laney's insistence on being able to walk through "the cutest little town" she'd ever seen, and Bronte's demand for wherever they went to have food, I was celebrating my birthday at the dive bar down the street from my apartment in my hometown of Galena, Illinois. We were all together. That was what mattered.

"So, how does it feel to be twenty-five?" Sam asked, tossing her long lavender-hued hair to the side.

I was the first one out of our little foursome to turn twenty-five, and we'd made a pact long ago to be together as often as possible. Birthdays, special occasions, the good, and the bad, we would be there for one another, always.

"I can rent a car now," I said, lifting my glass to the other girls. "But I don't feel any older or wiser after turning a quarter of a century."

Bronte scrunched up her button nose. "Maybe tomorrow."

Laney arched one perfectly sculpted eyebrow. "Or maybe next year."

I tossed her the bird.

As with any group of friends, we each had a role to play. Laney was the de facto leader, the most outgoing of us all. Bronte was the sweet one, everyone's conscience. Sam was the brainy one, the problem-solver. And me? I was the wild one.

I never backed down from a challenge and loved a good dare. I practiced yoga yet had never learned to hold my tongue. I changed my major three times and still wasn't sure what I wanted to be when I grew up.

"I, um…" I cleared my throat. "I opened up a savings account."

"No shit!" Laney crowed. "You actually read that article I sent you?"

Sam shifted in her seat to see past Bronte to Laney. "What article?"

"It was about money management and retirement. My dad sent it to me…you know him." Laney rolled her eyes. "But I thought it was helpful, so I sent it to this one," she said, tipping her chin in my direction.

"What did it say?" Bronte asked.

"It explained how much you should be saving every month." I skipped over the fact that even though I'd opened the account, it didn't actually mean I had any money to save. And I still didn't quite have a hold on the whole compound interest thing yet.

Sam poked my shoulder with her index finger. "Look at you, being all adult-like. Turning over a new leaf, huh?"

"Yeah," Laney added. "I'm glad you don't have your money buried in a jar in your backyard."

I gave in to a laugh. She wasn't far from the truth.

"Tell me—" Bronte started, propping her elbows up on the table, but the uneven legs wobbled, and her still-full gin and tonic spilled over. Sam grabbed a couple napkins to soak it up, while Laney bit her bottom lip, probably trying to rein in her booming laugh before it started.

I snickered. "You were saying?"

Bronte's clumsiness borderlined on a sitcom gag, but after all these years, we were used to it. "I was saying, what's your goal for this year?"

"My goal?" I gathered my long hair over my shoulder and started to braid it. "You're funny."

Sam sat back against the booth. "It doesn't have to be a goal. Maybe a wish?"

Bronte shook her head. "A goal," she repeated, digging through her purse. "Let me just get..."

"Please don't." Laney reached her arm over to stop Bronte from pulling out what would assuredly be a pen and paper from her purse to make some kind of list or plan or contract. Bronte was the only one to ever actually stick to New Year's resolutions. "We're celebrating. And I only have twenty-four hours before I need to be back in California, so I'm not wasting them on whatever test you're about to give us."

Bronte tucked a chunk of dark hair behind her ear. "Not a test. I thought we could all come up with something to focus on for this coming year, you know, like a—"

"This is not *Sisterhood of the Traveling Pants.*" Laney sliced her hand through the air. "This is a Friday night with cheap drinks and three of the people I love most in the world." She lifted her vodka and soda. "So, drink up."

I raised my glass. "Agreed."

"Here's to one more year older," Sam said.

"And one more year together," Bronte added.

"And life, liberty, and the pursuit of happiness." Laney threw back her drink and then waited, watching as the rest of us finished ours.

Sam sputtered a cough as Bronte smacked her lips. I

swiped my hand over my mouth, shimmying as the liquor settled in my belly. "Round two?"

"Yeah, but first, for posterity..." Laney stood up and leaned over to the booth next to us where a group of guys sat. They all gazed at her with cartoon heart eyes, nodding at whatever she said, and raised their hands to her, fighting over who would take her cell phone.

Laney handed it off to the one on the end, and he stood, grinning as if she'd knighted him, then waved to us. "Come on. Picture."

We scooched out of the booth and rounded to the front of the table.

"Looking good, ladies," the guy said, turning the phone sideways as the four of us linked arms.

"Happy birthday on three," Sam chirped, from her position at the end. "One."

Bronte kissed my cheek. "It's going to be a good year for you, I know it."

"Two."

"It's going to be a good night!" Laney said with a big laugh, dipping her head down to reduce the height difference between us.

"Three! Happy birthday, Gemma!"

After a lot of drinks courtesy of the guy Laney had wrapped around her finger, we staggered, giggled, and danced our way back to my apartment, arm in arm, where we fell asleep huddled together on the floor in a heap of blankets and pillows.

The next day, Bronte forced everyone up. She and Sam were both nerds who liked visiting museums, so they had an "education-forward" week-long road trip planned for their summer vacation, and Laney had a flight to catch.

Once everyone was gone, and I was left alone, my phone

buzzed with a text. I barked out a laugh at the picture Laney sent from last night—all of us in various drunk poses—with the caption **THE FOUR HORSEWOMEN OF THE APOCALYPSE.**

Bronte and Sam responded with various emojis while I sent back on line.

Miss you clowns already

I wasn't so much hungover as lonely without my girls. Needing some water, I trudged to the kitchen to fill up a glass then checked in on the boys. My pet turtle, Leonardo, crunched on some lettuce. Spot, the goldfish, completed yet another circle in its bowl. George sunbathed in the slanted light from the window, and I bent to pet him as Bronte's words repeated in my ears.

It's going to be a good year for you, I know it.

I huffed and stood back up, the browning leaves of my plants silently heckling me.

It's going to be a good year for you.

It wasn't as if last year had been so bad; it just hadn't been great. Here I was at twenty-five, trailing after my best friends, who all seemed to be so far ahead of me in life. I had nothing but a few dollars in savings and a permanent fear of commitment, while they had boyfriends and jobs with benefits and *plans*.

Staring down the barrel of a quarter-life crisis, what was a girl to do?

CHAPTER TWO

The sun set into an orange and purple haze, but the August heat still simmered in the air. I rolled my bicycle into a driveway at the end of a large suburban development and rested it on the kickstand before removing my helmet to study the home in front of me. It dwarfed the rest of the houses in the cul-de-sac. Between the tall pillars casting long, dark shadows on the lawn, the carefully carved wood porch, pristine white paint, and high windows surrounded by dark-green shutters, the house looked like something out of a television show where house hunters who walked dogs for a living bought.

But I actually had walked dogs for a while, and I could never in a million years afford this place.

A light turned on in a second-story window, shaking me out of the reverie, and I combed my fingers through my hair, trying unsuccessfully to tame what the humidity did to it. After digging into my large knit bag to pull out a skirt, I glanced around to make sure the coast was clear then stripped off my shorts for a costume change. By the time I hoofed it up the long driveway, sweat dotted my upper lip in the few seconds it took to reach the door, and it flung open before I had a chance to knock.

"Gemma Rose Turney, where have you been?" My mother stood with her hands on the waist of her yellow cocktail dress, a diamond solitaire necklace winking at me. With her glossy chestnut hair and wrinkle-free face, no one—sometimes not even me—believed she was forty-five years old.

I wiped my brow. "Nice to see you too, Mom."

"We've been waiting for you. What were you doing?"

"I was—"

"Nevermind." She dragged me inside by the wrist and inspected me, picking at the neon-green tank top with a big peace sign in the middle. "What are you wearing? You could have at least worn a bra."

"No one's in for a nip slip, if that's what you're worried about."

She scoffed but gentled her tone as she pressed her hands to my cheeks, kissing my forehead. "And put your hair up. Your bangs are always covering your beautiful face."

I followed her orders, tying my long hair up in a messy bun, but just when I thought she'd let me off the hook, my mom wrinkled her nose. "What's that smell?"

I sniffed myself. "What smell?"

"You smell...like outside."

"Outside? How does someone smell of outside?"

She batted at the air. "It smells like dry air or something."

"That's the smell of nature, Mom."

"Well, I don't like it."

Mumbling a weak protest, I begrudingly found tinted lip balm and my cruelty-free vanilla body spray in my bag. I hastily swiped on both and spun around to face my reflection in the mirror, next to my mother. "There. Satisfied?"

With the same brown eyes, cheekbones, and nose, we were practically twins. We were even the same height, barely scraping 5'3", but she always wore heels to make up the difference.

"I love you, honey," she said, smiling. Her shoulders rose and fell with a contented breath. "I'm so happy you're here."

I couldn't help how my eyebrow ticked up suspiciously at the emotion in her voice, but before I could ask about it, she tucked my hand in hers to wind through the house. We stopped at a sitting room with uncomfortable-looking wing-back chairs and a grand piano. A dozen people filled the space, laughing and drinking.

"I didn't know this was a party." A tiny whine escaped the back of my throat as I recognized how underdressed I was now.

"I thought I told you," my mom said absently, while waving to Frank, who was making drinks at a small bar in the corner.

I shook my head. She hadn't told me. I wasn't the only flighty one in our family of two.

Frank made his way over to us and slung his arm around my shoulders, offering me a light-colored drink. "Gemma, how are you?"

"Good." I accepted the glass tumbler before circling my finger in the air. "Nice digs you got here."

He kissed my cheeks and ruffled my hair. "Took you long enough to come visit."

Frank, with salt-and-pepper hair and a thick middle, wore his age, unlike my mother's usual choice in men. I'd taken an immediate liking to him when we met this past New Year's Day. We had been at a little Thai place and when my mom couldn't decide what she wanted, he ordered one of almost everything and made sure it wasn't spicy. "Your mother can't handle spice," Frank had told me as if I didn't know, and then added with a grin, "Except for me." I'd gotten a good laugh and understood why my mom had fallen for him. With his kind brown eyes and semi-permanent jovial smile, there wasn't much to dislike.

I took a swig of the drink, sucking in a quick breath through my teeth. It was fruity but really strong. "What is this?"

"Pitorro, it's like our version of moonshine. I learned to make it from my *abuelo.*"

I ventured another sip.

"It'll put hair on your chest," he said proudly.

"Great. Exactly what I need."

When my mom gazed up at Frank with one arm around his waist, he kissed her nose. "Want some, *mi vida*?"

"No, thank you. I learned my lesson the first time."

I pointed around the room. "What's this all about, anyway?"

Mom and Frank smiled at each other, sharing a secret with their eyes, and I gasped. "Are you pregnant?"

He guffawed as my mother frowned. "Don't be ridiculous."

"Then what is it?"

Frank winked at me then tugged on my mom's hand, backing up three steps to the landing. "Excuse me, everybody. Excuse me." The crowd all turned their attention to the pair. "We want to thank everyone for coming tonight. You're all our closest family and friends, and we want you to be the first to know—"

"We're getting married!" my mom shrieked, showing off her left hand. A sparkling cupcake of a diamond sat on her ring finger, and the party erupted into congratulatory shouts. Everyone rushed forward, hugging and kissing the newly engaged couple.

I, on the other hand, soaked up the mild burn of alcohol at the back of my tongue after another sip of pitorro. My mother was a hopeless romantic, and a wedding was nothing new but no less aggravating.

I loved Frank, which was exactly why I wasn't happy about them getting married.

When the crowd finally dispersed, my mother motioned me over. I tossed back the rest of the pitorro in one gulp and choked as it slid down my throat. I wiped my mouth. "Married? Whatever happened to living in sin?"

She ignored the comment and tucked me under her arm, directing me a few feet to a man by the piano. Given that his back was to us, I could only make out his height and shaggy hair.

"Gemmie, since you'll be my maid of honor, I want you to meet Jason Mitchell. He'll be the best man." At the mention of his name, he turned around, and Mom thrust me forward like a prized pig. "Jason, this is my daughter, Gemma." She smoothed down some flyaways from my bun. "She's beautiful, isn't she?"

I looked up, up, up to the man in front of me to find cool blue eyes assessing me from the top of my head to feet and back again. The corner of his mouth quirked in a tediously self-assured way as he stuck out his hand. "Nice to meet you."

He was much younger than Frank, probably around my age, and I briefly wondered why he would be the best man. But it didn't matter. I didn't really care. He had that preppy East Coast collegiate look about him, the type of guy I purposefully avoided. Tall and tanned with a jaw that could cut glass.

Gross.

His thick ashy-blond hair, long enough to tickle his earlobes and curl at the ends, was the only thing unkempt about him.

Ugh.

He probably played lacrosse or owned a boat, maybe both, and my skin prickled with bad memories.

Mom nudged me back into reality, and I shook his hand, trying to keep the reflexive disdain from my voice. "Yeah, you too."

Jason's gaze dropped to our clasped hands, his face morphing from arrogance to surprise, but I wasn't at all interested in any more conversation and released our handshake.

Mom clapped in delight. "We're going to have so much fun together. Come on, you two, grab your seats for dinner. I put you next to each other at the table."

She all but skipped away as I stood in place, frozen between annoyance and disbelief. She was getting married *again*, and I'd apparently have to spend time with a guy who carried the calling card for everything I hated most. "I need another drink."

"I can get it for you," he offered, reaching for my glass, but I snatched it away.

"Nope."

He cocked his head, his brow furrowing in a question I didn't care to answer.

"I'm good." I whirled away from him, ignoring the stare I felt on my back as I uncorked the tall jar of pitorro and took a whiff of the coconut-and-almond scent before pouring two fingers worth of the alcohol into my glass.

After a sip, I pivoted around, catching Jason's attention zip back to the two men in front of him, and I inhaled a breath meant to calm me. It didn't.

To get to the dining room, I had to pass the trio currently blocking it, and the closer I got to them, the more details I overheard of their conversation.

"What do you say, Jay?" the man with thinning carrot-colored hair asked.

He shrugged. "Yeah, whatever. I don't care."

"Great, I'll call for the stripper." The bald-headed man slapped Jason's back.

I rolled my eyes. "Excuse me."

The bald guy smiled down at me next to him. "Well, hello there."

Jason, at least, had the decency to appear a little embarrassed. "We were talking about the bachelor party."

I shrugged and motioned to the dining room, silently telling the big brute in front of me to move.

Carrot top checked me out, his eyes lighting ever so slightly. "Who might you be?"

"The tooth fairy."

Carrot top winked, mistaking my sarcasm for flirtation. "Well, you certainly fit the bill, huh? I'm Howie."

The bald one tipped his chin to me. "Derek."

"Great. I need to get through."

Derek glanced over his shoulder and shifted as if just now realizing he took up so much room I couldn't get by. I huffed. It was the story of mankind.

Finally seated at the long mahogany table, I grabbed my cell phone to text the girls about my mom. I sipped the pitorro with one hand and thumbed out the message with the other.

Moments later, the chair next to me squeaked as Jason leaned down. "You better slow down."

I angled away from him, the temper I kept under wraps quickly unraveling. "What?"

He pointedly shot his gaze to the glass in my hand. "That'll knock you on your ass if you aren't careful."

His unwanted advice grated on the last of my nerves, and I

plopped my phone back into my bag with a forceful flick of my wrist. "I'll be fine."

"You probably think—"

I whipped my head toward him so fast, the bun on the top of my head fell lopsided. "You're going to tell me what I think?"

Men and their suggestions. I fucking hated it.

He jerked back, and I felt some satisfaction in the flash of remorse that crossed his features. "What? No." He ran a big hand over his jaw then shook his head. "Why are you so…"

"So what?" I raised my eyebrows, waiting for him to fill in the blank, ready to fire back, but Frank stood up, calling everyone's attention to him as flutes of champagne were passed around the table.

"Once again, we want to thank you all for coming here tonight, and we hope you enjoy the feast. But first, I want to thank you, Caroline." He faced my mother. "I didn't think I could love again until you showed up at Angelo's in that red dress, remember?"

My mom chided him before covering her smile with delicate, manicured fingers.

"I thought I had died," he said, painting a picture with his hands as he spoke. "There was an angel standing in front of me. And now, I am going to marry her. I'm the luckiest bastard in the world. To my future wife, Caroline."

Glasses clinked around the table, and Jason held his water up to mine. Without saying a word, I tapped my pitorro against it then drained my glass to spite him. He watched me with unblinking eyes, and I slanted my chair, needing to escape his icy blue stare and the column of his throat as he swallowed.

Perfection like that was nauseating.

As everyone helped themselves to the prepared catered food, I spied my mother at the head of the table, nibbling on dainty bites of the chicken and mushrooms. She motioned for me to eat, but instead of picking up a fork, I picked up my flute of champagne.

Jason cleared his throat next to me, and I cut my eyes to him over the delicate glass.

"Going in tonight, huh?"

I ignored him.

"Might want to hydrate." He pointed to my water with his knife.

"Bold move, telling a complete stranger what to do." By nature, I tended to be contrarian, and I wasn't holding back with Jason. Everything about him irritated me, from his tone of voice to the way his knee bumped against mine. Guys like him always took up so much fucking space. I hated it.

He twisted in his seat, fixing a congenial smile on his face that didn't quite fit. "You better eat. You're going to get sick."

I clucked my tongue. "I don't eat things with a mother."

"Don't tell me you're a vegetarian." He pursed his lips like he might laugh, and I hated him even more for making me notice his mouth.

I set down the empty champagne flute with a thunk. "I'm vegan."

"Really?"

"Yes, really."

He shoved a piece of bread into his mouth, saying something under his breath that I didn't catch, but I knew it wasn't complimentary. His jaw worked as he chewed, and I forced my attention away from the shadow of stubble on his chin.

One of Caroline's friends leaned forward across the table. "Gemma, your mother told me you'll be the maid of honor."

"Yeah." I nodded, plucking up a stalk of asparagus with my fingers to bite it.

"Aren't you excited? Weddings are so fun, and with your

mother as the bride, I'm sure everything will be beyond elegant."

"I'm sure."

The woman's smile melted at my deadpan response, and she went back to her food.

"You don't sound too excited." Jason elbowed me like we were buddies. We absolutely were not.

I offered him a wry smile. "Fourth time's the charm, right?"

When he studied my face, I refused to shrink under the weight of his eyes. "Did anyone ever tell you you've got a bad attitude?"

"I'm sorry, I think I misheard you?" I tilted my head, aiming my asparagus at him. "It sounded like you said I have a bad attitude."

"You're being a little rude." He narrowed his gaze at me like I was a misbehaving child, and a flash of heat scorched my spine. All I could see was red. But this asshole continued cutting up his food as if nothing had happened.

"*I* am being rude?" I shot back in a whisper-shout. "Don't you think calling me rude is a little rude?"

He considered me with one squinted eye before motioned to his plate with his fork. "You should try this. It's so good."

I clenched my jaw, annoyed with myself for not being able to squash my confrontational impulses and tired of him for continuing to play this stupid game. And for looking so goddamn good while he did it.

With each forkful up to his mouth, the muscles in his arm tightened and released. The veins in his forearm and hand stuck out, strong and masculine. A damn shame.

"I wonder if this chicken had any little eggs in her nest. Or maybe a rooster at home," he mused.

I grabbed a roll, fantasizing about stuffing it down his throat. "Don't antagonize me."

"Is that what you *think* I'm doing?" He flashed me a crooked grin, calling back my unfinished words from a few minutes ago, but this time, I didn't take the bait.

Instead I settled for silence.

Because I could be an adult about this.

CHAPTER THREE

Jason

After the last of the guests had said their goodbyes, I headed to the kitchen to steal some leftover cream puff pastries for the road while a very bad version of "Heart and Soul" drifted throughout the house.

Quietly padding down the hall, I caught sight of Gemma at the piano, her mother next to her on the bench.

"Did you have fun tonight?" Caroline asked her.

I stayed close to the wall, eavesdropping. *Fun* wouldn't be the word I'd use to describe the night.

"Yeah. Fun." Gemma kept her fingers on the keys, swaying, a little tipsy, and even though we were practically strangers, it was easy to hear the lie in her voice.

"When's the big day?" she asked.

"Next month."

The piano silenced. "Why so fast? You've only been with this guy a couple of months."

I hated to admit it, but I thought Frank was moving a little fast too. Although, I couldn't begrudge my godfather happiness.

"Don't say 'this guy' like he's some stranger on the street," Caroline said. "I love Frank very much." She wrapped her arms around Gemma, pressing their cheeks together. "Honey, I know you don't understand, but I truly believe Frank is the one I will spend the rest of my life with. I just can't live—"

"A day without him as your husband," Gemma finished for her mom as if she'd heard that line before.

"Frank's different," Caroline said, so quietly I had to lean almost around the corner to hear. I knew I shouldn't be listening in on this private moment, but I couldn't help it. Something about Gemma needled me, like a side stitch after a long run. I couldn't get a handle on her, and I wanted to know more, despite her obvious prickly nature.

She wasn't going to give me *any* information about herself freely, so I had to take it where I could get it. By skulking around corners like a creep.

"Frank is a good man. I love him and trust him," Caroline went on. "I hope you do too."

"I..." Gemma left her sentence unfinished, and I was oddly disappointed. What was it about Frank or about this marriage that she didn't like? But Gemma only rested her head on her mom's shoulder. "Just tell me when and where."

Caroline held her daughter's hand. "September 30th, at the country club."

"Marrying Frank does have its perks, huh?"

"Hey. You, of all people, should know that's not what it's about." Caroline lifted her shoulder so Gemma was forced to face her, and I ducked back into the shadows to remain unseen. "One day, you'll find somebody as wonderful as Frank."

"Don't hold your breath."

I had to agree with that one. I didn't know who would be able to put up with Gemma. Maybe an alligator wrestler or bounty hunter.

Caroline stood, calling out, "Jason, can you give Gemmie a ride home?"

I startled at almost being caught snooping on them and shuffled back a few steps, trying to toss my voice to sound farther away. "Sure."

"Never mind!" Gemma yelled back. "I don't need a ride."

"Yes, you do," Caroline said, as I sauntered down the hall, all cool and collected, flipping my car keys around my index finger. Gemma heaved a sigh in my direction.

"It's after eleven," Caroline told her, "and you have a *bicycle*." She said bicycle like it was a whale and Gemma was going to *Free Willy* home.

"I've ridden it at night before." Gemma folded her arms. "I'm good, I don't need a ride."

Though I wasn't too excited about the prospect of spending any more time alone with the she-wolf, I didn't like the idea of Gemma on a bicycle at night. I'd rather see her home safe than hurt. "Ready?"

"No."

"Yes, she's ready," Caroline told me as Gemma's shoulders drooped in compliance. Doing what she was told for the first time tonight.

Frank ambled over to my side, and we hugged before I kissed Caroline's cheek.

"Take care of my daughter," she said, pressing her hand to my chest.

"Of course." I smiled, genuinely, at her, and Gemma mumbled something that sounded like "too pretty for his own good" as she followed me outside to my car.

"What's this? The Batmobile?"

"I wish." I unlocked the doors. "It's a Mercedes." Then I tipped my chin to her bicycle. "What's this?"

"My bike."

"I can see that. I meant, why do you have it?"

"I rode it here."

I raised one eyebrow, and she stared at me with so much disdain a lesser man might have crumbled. Such attitude for such a little person.

"My car went to the junkyard a few months ago, and I bought a bike instead. Good enough reason?"

I lifted a shoulder. "That's not going in my car."

"What am I supposed to do with it?"

Pretending not to hear the question, I dropped into the driver's seat. She could leave it here for all I cared, but my car didn't have room for it.

"You know what? Thanks, but no thanks. I'll ride home." She sat on the bike a little wobbly and rode a few feet down the driveway then fell over.

I stomped over to her. "Get in the car."

"No, I'm fine."

I hauled her up with one hand on her elbow. "I told you not to drink so much."

She ignored me, reaching for her bike.

"Look at you. You can't even walk right."

She stuck out her tongue at me. It was like dealing with a toddler.

"Real mature, Gemmie."

"Don't call me that," she snarled.

"Don't act like a child," I snapped back.

She started off again, but in a few quick steps, I blocked her, my hands over hers on the handlebars. "Get in the car."

Neither of us moved from our stand-off.

"Gemma." It was the first time I'd used her name. I hated how much I liked saying it. Worse yet, the way her eyes widened slightly, as if she liked it too. "Get. In. The. Car."

"When. You. Ask. Nicely."

I laughed through my nose. "No."

She tried to get away from me, but with my knees on either side of her front tire, she didn't have any leverage.

"Just get in the goddamn car," I said after a while, shaking the bike a bit so Gemma lost her balance, stumbling off of it

"You're so nice." She hobbled up, and I picked her bike up. "A real prince."

"And you're a real pain in the ass."

We stalked back to my car, where I somehow finagled the bicycle into the back, then drove to Gemma's place in silence, only speaking for directions.

"Right here is fine," she mumbled when I pulled up to her apartment complex.

As soon as I stopped the car, she hopped out, but I took my time removing the bike from the back, earning me more angry grumbles. She snatched it from me as soon as I lowered it to the ground. "You know your car is ridiculous, right?"

Leaning against it, I crossed my arms. That thorn in my side was feeling more and more like a knife. "Okay."

"No one needs something with so many bells and whistles. It probably has terrible gas mileage."

"Okay."

Obviously annoyed, Gemma worked her jaw back and forth for a moment before she dragged her bike up the sidewalk. She had trouble getting it in the door, and I bit back a laugh. "Need help?"

"No." For the fifth time, she tried and failed to hold the door open and get her bike inside.

"Okay."

"Stop saying okay, and get over here!"

"Okay."

When I reached the door, I easily lifted the bike and motioned inside. "After you."

Gemma's second-floor walk-up apartment was a hole. Small, old, and in need of a good cleaning. I set the bike down and stuck my hands in my pockets, afraid to touch anything. "Nice place."

"I'm sure that was sarcastic, but I will say thank you anyway," she said, clicking on a few lamps.

How was there no overhead lighting anywhere? I blinked into the sudden brightness then spun in a slow circle. Sketches and watercolor paintings were scattered on the floor, and I admired one black-and-white image of a Joshua tree. She had a drying rack full of clothes off to the side, a well-worn brown couch against the far wall, and an ancient television, which sat on top of what appeared to be a table made entirely out of painted soda cans. Homemade picture frames clung to the pea-green walls. I fingered one made from popsicle sticks. It held a picture of Gemma surrounded by little kids, who had paint smeared on their faces and hands. She was in the middle of the group with her arms around them, her own face beaming through streaks of orange and blue paint.

An angry hiss sounded from the corner, not even a foot away, and I jumped. A heap of fur lay on top of a bookshelf, and I slowly backed away from it. "What the fu—what is that?"

"George," Gemma answered over her shoulder, opening cat treats. The lump of gray fur leaped down to the floor, and she petted its head.

"*What* is it?"

"A cat," she said as if it should be clear.

On cue, the thing rolled around to glare at me, one-eyed and ugly.

Gemma picked him up. "This is Mr. George Clooney. I rescued him."

"I hate cats." I backed farther away, my hands up. "I don't trust them."

George Clooney bounded into another room after what sounded like an offended hiss.

"That's stupid. What if I said I don't trust..." Gemma coasted her gaze around the apartment as if she could find the end of her sentence on the walls. Then her eyes landed on me, and she waved her hand down the length of my body. "I don't trust anyone who wears short-sleeved button-downs?"

"That's the best you could come up with?"

"I mean...you look like a child. Like you should have a pocket protector."

She was lying. I could tell from the way her attention snagged on my chest, where I knew the snug button-down fit me just right. And I'd be lying if I said I didn't work out for this exact reason. For this exact moment.

With her angry gaze on me.

And that knife in my side shifted a few inches, to the center, hitting right under my breastbone.

"I left it at my math club meeting," I said. "What about you? I'm surprised you even shave. I thought you nature fanatics didn't do that."

"I'm a vegan and an environmentalist. Whether I choose to shave or not is my choice, not society's. And certainly not because some guy decided it was sexy or not." She aimed her words at me like darts. "Especially you."

"Especially me?" I repeated, but she twirled away, toward the kitchen.

I didn't know what exactly it was about me that pissed Gemma off so much. When Caroline introduced us, Gemma had barely met my eyes for 0.2 seconds before she'd judged me. Even as we shook hands, her fingers small and delicate in mine, exchanging what felt like static electricity so the hairs on my arm rose, she had still pouted, all huffy and harsh-eyed. We exchanged a few words, and I was man enough to admit it was partially my fault for instigating it at some points. But she put me on the defensive.

And I evidently had some new masochistic streak keeping me firmly planted in her apartment.

I watched as she let her hair down, brown and golden strands blending together to create an almost copper color that couldn't quite decide if it was curly or straight or something in between. She ran her fingers through it—strangely enough, something I wanted to do too—before feeding a goldfish that swam back and forth in a small bowl on the kitchen counter. Next, she grabbed a banana out of a hanging fruit basket and tossed the peel into a bucket piled up with garbage by the sink.

I leaned against the archway of the kitchen. "What's that?"

"A compost pile."

"You're a vegan, and you have a compost heap?"

"Yeah," she snipped with a glance over her shoulder. Her tank top fluttered with the movement, the outer curve of her breast peeking from the side—of course she wouldn't wear a bra—and I forced my gaze to the floor so I wouldn't stare. "I have to make up for the huge carbon footprint you're leaving."

"There's nothing wrong with eating meat."

"Except for the fact that those animals are given chemicals from birth to make them grow much bigger than they're supposed to be, kept in cages and pens too small so they become sick and overcrowded, and then, finally, slaughtered in the most inhumane manner possible."

I lifted my head in time to see her break the banana in half, giving some to a turtle that crawled around a terrarium in the space where the microwave should be above the stove. The other half, Gemma ate.

I could not believe her.

I couldn't believe she was the daughter of the stately Caroline. I couldn't believe she lived like this, that she did and said whatever the hell she wanted, and that she rode a bicycle, for Christ's sake.

I couldn't believe how goddamn attracted I was to her.

"Thanks for dropping me off and everything." Gemma's voice lifted my focus from the curve of her ass in her tight skirt, my self-control long gone. "But I have to get up early tomorrow, so if you will…" She pivoted around and ushered me to the front of her apartment.

"I have one question."

"What?"

I stood in her open doorway, facing her. "What's your deal with this wedding?"

She slumped against the doorframe. "What're you talking about?"

"Frank's like a father to me, and I want him to be happy. You, on the other hand, are practically foaming at the mouth over these nuptials."

"You have a real way with words."

I quirked a brow at her. Immature as it was, I really, *really* enjoyed getting a rise out of her.

"Not that I should have to explain myself to you," she said, dragging her hair over her shoulder to play with a few ends. "But I'm cynical about my mother's marriages."

"You don't say." When she sneered at me, I grinned down at her. "I'm sorry," I apologized, completely insincere. "Go on."

She didn't say anything, and I didn't move from my spot.

Another stand-off.

I anchored my arms across my chest, gratification warming my blood at how her dark eyes stayed there. I cleared my throat, calling her attention back to my face, unable to hide my knowing smile.

She straightened up, an annoyed curl rounding her lips.

"Husband number one, my father, knocked up my mother when she was nineteen, married her, then ran out on us when I was a year old. Last I heard, he'd found himself a new family in Arizona somewhere. Then there were a few boyfriends who came close to attaining husband number two status, but that glory went to Wayne. He showed up in time for my ninth birthday party with a pet hamster to win me over. He was a good guy, but gone by my twelfth birthday. He left a nice card, though. And this last husband was a young Frenchman, Renard Colbert. She met him at an art gallery I was working in. He was cute, but totally worthless. Did nothing but smoke cigarettes and read poetry all day. He was... *Comment dites-vous* asshole?"

I stepped toward her, keeping my voice casual. "So, what you're saying is, you have daddy issues?"

Gemma's skin turned a pretty pink, and she fisted her hands at her sides. A little lightning bolt. "It's a shame."

"What's a shame?" I tipped my head to the side, genuinely curious at what might come out of her mouth next.

She placed her hand on my bicep and leaned in close, on the balls of her feet. Even though she was a whole foot shorter than me, she made up for it with sheer sass. "It's a shame you're so gorgeous and such a dickhead."

"You think I'm gorgeous?"

"Fucking douche," she grumbled, dropping her chin toward her chest.

I ran my hand over my mouth and jaw. "You've got quite a mouth on you. I can't believe Caroline lets you get away with it."

"I'm a grown woman. I don't need to 'get away' with anything."

I pushed my hands into my pockets so I didn't grab hold of

her and do something really stupid like kissing that mouth of hers.

No matter how appealing Gemma was, she clearly had a lot of baggage, and I wasn't interested in being tied to it for this wedding. "You seem to be making some pretty dumb decisions for being so grown up."

Her eyes narrowed. "I'm not dumb."

"I didn't say you were dumb."

"You insinuated."

"You don't think getting drunk at your mother's engagement party is dumb?"

"I wasn't drunk."

She'd had so much alcohol tonight she couldn't even sit on her bike, but pointing that out would only continue the argument. "Can't you admit when you're wrong?"

"Yes, I can, but I'm not wrong." She folded her arms over her chest.

"Okay, whatever you say."

"Stop saying okay!"

When I gave her one of my best smiles in return, she growled.

"You're infuriating."

"You aren't exactly a ray of sunshine either." I lowered my face to hers so we were eye to eye, our lips were an inch apart. With her breath hot on my cheeks, it was hard to concentrate, but I soldiered on. "Let me give you a piece of advice," I said in an almost-whisper, recalling how I'd spotted her quick change at the bottom of the driveway earlier. "If you're going to strip in public, make sure no one is around."

She responded by slamming the door in my face. Then adding through it, "Pretentious bastard!"

Yep, little ray of sunshine, she was.

The next morning, I woke up with a headache from hell. George didn't move from his spot on the comforter, merely opened his lone eye before going back to sleep. I pushed off the bed, the argument I'd had with Jason last night still fresh, like the sleep lines on my cheek.

After brushing my teeth, I stared into the mirror with slightly bloodshot eyes, only to have my brain ransacked by the image of steely-blue ones, the color of winter. I groaned, my skin warming at the thought of my hand engulfed by his long fingers.

Ugh. I hated him.

Hated everything about him, from his stupid perfect face to his cocky swagger.

He was everything I couldn't stand in a man, and yet I spent the better part of last night trying to forget the tangy smell of his cologne and how heavy his attention felt when he towered over me, his palm smoothing over his lips just before he said, "You've got quite a mouth on you."

And I hated that I wanted to put my mouth on him.

George snuck up behind me, purring, and I shook away the shame of second-guessing myself. Guys like him brought all my insecurities to the surface. Sure, he was handsome, but he was also arrogant, argumentative, and an asshole. He gave me that smug half-smirk, and I knew all I needed to know.

Bending to skim my hand along George's spine, I dropped my voice to mock Jason. "Can't you just admit you're wrong?"

George's tail swished, uninterested in my impression.

"All right. Time for breakfast."

In the kitchen, I said good morning to Spot and Leonardo, who poked his head out of his shell. "You like me, right?"

The turtle chomped his mouth open and closed.

"I'll take that as a yes." I patted his shell before swallowing an Advil with a gulp of orange juice then headed off to work. The humidity was on the rise already, and by the time I hopped off my bike in front of Bare Necessities, I was a hot, sweaty mess. A bell above me rang when I opened the door to the little corner store that sold all-natural products.

"Finally, Gem! I need your help," my boss called from the back of the store, and I strolled to the storage room, where he jumped down from a small stepladder.

"Morning."

Alex turned, their platinum hair styled exactly right, while their face was done up all wrong.

"Uh... What's on your face?"

"Trying out the new line of vegan cosmetics. Too thick?"

"Way too thick."

Alex pointed to a shelf. "Grab those boxes for me, please." I did so as Alex washed their face off at the sink. "I have to do some paperwork this morning. Can you restock?"

"Sure."

After patting their face dry, they walked alongside me to the front. "You look tired."

"I am." I set the boxes on the floor before dropping my

arms onto the counter, next to the folders and notebooks Alex used for accounting.

"What happened?"

I pressed my cheek to the cool wood of the counter. "My mom's getting married. Again."

"What number is that?"

"Four."

"Good for her. But why are you so tired?"

I stifled a yawn. "I had a little too much to drink."

They handed me a small pill bottle from under the register. "It's ginseng."

"I'm the maid of honor," I said without any pretext.

"Okay." They passed me an aluminum water bottle next. "What's the problem with that?"

"The best man is a total tool bag."

"How old is he?"

"I don't know. Maybe twenty-eight or twenty-nine."

"No." They laughed. "I mean the guy your mom is marrying? How old is he?"

"In his fifties, I guess." I opened the ginseng and sank to the floor, ready for a nap even though it wasn't even ten in the morning.

"What's a kid doing hanging out with a fifty-year-old?"

"I'm twenty-five." I swallowed the herbs with water. "And I hang out with you."

"I'm not fifty."

"Thirty-five...fifty. Close enough."

"Hey!" Alex whacked the top of my head with their pencil. "So, what's the big deal?"

"The big deal is he's a know-it-all who drives a Mercedes-Benz."

"A Mercedes? Sounds nice."

"And he doesn't like cats."

Alex sniffed. "I don't like cats."

"He wore a short-sleeve button-down. Like a Boy Scout."

"Always prepared. Who doesn't like Boy Scouts?"

I glared up at Alex. "Whose side are you on here?"

They shrugged. "I don't understand the problem."

"The problem is he's too good-looking."

"How dare he!" Alex tossed me a smile then took their place back behind the counter.

From my place on the floor, I raised my fist to the sky in anger. "He should be in magazines. That's the problem. He's arrogant and a bully and incredibly hot."

Alex mumbled something, probably nibbling on their pencil, and I moved to peek up at my boss. "What? What are you saying?"

They flicked their pencil out from between their teeth. "I said, it doesn't sound like a problem to me. Sounds more like an opportunity."

"I'm going to take this opportunity to rest my head. Wake me in ten minutes." I closed my eyes, my head on top of the vegan protein bars I needed to put away.

CHAPTER FIVE

Jason

Santos & Mitchell Engineering Group buzzed about the CEO's engagement. Balloons and flowers covered Frank's office. A few men sat around drinking beer and eating hoagies and chicken wings, while I had my feet propped up on a chair, watching ESPN on a flat-screen mounted on the wall. Frank seized a chair next to me and offered me a beer, but I shook his head, biting into a sub.

Frank drank the Sam Adams himself. "I assume you got Gemma home safe and sound last night."

I nodded.

"Spitfire, isn't she?"

"That's one way to put it."

Frank's laughter boomed in my ear. "You don't like each other or what?" When I didn't answer, he slapped my shoulder. "Cat got your tongue?"

"We're not exactly peas in a pod if that's what you were hoping for."

He sipped from his beer. "She looks just like her mother, doesn't she? A knockout. She and Caroline could be twins."

I continued to eat, my attention on the TV. I'd spent most of last night bouncing a tennis ball off my bedroom wall, trying to release some tension. And when that didn't work, I closed my eyes and took my dick in my hand, hating myself for coming with Gemma's face in the front of my mind. She was a real knockout who had a mean one-two with words.

"Gemma's nothing like Caroline."

Frank nodded. "That's why I like her so much. You could learn a little something from Gem."

I almost choked on my sandwich. "I could learn from her?"

"Yeah." He smacked my back a few times as I coughed. "You need to have a little fun in your life."

"I have fun," I said, reaching for a water bottle.

He stole a chip from my plate and shoved it into his mouth. "When? With who?"

"My friends."

Frank snuffed out a laugh. "Your friends? You have two friends, Kevin and Luke. I mean girlfriends."

I wiped a bit of mayo from the corner of my mouth. "You know I don't have any. Nor do I want one right now."

I prayed for a distraction from having this conversation again. I didn't want to commit to just any woman simply because it'd make Frank happy or because I feared being alone. If or when I chose to settle down, I would. Until then, I liked my life fine the way it was.

Thankfully, a buzzer on Frank's office phone rang, followed by a voice. "Mr. Santos, you have a special delivery."

The men in the room whistled as Frank pressed a button on his phone. "Send it in." Then he glanced back to me. "You need to loosen up, kid." Moments later, his office door opened, and a Marilyn Monroe look-alike sauntered in. "Right on time, Miss Monroe. My friend Jason needs to have some fun."

The woman swirled around to where Frank pointed.

"Anything you say, Mr. Santos," she cooed. Marilyn pursed her lips and winked at me before swaying over to my lap.

Hours later, I pulled into my garage, well after my usual time getting home from work. I lazily unknotted my tie as I winded my way through the back door in the garage and then into the kitchen, which was decked out in state-of-the-art appliances. I grabbed milk out of the refrigerator and drank it straight from the carton because I could.

Once I put the milk back in place, I paused a moment at the picture held up by a magnet on the fridge, the same usual pang of longing burning in my chest. The photo was of me with my parents, huddled together on a blanket outside, a picnic set between us. I shared my father's nose and smile but had the same color of eyes and hair as my mother. It was the only picture I displayed of them in the whole house. All the rest of the family photos and mementos were stored in a few boxes, where I didn't have to face them every day.

Upstairs, I swung open the double doors to my bedroom and sat on the California king-size bed, stripping off my shirt to rub at the lipstick marks on the collar before tossing it in the laundry. I took off my slacks and stepped inside the walk-in closet. My work clothes hung neatly on racks, while folded jeans, shorts, and shirts stacked the shelves. Sneakers and shoes were piled underneath. The entire right side of the closet was barren.

What could I say? I didn't like clutter.

I pulled on a T-shirt and mesh shorts and slipped on a pair of sneakers. Closing the closet doors, I considered my bedroom. It was empty. Save for the bed and miscellaneous gray chair and lamp in the corner of the room. I could admit to myself that my bedroom was empty.

The whole house, really.

I worked hard for the things I wanted. I had a big house, a lot of toys, and a few women to fill up my nights. But still, the fact remained, my bedroom was empty.

But it's not like I was upset about it.

Not really.

And I definitely didn't feel the knife in my chest that some little spitfire drove in there last night.

Not at all.

Aiming to relieve tension in a way that didn't involve my hand wrapped around my cock again, I ended up in the driveway, shooting hoops until my cell phone rang. I glanced at the number before answering. "Hey, Bridge."

"Hi, handsome," she said in her typical purr. But for some reason, tonight, I didn't find it as inviting as usual.

"What's up?"

"It's Friday." I ignored the comment, and she continued, in a sweeter voice, "Are we hanging out tonight?"

"Uh, yeah, I guess."

"Let's go out to dinner," she suggested.

"Um…" I took a one-handed shot and missed. "I don't know. I'm pretty tired."

"But we never go out anywhere."

I tried to remember Bridget's pursed lips and her full hips, but I couldn't conjure the images at the moment.

"Come on, baby."

The pet name grated on me, and the ball got away, rolling into the next-door neighbor's yard. "We went out the other week for ice cream."

"I mean on a real date," she said.

I grabbed the ball and rested it against my hip, remembering Gemma's dark eyes pinning me in place at her apartment, that disaster she called a home. I didn't know why I liked it so much. "How about we watch a movie or something at your house?"

"My pick?"

"Your pick," I agreed, although I could barely scrape up a

fraction of the excitement I used to feel about Bridget. It still paled in comparison to last night and what it felt like to spare with Gemma. But there was no way I was going there. "I'll be over around nine."

"I'll make cupcakes. Chocolate-filled," she said, back to her bedroom voice.

"Sure. Sounds great."

"Can't wait to see you."

I hung up and tossed the phone on the grass then took a step back for a shot. I missed.

CHAPTER SIX

The last week of August flew by in a blur of wedding planning. My mother dragged me along to appointments for invitations, decorations, hairstyling, and now the biggest of them all.

The wedding gown.

She swept open a pink curtain and posed gloriously in the doorframe of the bridal salon dressing room. A long cream dress with a boat neck showed off her thin frame. "So, how do I look?"

I put down the bridal magazine and took in the bride-to-be. "Great."

"You think so?" She twisted in front of a mirror, admiring herself from all angles.

"You look beautiful, Mom," I said sincerely.

My mom had come from a family of money in Chicago, but when she got pregnant before she was married, they kicked her out. Since then, it had always been us against the world.

The sales attendant appeared to explain the bustle to me, but I only half listened as Mom continued to fiddle with the dress, inspecting every detail, pointing out any possible snag or stain before the attendant left with a paper full of notes and a tape measure around her neck.

My mom spun toward to me. Even in the drab light of the dressing room, she sparkled. "Frank and I want to take you and Jason to brunch tomorrow."

I wrinkled my nose. I'd gotten away with not having to interact with him so far, and I hoped to hold off until the actual big day.

"We'll pick you up at eleven." She beamed. "He's cute, isn't he? Frank speaks so highly of—"

I opened the magazine back up with an irritated flick of the wrist. "All right, all right. You don't have to try so hard. I know you did this to set me up with him."

"Did what? Get engaged?"

"No. The maid of honor, best man thing. I'm not interested."

"First of all," Mom said, sliding the brightly color page full of bouquets out from my grasp, "who else would I have as my maid of honor besides my daughter, who is, most of the time, wonderful, caring, and lovely? And second of all, I had nothing to do with Frank's choice of best man." She sat down, wiggling into the few inches between me and the arm of the lounger.

I shifted over, but there wasn't enough room, so she hoisted me into her lap. I wrapped my arm around her shoulders.

"Some things never change," she said with a laugh, then more seriously, "Frank practically raised Jason, so I would assume he would be the only choice to stand next to him on our wedding day. And yes, I thought maybe you two would hit it off, but I'm not going to force you to do anything you don't want to." She held my hand in her own, her eyes drooping like a puppy's. "If you don't want to be my maid of honor, you don't have to."

I blew out a guilt-ridden breath. "You're not forcing me to do anything. I'm happy to be your maid of honor."

My mom perked up, squeezing my middle until I squeaked out a giggle.

As if I was ever really going to say no to her. "And I'll go to brunch tomorrow."

She pulled me to stand up next to her, looping our arms together. "This time, Gemmie, I'm going to do it right. With the right man, for the right reasons. I only want you to be happy for me."

"I am happy for you, Mom." I smiled at her reflection in the mirror. "Very happy."

———

By the time Frank, my mom, and I arrived at the café, Jason was already seated at a table outside. He stood up and slid his aviators off before shaking hands with Frank, who asked, "Were you waiting long?"

"About ten minutes," Jason answered, kissing Mom on the cheek. "How are you?"

She smiled widely, petting his jaw in a motherly fashion. I wanted to puke. "I'm fine, thank you," she said. "I'm sorry we're late. Gemma was running behind this morning."

Jason turned, peering down his nose at me. My sour feelings hadn't lessened, but I refused to get into it with him again.

I was a lady.

We settled into our seats as a waitress appeared at the table. "My name is Jessica, and I'll be serving you today." She smiled politely, writing down everyone's order until her sights landed on Jason. She smoothed her apron over her hips, color rising in her cheeks as she smiled brightly at him. He played along with her flirtations, sliding his sunglasses back on, covering up his steely-eyed gaze.

In my head, I stabbed him right through his eyes as he

ordered his omelet with a side of bacon. His mouth quirking up in a way that I *knew* was on purpose. Eating meat just to piss me off.

Well, it was goddamn working.

"You let me know if you need anything," Jessica said to the table, though her attention fixated solely on Jason.

"We will. Thank you, Jessica."

My mom opened her napkin. "Seems like you're quite popular with women, Jason."

He only shrugged, his knee bumping against mine as he shifted in his seat. And it might as well have been an electrical shock by the way we both jumped at the touch.

Frank wiped his forehead with a handkerchief. "Gem, how do you ride your bike around in this heat?"

Out of the corner of my eye, I noticed Jason place his elbow on the table, his hand at his chin, almost as if he was interested in my answer. I angled away from him. "It's not bad. You get a nice draft."

Jessica arrived with our drinks, and after passing them out, she placed her hand on the back of Jason's chair. "I love your hair."

He ran his hand through it, the tips curling around his fingers. "Thank you. I grew it myself."

She giggled, a bit over the top, and I snorted, rolling my eyes. His knee bumped mine again, and what the fuck was with this guy? He might've been eighteen feet tall, but he didn't need to continually man spread.

"What about you?" he asked Jessica. "Is that your natural color?" When she nodded, tugging at the black-as-night strands, he smiled. "It's beautiful."

I hate that he smiled at her. A real smile. Blinding in its perfection.

"Could I get more water?" I cut in.

Jessica didn't seem to hear me as she backed away from the table, still only speaking to Jason. "I'll be back with your food in a little while."

"Excuse me," I called after her. "Jessica!"

She didn't acknowledge me.

Frank guzzled down his drink. "So, Gemmie, I know you and your mom went dress shopping yesterday, but she won't tell me anything about it."

"Sorry, Frank. All I can say is that she'll be the most beautiful bride," I said, and Jason was looking at me again, the weight of his stare perceptible even through his shades.

Mom reached across the table to cover my hand, smiling, and I was about to tell her how thankful I was to have her as my mom, but Jason cut me off.

"Gemma isn't a name you hear very often. Where did it come from, Caroline?"

I lolled my head to the side, bored with him, although my mother sat up tall. "Well, when Gemmie was born, she arrived with that gorgeous tawny hair in a ring around her head like a crown. I wanted to give her a name fit for a princess. But instead of a princess, I got a—"

"A hipster," he interjected.

I curled my lip at him. "I'm not a hipster."

"A hipster?" My mom arched her brow at Frank as if for back-up, but he only fanned himself with his napkin, not paying much attention to the conversation, and she pressed her hand to her chest. "Forgive me for being *an old*," she said with a pointed look at me because that was our inside joke. "But my daughter doesn't strike me as a hipster."

Jason opened his mouth to speak, and without thinking, I slapped my hand over it. I didn't want to hear any more of his passive aggressive taunts. "Exactly. Hipsters wear skinny jeans, listen to jazz music, and read Tolstoy for fun. I'm not a hipster."

My mom nodded. "Right. If anything, she's a hippie."

Jason nipped my palm, and I yanked it away, a fissure of pleasure throbbing between my legs. One little pinch of his teeth, and my skin was on fire. I'd hate to know what would happen if I had the full force of his mouth on me.

But I got a hint of it when he licked his bottom lip, his tongue lingering as if he could taste me there. It was obscene, really, the way his tongue stroked back and forth a moment before his top teeth scraped over it. And I wasn't only throbbing, now I was wet too. Like he knew, one sandy eyebrow raised in a challenge.

Trying to gain some control of the situation, I faced forward, only to be taken by surprise when his hand skimmed my collarbone. I sucked in a breath as his fingertips traced my shoulder, gently brushing back my hair, then toying with the thin strap of my sundress. I felt a blush crawl up from my chest to my neck as the pad of his thumb dragged over my pulse point, his fingertips pressing into my skin ever so lightly.

And I liked it.

But I hated him.

"Sorry," he said after an eternity. He shook his head like he was coming out of a trance. "Your hair was caught in your necklace."

"Honey, why are you all red?" My mom asked, oblivious. "No need to be embarrassed. You know I love that you're basically a reincarnated man who lived and died on some commune from eating poison berries."

I let out a reluctant laugh at her teasing, grateful to clear the tension simmering on this side of the table.

"Yeah, I love you're into all that environmental stuff,"

Frank agreed. "In fact, we're working on a new housing development that's all green. Right, Jason?"

"Yeah." He cleared his throat. "Yes."

I tied my hair up in a messy knot, unable to cool down. "I didn't know you two worked together."

"He is the Mitchell in Santos & Mitchell Engineering Group. Jason's father and I started the company many years ago." Frank unbuttoned the top button of his shirt. "In fact, Jason'll become the CEO when I retire."

"In a hundred years," Jason said, waving his hand noncommittally, and if I wasn't so turned inside out, I might've been impressed.

Frank went on. "I've never known anyone as smart as this kid, except maybe his dad." His face was bright with pride as he spoke to me. "Undergraduate in architectural engineering and an MBA. He's transforming us into a green company, and his new development will be the first in the state built with completely renewable energy. Tell her about it, Jay."

"No, I'm sure she doesn't want to hear it."

I lifted my attention from the seam of my dress. "I do, actually. Tell me."

He shifted forward, one elbow on the table, the other on his knee. "We're looking at land over by—"

"Here we are!" Jessica appeared with a tray full of plates, interrupting Jason, and I tried to ignore my disappointment. She served everyone and, yet again, stuck next to his chair. This time, she placed her hand on his shoulder. Bold.

If I didn't want to shove her fake eyelashes down her throat, I would have appreciated a woman making the first move.

"I hope you enjoy your food," she said. "I'll be back to check on you in a few minutes."

I held up my empty glass. "Could I have—"

She kept walking.

"Can you stop dazzling her?" I thumped my glass on the table and glared at Jason. "I'd like some water."

Without turning away from me, he called out, "Excuse me, Jessica?"

She immediately spun around. "Yes?"

I let out a huge guffaw.

He lifted my glass. "We'll need some more water, please, when you get a chance."

"Absolutely. I'll be right back." Jessica scurried away and returned in a minute with a pitcher of water. She kept her hand on the back of Jason's chair, shoving her boobs right up in his face as she leaned across him to fill up everyone's glass before leaving the pitcher next to his plate.

"Un—fucking—believable," I mumbled, and Jason clucked his tongue, leaning into my space.

"There's that mouth again."

I hoped I wasn't still blushing, and I chanced a glance to the other side of the table. Frank and my mom were occupied in wiping off maple syrup from his shirt.

"My mouth? What about yours? You bit me."

A shadow of an overly pleased grin appeared but was almost immediately wiped away with his palm. "What? You want me to apologize? I didn't realize your sensibilities were so delicate."

"I'm not delicate. I just don't like —"

"What?" he asked, so close I could smell the orange juice on his breath. "You don't like my teeth on you? Then don't put your hands on me unless you're ready to handle the consequences."

My jaw dropped open as my brain went blank, completely unable to come up with a retort. I rubbed my thighs together, hoping to relieve the pressure building there.

"Go on, eat," he said, nudging me. "Your weird fake eggs and toast will get cold."

Even as he made fun of my food, my mind still reeled from his threat. It almost sounded like he *wanted* me to touch him just so he could follow through.

But it would be a cold day in hell when that happened.

I only had to get my body to fall in line.

While Jason, Frank, and my mom talked about whatever-the-hell, I worked on cooling my hormones. Horny little bastards, they were. At end of the meal, Jessica returned with the check.

"I can take this when you're ready." She bent down to Jason's ear, whispering something. And then, "Call me."

Jason watched her walk away, and I gripped my fork like a weapon.

"She's cute," my mom observed.

"A little forward and not very good at her job, but whatever." I bit into a piece of cantaloupe, and Jason tilted his head in silence as I chewed and swallowed.

"Jealous?"

"Of Jessica? No, I'm not jealous of the waitress throwing herself at you."

"Okay," he said with a sarcastic chuckle, and I tried to remember where the arteries in legs were. All it would take would be one quick stab, and he'd come tumbling down.

Frank reached for the check, but Jason batted his hand away and stuck his credit card in the holder before passing it to another waiter as he walked by. When Jessica returned with it a minute later, she seemed a bit put out, yet he signed the receipt without any further flirtations. "Everybody ready to go?"

Frank helped Caroline up and led us to the parking lot,

where Jason pressed a button on his key fob. The lights flickered on his truck.

I stopped in my tracks. "You've got to be kidding me."

"What, sweetheart?" Frank asked, opening the passenger side door of his car.

"First, the sports car, and now, a truck?"

Jason stepped next to me. "What's this scowl for now?"

"Have you ever thought about the gallons of oil you're burning through every day? The amount of carbon dioxide you're putting into the atmosphere? Almost nine thousand grams of—"

"And there it is," he grumbled.

"There what is? You really don't—"

Frank cut me off. "Jay, you're coming to the picnic tomorrow, right?"

When he nodded, Mom smacked her forehead. "Gemmie, I forgot to tell you about that. We're having—"

"A picnic. Yeah, I deduced that from what Frank said."

"Deduced." Jason rocked back on his heels. "Good use of vocabulary words."

I should've gone for the femoral when I had the chance. "I don't have a master's degree but at least—"

Mom grabbed me by the shoulders. "I'm sorry. I forgot with all the wedding planning and everything. You can come, right?"

"I'm supposed to work at the store tomorrow. Alex has the day off."

"But tomorrow's Labor Day."

"So?"

She rubbed my back. "You get that many customers that you need to stay open on Labor Day?"

I shied away from her, annoyed at her patronizing tone.

"Yes, we get enough customers to stay open on Labor Day. Where else would people get their tofu hot dogs?"

Frank choked at that. "Who eats tofu hot dogs?"

"All right." Jason clapped. "On that note. I'm gonna head out." He kissed my mom's cheek then shook Frank's hand before heading to his truck.

"Besides, I don't want to ride my bike there again," I said, returning back to my conversation with my mother.

"That's not a problem. Jason'll take you. Hey, you'll pick Gemma up tomorrow, right?" Frank said, and Jason paused with one foot in the open door of his truck.

"Uh…"

Frank lowered his voice. "You can pick Gemma up at her work and bring her to the picnic tomorrow."

When he started to argue, Frank straightened his features in a way that had Jason's shoulders dropping in compliance, and wasn't that interesting. The lion could be tamed.

"Sure. I can pick her up tomorrow." He faced me. "I'll pick you up at six o'clock."

And with that, he drove off, and I stared after the exhaust. "He doesn't even know where I work."

Frank chuckled, wrapping a big arm around me. "Oh, he knows. Don't worry."

CHAPTER SEVEN

Labor Day was unbearable. Swelteringly hot. No one in their right mind left the air conditioning unless they were lucky enough to find a pool. Unfortunately, I had neither of those luxuries as I sat behind the counter at Bare Necessities, feet up and fanning myself with a piece of a cardboard box I'd ripped off.

The bell above the door chimed. I knew it was Jason. And he was five minutes early.

He lazily strutted down the aisles, regarding all the merchandise with his aviators still on, picking up random items to study before putting them back down. Like a character in some kind of 80s movie, he stopped in front of the counter, took off his shades to hook them on his shirt, and combed his fingers through his hair. "Nice store you got here."

"Nice swimsuit you got there."

He glanced down at his green swim trunks dotted with pink whales. "You like?"

I ignored the double meaning behind the question. "You're early."

"I know. Better than being late."

I hung my head back, trying to get a little more air. I was

not going to let him get to me today. The stagnant heat was bad enough without adding his bullshit hot air.

"It's a furnace in here. Why isn't the air conditioning on?"

I dragged my focus up to Jason as he tugged at his shirt. A sliver of taught stomach revealed itself with every pull as he aired himself out. "We don't have any. Saves power."

"No wonder you don't have any customers." He shook his head and pursed his lips in that annoying way he had. "You could invest in eco-friendly HVAC products." He held his hand up, listing them off on his fingers. "Get a programmable thermostat. Reseal the heating and cooling ducts. Get ceiling fans. Do you have radiant heat barriers?"

Of course, he had to know everything about everything when I had no idea what radiant heat barriers were. I stood up with a huff and used a band to tie my now frizzy hair back. A few beads of sweat gathered from my neck and fell in a line down to my collarbone, sinking between my breasts. I swiped at it then pushed out my bottom lip, blowing air onto my face, sending my bangs flailing above my head. After tossing the wilted cardboard onto the counter, I finally faced him, catching him gawking. "What? I know I look awful. It's the humidity."

He shrugged, his eyes openly roaming over me. With my woven cover-up on over my favorite paisley-print bikini, there wasn't a whole lot hiding me. I snagged my bag and elbowed him on purpose as I passed by to lock up.

Outside, I had to jump up into the truck. "No Mercedes today?"

"Nope." He turned out of the parking lot and into the street. "Seat belt, please."

I buckled in. "Concerned with safety, but not pollution."

"A car can kill you in a second. Global warming will take a few hundred years."

"That's disgustingly selfish. What about the future? The next generations?"

"I'm doing my part." He flicked on the radio before I could argue, and emo music blared through the speakers.

"It's too loud," I shouted at him, reaching for the dial, but he caught my hand, his fingers big and warm around mine. There was that ever-present heat, maybe friction from all the animosity. It had to be that. I couldn't stand to think of the opposite.

Halted at the stop sign, we faced each other. His cool eyes contained a hidden depth, and the more I wondered what his secrets might be, the more I lost myself in the miles and miles of blue. I was slowly sinking into them. Into him.

I had to find a way out.

A car behind us honked, and we instantly released our hands. He turned the volume down, but neither of us spoke as we listened to the roaring song.

Jason made a left, quietly singing along to the radio. His voice was low and smooth, and I pretended not to notice. "Never placed you as a Paramore fan."

He lifted one shoulder then glanced in my direction as I shielded my eyes from the sun. "Forget sunglasses?"

"Lost them."

Without pause, he held out his mirrored aviators, but I hesitated. "Put them on."

I squinted out of the windshield. "No. I'm fine."

He dropped them in my lap. "Put them on. You'll hurt your eyes squinting like that."

"Are you always so bossy?"

"Are you always so difficult?"

After a few moments, I gave in and slid them on. "How do I look?"

He did a double take then a slow, crooked smile unfurled across his lips. "It's a shame."

"What?"

"It's a shame you're so damn gorgeous yet so incredibly annoying."

My mouth dropped in amusement at his stolen insult, and I punched him in the arm.

"Hey." He grabbed his shoulder. "That hurt."

"That didn't hurt, you weenie."

He stopped at a red light and tossed me a look. "Weenie? Really?"

My smile unwittingly transformed into a giggle. Then he grinned, his teeth all gleaming, his eyes shining. Honestly, the audacity of being so good-looking was off the charts.

Arriving at Frank's house, Jason parked on the grass alongside the already crowded driveway. He jumped out and sauntered around to the passenger side, holding his hand out to me when I opened my door. My eyebrows shot up in surprise, and he nodded back toward the house.

"I'm being a gentleman. Come on."

Memories I'd rather keep locked away suddenly flashed in my mind, and I bit my lip, frozen in time, seven years ago.

A newly minted college freshman exploring the social scene. A frat house with a guy, not so unlike the one in front of me now, offering to be a gentleman, to take my hand and get me a drink. Little did I know what would be in that drink. Thank the universe, Bronte, Sam, and Laney had seen it, and they had saved me. We'd gone from near-strangers to best friends in a matter of minutes.

And all because of a pretty boy with a nice smile.

"Gemma, you okay?" Jason asked, stepping closer to drop his hand on the seat next to my knee.

I shook myself out of my years' old nightmare and into the present. "Yeah, fine."

"Are you sure? You look a little pale all of a sudden." When he reached for me again, I backed away.

I hated that instinctive reaction, yet sometimes fight-or-flight mode took over. Most of the time, I used my words to fight, but on occasion, my body preferred the flight.

"Sorry," he said quickly, although he seemed to apologize out of confusion rather than any real emotion.

"It's fine." I bypassed him and hopped out of the truck on my own. "I'm fine. Really."

Jason trailed me for a few steps before reaching for me, loosely holding on to my wrist. "Is it the party? The wedding?"

Back in fight mode, I rolled my eyes. "No. It's nothing. Don't worry about it."

He stopped me when I tried to walk away. "You don't have to do this, you know. The party, the wedding, the whole tough girl thing..." He gestured his arm in a circle as if he could encompass my aura. "You don't have to argue with me. We could get along, if you want to."

Standing in front of this man, an actual gentleman who showed no signs of bad behavior—besides the pseudo-cocky thing which I hated myself for being into—I thought about the roadblocks I'd put up about certain guys. If they looked like *him* or had any kind of resemblance, I immediately wrote them off. Even though Jason and his stupidly arrogant grin did have some physical similarities with my real-life nightmare, he was also concerned for my well-being and treated those around him, especially my mom, like gold.

I didn't want to hold on to my trauma any longer. I had to release it, stop letting it get in my way. So, I did the only logical thing. I poked Jason in his hard chest. "Then let's get along."

He licked his lips and pulled himself up to his full height. I hadn't noticed he'd bent his knees to sink down, closer to me, but now that I did, my heart stumbled over itself as I followed him into the party in Frank's backyard.

The place was brimming with noise. Guests sat at tables with umbrellas, eating hot dogs and potato salad. Jason knew most of them as he waved and said hello. A DJ, set up next to a kidney-bean-shaped pool where a few inflatable dolphins and noodles floated, played classics from the 70s and 80s.

I took it all in. "What a tremendous waste of resources."

Jason tipped his chin to the water. "But since it's already wasted, you might as well get some use out of it."

I nudged him with my shoulder. "For the first time, I think I agree with you."

We made our way to Frank, who manned the grill in an apron with the body of a busty, half-naked lady on it.

"There you are." He threw his arm around me. "I was waiting for this pretty girl to take a dip in the pool with me."

"You got it, but I'm a little hungry. Got anything on there for me?"

"Go grab a plate from your mother. I have a veggie burger with your name on it."

I headed toward the house, not even out of earshot as Frank said to Jason, "They're disgusting. I don't know how she eats them."

Then Jason laughed. He had a great laugh, the bastard.

CHAPTER EIGHT

Jason

By the time everyone had finished eating, the sky had turned pink, the heat of the day burned off, and an easy summer breeze took its place. Some guests lounged around playing cards, while others danced to disco music.

I'd spent most of the day watching Gemma. Like some lovesick dope.

She wasn't as surly as she would like people to believe. Gemma dutifully stood by her mother when Caroline called, always smiling demurely, if not a little embarrassed, when Caroline bragged about her. But she played the part of a prickly cactus well. A good-looking cactus, but a cactus none the less.

Now, she floated on an inner tube, her head back toward the sky, eyes closed so I could admire her all I wanted. I soaked up the sun-kissed freckles on her shoulders, the miles of creamy golden skin along her toned legs, and that itty bitty thing she called a bathing suit. Gem was pocket-sized, and yet the hot pink print triangles barely covered her breasts.

Jesus. Those breast, small but perky, I'd be able to cover them completely with my hands like they were mine to own and to do with what I pleased. To kiss, suck, lick, *bite*.

Curling my fingers into fists at my side, I stalked over to the side of the pool and crouched down. "Hey, you."

When she didn't pick her head up, I flicked water onto the side of her face.

She gasped and paddled around, her face morphing from annoyance to what looked like desire and back to annoyance.

"Hey."

"You're looking a little red," I teased, flicking more water in her direction. "Let me guess, you don't believe in sunscreen either."

"There is a wedding coming up, remember?" She held up her arm, studying her skin. "I can't look like the abominable snowman walking down the aisle."

I hummed, raking my gaze over her, taking my time at the dip of her belly button and the slight swell of her hips, the hidden place between her thighs. When I brought my eyes back up to her face, caught openly ogling her, the corner of her mouth ticked with a sardonic smile.

And I blinked away, heat rising in my cheeks. "You look nothing like the abominable snowman. You don't have near enough fur."

Her laugh surprised me, and I brought my attention back to her, giving into my own grin.

"You coming in or what?" she asked, fluttering her feet in the water. "I'm sure you didn't wear those whales to sit around in."

I stood up to strip off my shirt, and Gem huffed out a mix of a gag and sigh. "What?"

"Of course you look like that." She flailed her hand. "You look like a commercial for a home gym or protein shake. God. What is it with you? You have to be so perfect all the time?"

I snickered and set my cell phone down next to my sneakers as she continued her tirade. Something about low riding shorts and being misted with sweat. I dove into the water, popping up next to her and shaking my hair free of water.

"Like a wild animal," she said, holding her hands up to block the spray.

I offered no response, only gave her a half grin, and I could feel her giving into me. Little by little, I was cracking that hard shell of hers.

Ducking back under the water, I swam to the other end of the pool and propped a small basketball hoop on the edge. "Want a game?"

"Sure." She slipped off the inner tube, raising her hands up for the orange ball, and when I tossed it to her, she made a big display of catching it. "All right, big guy. Ready to lose?"

I moved toward her, the water cold enough to draw out goosebumps along my skin. "I don't know about that, little girl. I should tell you, I'm pretty good at basketball. I played through high school and college."

Even though I stood in front of Gemma, she struggled to tread water in one spot, and I curved my hands around her hips to help her stay up. She used the opportunity to place her fingers on my shoulder for leverage, her voice like a siren calling out to me. "I should tell you, I don't play by the rules."

Then she splashed me and took off, though I caught her easily by the ankle and pulled her back before stealing the ball. I sank the shot. "That's one, Gemmie."

She grabbed the ball back, undeterred. "Play to ten?"

When I nodded, she threw the ball as hard as she could toward the net, but it bounced off the backboard and settled a few feet away. We both lunged for it, though my arm outstretched hers by a mile, and I easily sank another point.

The game ended almost as fast as it began, and I circled Gem like a shark. "Ten-zip. Who's the loser now?"

Obviously not one to give in, she swam over to the side of the pool to catch her breath. "Double or nothing?"

I dropped my arm alongside hers on the concrete edge. "We didn't bet anything."

"Okay." She pushed her wet hair out of her face when a thought struck her. "If I win, you ride a bike for one week."

I huffed. "I don't own a bike."

She lifted her shoulder, the strings of her bikini top sticking to her neck. "I'm sure I can rustle one up for you."

I brushed the thin straps away with only my index finger, avoiding touching any other part of her. I knew from experience how soft her skin was, how sweet she smelled, and with the soft heat in her gaze, I had trouble moving away from her.

But I did.

Because I was a gentleman.

Who absolutely would not nibble on any part of her, no matter how delicious she looked.

"All right," I said, "if I win, you have dinner with me. Cheeseburgers."

"Ew. No. No way, Jason."

Even in that whiney tone, I loved hearing her say my name.

I tugged on a wet clump of her hair. "I'm kidding. No cheeseburgers, but if you win, you won't have to worry about it." When she didn't reply, I sucked air through my teeth. "Or say you're afraid to lose. It's fine. I won't gloat."

Her nostrils flared at the challenge, and I gave her a big grin, knowing I'd just won a date.

"Look, I'll even give you a free shot." I backed off, motioning to the basket, and she swam up to dunk the basketball in.

"Cheap point, Gemmie," I chastised, then dove under the water to grab her legs. She let out a shriek of laughter as I yanked her down. I came up with the ball in hand and scored while she resurfaced, sputtering, wiping her hair out of her eyes. "Tie game."

As she fixed her bikini top back in place from my rough-housing, I caught sight of a dark pink nipple. And I was glad the water was so cold, keeping my blood cool and my dick from tenting.

When she lifted her head, she caught my staring again. But this time, I narrowed my eyes. I was playing to win.

"I didn't think you were the rule-breaking kind, Jason."

"You should know I have a one track mind. When there's something I want, I don't stop until I have it." Then I tossed her the ball, but she was clearly caught off guard by my words and missed the catch. She had to swim after it, and I easily blocked her next shot.

We went back and forth, more grab-handing than shots taken, and by the end, I was backed up against the pool wall, holding the ball above my head while Gemma clawed at it. "Game point." I tossed her a dark smile then lobbed it over her head and scored before holding my hands around my mouth like a game announcer. "From the three-point line!"

She slapped the water. "It's like playing with an octopus. Legs and arms everywhere."

"Come on now, Gemmie. Don't be a sore loser."

"I am not a sore loser." She glared up at me through her wet eyelashes. "Best out of five?"

"I don't know." I checked an imaginary watch on my wrist. "It's getting pretty late."

She ignored the fact that the floodlights over the pool had turned on to illuminate us, the sky almost navy now, and pushed at my shoulder. "Come on."

"If you insist on continuing to be embarrassed like this—"

"You're so arrogant."

I moved close, so close I could see individual flecks of

amber in her irises, and I lowered myself so my chin dipped into the water. Reaching for her waist, I whispered, "But you kind of like it, huh?"

Her only reaction was her throat bobbing on a swallow, and I snatched the ball from her. "One more game, then."

By the time we finished playing, the moon was high above and most of the guests had left. As Gemma wrung her hair out, I snagged towels from a small outdoor shed, and when my phone rang, I nodded toward it. "Can you grab that for me?"

She picked it up, her lips pinching at the name on the screen before exchanging it for a towel.

I rubbed at the back of my neck when I saw it was Bridget. I'd honestly forgotten she even existed for a while. When I was around Gemma, I was sucked into her atmosphere. There was nothing but her and her hot, bright light.

"Hey, Bridge," I said, my voice calmer than I felt as I watched Gemma wrap herself up in a towel. I had trouble paying attention to Bridget asking me where I was and if I wanted to hang out, especially when Gemma not so subtly stepped closer to me. "I'm at a picnic," I told Bridget. "We'll talk later, okay?"

When I hung up, I scrubbed my hand over my head, unsure how to play this since Gemma appeared so curious. Before I even got a chance to explain, she said, "Bridget?"

"A friend."

She nodded slowly, suspiciously.

"Why? You have that jealous look in your eyes again."

"Jealous?" She huffed. "It feels like you're projecting. Like you want me to be jealous."

She had me there.

I didn't necessarily want her to be jealous, but I wanted her to acknowledge this...whatever it was between us.

"So," I said, completely blowing off her last statement. "You and I have a date. When'll it be?"

"No, thanks. I'll pass."

"You can't pass." I ran the towel over my chest and torso. Gem's focus followed. "That was the bet. You lost three games. I told you it wouldn't include cows."

She pretended to puke.

"It's really not that bad. You couldn't have always been against meat. You must've had it at some point in your life."

Turning her hair upside down to run her fingers through it, she said, "Not since I could think for myself."

I tilted my head so I was upside down too. "When was that? Last year?"

She flipped her hair back and stood tall, yet she still had to crane her neck to meet my eyes. There was something about how petite she was that I really, *really* liked. A desire to toss her over my shoulder—she couldn't weigh more than a sack of potatoes—and bring her back to my cave where I could make a home between her legs took over. Though she'd probably hate that since my cave would undoubtedly be cleaner than her apartment.

"I haven't eaten meat in twenty years," she said, draping her towel around her shoulders.

"Are you cold?"

"Not really." But her shiver gave her away, and I held my hand out.

"Let's get you warmed up." I failed at biting back a smile when she laced her fingers with mine. Those prickly needles were retracting one by one. All my little cactus required was some sun and fun.

I escorted her inside the house and into the kitchen, where I sat her at the massive kitchen island then proceeded to make coffee.

"You know this place well," she said, touching the brass pots and pans hanging above her head.

"I would hope so. I used to live here."

"Yeah?"

I nodded, retrieving two mugs from a shelf above my head.

"Is Frank your long-lost uncle or something?"

"Kinda. He and my dad met in college. They were best friends." I poured the coffee and carefully carried it over to the island before opening up the refrigerator. "Do you want cream?"

She pointed at her chest. "No animal products, remember?"

"Oh yeah. Sorry." I cringed and rummaged inside the fridge. "Uh...there's..." I pulled out a plastic tub. "Can't Believe It's Not Butter?"

She laughed and shook her head. "Sugar is fine."

I handed her the little cup filled with sugar, and she proceeded to dump about a dozen spoonfuls into her cup. I watched, shaking my head in amusement.

"What?" She pushed the sugar back my way. "I like it really sweet." Then she held her steaming mug between her hands. "So, why did you live here and not with your parents?"

Keeping my attention on my spoon, I stirred cream into my coffee until it was light brown. "My parents died when I was thirteen, and I moved in here with Frank."

Gemma covered her face with her hands. "Oh my god, Jason. I'm so sorry. I didn't know. I shouldn't have asked."

"It's okay." I tugged on her fingers until she lowered her hands, then casually sipped my coffee. It was a long time ago, and though it still hurt, I wasn't comfortable with sympathy from other people. I never knew what to say. "Frank's wife had passed away a few months before. We helped each other through it."

She pushed out her bottom lip. "I feel so stupid. I didn't know."

"It's okay. Sometimes it feels like a hundred years ago. My life is so different now than it was then." I folded my body over the counter, so my face was centimeters from hers. "But," I said pointedly, "maybe if you weren't so judgmental, you'd have taken some time to get to know me."

She brought her hands to her chest, in fake outrage. "Me, judgmental?"

"Is there someone else in this room who called me pretentious?"

She opened her mouth but her jaw only flapped a few times. I loved when I rendered her speechless. When I could get this woman who wielded her words like a sword to shut up.

I breathed her in, coffee and chlorine enveloping us in an odd but wonderful mixture, and as it seeped deep into my lungs I was sure I'd always associate these scents with her. She closed her eyes like it was too much for her.

It was a little too much for me too, and yet I couldn't drag myself away.

After a long minute, her eyelids fluttered open, offering me a barely perceptible nod.

You feel this too?

When we finished our coffees, Gemma found her cover-up and bag on her way outside. Caroline and Frank were drinking wine on a swing. All the other guests had left, leaving their evidence on the ground.

"Hey, we didn't know you were still here." Caroline lifted her head off Frank's shoulder.

"We're leaving now." I tossed my keys in my hand. "But this needs to be cleaned up. I can stay."

"Yeah," Gemma agreed, grabbing up a few napkins from a table.

Caroline stood up, taking the trash from her. "No, no, go home. It's past midnight. You need your sleep. Your classes start this week."

"Classes?" Frank asked, scratching his stomach.

Gemma threw two soda cans into the recycling bin. "I run an after-school art program that's a couple days a week."

"Oh, well then, get going. We'll clean up tomorrow. This stuff isn't going anywhere," Frank said, and Caroline chased us out, waving and blowing kisses.

I opened the truck's door for Gemma. "I didn't know you were an art teacher."

She imitated me in an absurdly low voice. "Maybe you should take time to get to know me," then she closed the door on my chuckle. She dozed off on the ride home, only to wake up when I tapped her nose.

"Home already?" She yawned.

I nodded. "Now, what about that cheeseburger?"

"Not a funny joke."

"No meat." I drew an X over my heart. "Promise. But you'll still come over for dinner? Sometime this week?"

She gave in after a long moment that had me holding my breath. "Yeah, okay. I teach yoga Tuesday and Thursday nights."

"That's quite a schedule you got, between the weird tofu shop, art class, yoga, and all the saving the world. Can you even fit me in?"

Her answer was garbled with another yawn. "I guess I could try."

"Said so enthusiastically. Where's your phone? I'll give you my number." When she took out a tiny cell phone from her bag, I practically yelped. "Where did you get this? It's archaic." I flipped it over in my hand. "Is this a first-generation? I can't believe it. How is it still running? What's the serial number on this? One?"

She quirked her lips to the side in a move I now knew meant she was fighting a laugh. "Don't make fun. It's been with me for many years."

I typed in my number and called my phone before she snatched hers back. "I don't like to throw away perfectly good items."

"Right. Yeah. Makes total sense. Should I send you smoke signals instead? That might be easier."

She opened her door and stuck one foot out. "No smoke signals. You'd have to burn down trees for that."

"Okay, no smoke signals. A carrier pigeon?"

She jumped down to the ground and turned, resting her chin on her arm on the top of the open window. My cold dead heart melted at her sleepy smile.

"As long as it's free-range. You know the address to send it to."

Tuesday morning was gray, and storm clouds loomed in the distance as I peddled to work. Bronte had texted the group thread earlier about her latest fight with her boyfriend, Hunter. They'd been together since college, and I had lost almost all my patience with the guy.

> You think it might be time to cut the cord?
> He's hot one day, cold the next. You don't
> need that.

I ducked inside the store when the rain began to fall. Alex greeted me with a wave of a dustrag. "A good day to get some cleaning done. How was it yesterday? Any customers?"

"A few." I put my bike and bag in the storage room, carrying a broom back to the front to help. "How was your day off?"

"Great. And thank you so much for working. We went hiking, had a picnic on the mountain, and had a little too much to drink. You know, the usual. Did you get to do anything fun last night?"

"I, uh…" My cell phone buzzed in my pocket with a message.

SAM

What do you want to do, B?

"Nothing good, then?" Alex asked, skirting around me and my phone in the middle of the floor.

"No, it was..."

BRONTE

I have to think about it.

You mean make a list?

BRONTE

YES

LANEY

LOL

"It was?"

I finally lifted my attention to Alex. "Sorry, what?"

They propped a hand on their hip, their eyelids highlighted in a shimmery yellow and white. "Your day, it was...?"

"Remember the guy I told you about?"

They crossed their arms, always ready for tea. "Jason, the Boy Scout. Yes, of course. What happened?"

That was when my phone vibrated with a group FaceTime call. It was the easiest way for all of us to chat together, and I immediately answered.

Alex rolled their eyes. "You know your boss is standing right here."

I stepped up next to them and adjusted the angle so we were both on screen. Bronte, Sam, and Laney all appeared in their boxes. "Hi!"

Alex took stole my broom to lean on it, grinning into the phone. "Hello, lovely ladies."

The girls all greeted them cheerfully, even Laney, who was still in bed, her naturally curly hair spread out on the pillow.

"Am I the only one who ever works?" I said, and Alex snorted behind me. The girls all had similar reactions. Laney was the social media manager for the Giants in San Francisco, Sam was currently working on her doctorate in psychology, and Bronte taught at a middle school.

"I only have five minutes before the bell rings," she said. "This is my free period."

Laney yawned. "You're the one who wanted a team huddle? It's not even seven here yet."

Bronte smiled sadly. "I miss you guys."

Sam frowned. "You all right?"

She only nodded, and Alex butted in, sticking their head in front of mine. "I was just trying to get the gossip from your friend here."

"What?" All three of the girls echoed the question, and I tugged the broom out from underneath Alex with a snarl.

Sam's eyes lit up. "Are you keeping secrets from us?"

"No."

Laney got up from her bed. "Okay, let's hear it."

Alex raised their hand. "She was about to tell me about Jason."

"The Boy Scout?" Bronte asked, moving closer to the screen.

"I don't know what's wrong with a Boy Scout," Alex said. "They're always prepared."

I groaned. "Can't you be like a regular boss and yell at me for not working?"

They scrunched their nose and popped out a hip. "I'm not a regular boss. I'm a cool boss."

Laney caught the *Mean Girls* reference. "You can't sit with us!"

Alex pointed to their glossy pink shirt, but before they could get another line out, Sam said, "So, what's the deal with the Boy Scout?"

When I hesitated, Bronte whined, "Come on, quick. I need to hear before all the kids come in."

Resting against the broom, I relayed the events from the previous night.

"So, you like him?" Sam asked.

"No. He's impossible."

Laney, now in her bathroom with a toothbrush in her mouth, said, "But you like him."

"We have nothing in common."

"But you like him. Honey, he's hot and single." Alex waved the dustrag above their head. "What's the problem?"

"Well," I started, setting my cell phone down against a jar of honey so I could pretend to sweep. "He might not be single. He got a phone call from someone named Bridget last night."

"Bridget?" Bronte repeated.

"Yep."

"Okay. And?" Laney spat out her toothpaste. "Are you going to ask him about it?"

I avoided the question, diligently sweeping.

"Gemma Rose," Alex chided, and the three girls oohed like I was in trouble.

"You sound like my mom when you say that."

"Good. Your mother's a queen. Are you going to call him?"

"I have a lot of stuff to do today. Yoga tonight."

"It's only a phone call," Sam said. "Are you afraid?"

When I didn't answer, Bronte practically cooed. "You are. You really like him. Gemma's in love."

"Hey, whoa. Don't get ahead of yourself."

Alex picked at my hair like a mother hen, pushing it behind

my ears just so. "Yeah, yeah, I know. You don't know how to commit. Daddy issues."

I plucked their fingers off where they fussed with my tank top. "That's what Jason said. That I have daddy issues."

Laney wrapped her hair up in a bun on the top of her head. "You do."

"*I* know that, but I don't want *him* to know that."

"I think you should call him right now," Laney suggested, and Alex agreed.

"I'll even give you a fifteen-minute break to do it."

I laughed, waving my arm around as if I wasn't already on a break.

"Yeah, you should definitely call him," Sam said.

Bronte pumped her fist, chanting, "Call him. Call him. Call him."

The girls and Alex joined in.

"Fine!" I gave in with a growl.

A loud buzzer rang out, and Bronte glanced toward the sound somewhere behind her before smiling back at her screen. "I can't wait to hear how it goes."

"Good luck," Sam said in her singsong voice.

Laney waved at the screen. "Send us a picture. I need to see this Boy Scout in the flesh."

With the FaceTime call ended, Alex folded their arms, foot tapping on the linoleum. After a short stare down, I pulled up Jason's contact and put my phone to my ear, pacing down the aisle. Alex tiptoed behind.

Jason picked up on the second ring. "Gemma."

"Jason."

"I'm glad you called."

When I pivoted around, I collided right into Alex's chest, and I nudged them out of the way as they bent down, trying to listen.

On his end, Jason said, "I assume you're calling to make good on our bet."

"You know what happens when you assume," I told him as Alex tripped on my heels, following so closely behind. I pushed their shoulder, and they grabbed my wrist, forcing me to hold the phone so they could hear as well. "I could be calling you because I have an engineering emergency."

"Okay, then. What's the emergency?"

"There's a huge pothole out front of the store that needs fixing."

"I'm a structural engineer. Call the mayor, she'll fix your potholes," Jason said, and I could hear the smile in his voice. "But first, do you want to come over tonight for dinner?"

Alex nodded enthusiastically, and I palmed their face. "Yeah, I'll come over. My class ends at seven."

"Call me when you're ready. I'll pick you up."

"You don't have to do that. I'll ride my bike as long as it's not raining. I'll call you for directions later."

"Okay. Bring a bib. I'm making ribs."

"Jason."

"I know. I know. No meat or cheese or anything that tastes good."

I placed the phone back to my ear, much to the chagrin of Alex. "Hey, don't knock it till you try it."

"Okay. Bye, Gem."

"Bye, Jason," I said, sucking my bottom lip between my teeth to keep from grinning as I ended the call.

"Look at you. You're like..." Alex circled their hands out in front of me. "Like a blooming flower, all glowing and rosy in the sun."

I rolled my eyes at the ridiculous romantic notion.

They shimmied "Feels good, doesn't it?"

"What?"

"To believe in happy endings." They pinched my arm in a way I always thought an older sibling might and then handed me the broom. "Now get to work."

CHAPTER TEN

Jason

Biting back a smile, I pocketed my cell phone, after hanging up with Gemma. Knowing how she blew hot and cold, I had to let her come to me. It wasn't easy, sitting around in my office all day, waiting to see if she'd contact me, but my patience paid off.

And now I'd have her all to myself.

There was something about her, uninhibited and carefree, so unlike myself, and I was desperate to know her. Be closer to her.

After losing my parents, I coped by walking a tight line. Death and grief were messy, and I liked things to be tidy and neat. Nothing out of place, nothing but perfection to hold myself together, to forget what I'd lost.

But Gemma was the opposite. She made me feel things I hadn't felt...maybe ever. From the first moment I laid eyes on her, I'd been undeniably attracted to her, but there was something else besides her pretty little mouth which drove me crazy. Something that called to me.

Something that made me want to forget my straight and narrow and follow her zigzag, even if it meant following her through a prickly desert.

I focused on my computer, trying to put Gemma out of my mind, though it wasn't easy with the memory of her in that tiny bikini. She was small but mighty. Lines of muscle contoured her stomach and legs, no doubt from her biking and yoga. I imagined wrapping her arms around my neck and lifting her up to kiss her bowed pink lips, quieting her constant arguing.

Better yet to have her mouth wrapped around my cock.

Gemma was like a summer storm, coming on suddenly, heat and wind threatening to sweep me away. And for once in my life, I was okay with getting caught in the rain.

As the day trudged on, the seconds slowed, the minutes stretching on forever once my four o'clock meeting extended from one hour into two. When I finally got home, I changed and headed out for a quick run to grind down the nerves determined to clog my windpipe and make me sound like a middle schooler whose voice hadn't changed yet, threatening the cool façade I carefully put on every day.

After working up a good sweat, I circled back to my house and slowed to a jog when I had it in my sights. A tall, curvy figure stood at the front door. With a grunt, I caught my breath, hands on my hips.

Bridget waved. "Hey, babe."

I brushed past her, wiping my face with the hem of my T-shirt. "What are you doing here?"

"I wanted to see you." Her dark hair sat in a high ponytail on the top of her head, her navy-blue dress clinging to her hourglass figure.

I'd always kept women at arm's length. Bridget was no different, so I ignored her sentiment. "How was your day? You had that big presentation, right?"

"Yeah, it went great. Exactly as planned," she said, leaning against the beveled doorframe. "Aren't you going to invite me in?"

I didn't want to be rude, even though I had no plans of keeping her here, and opened the door wider, gesturing her in. I flipped my sneakers off and tossed my phone and keys on a table next to the door.

"You look good," she mused, dropping her eyes to my drenched shirt, the sleeves cut off so it hung loose around my torso.

I knew that look. "What's up, Bridge?"

"Nothing," she murmured, cozying up next to me, her painted fingernail dragging along my shoulder. I stared down at her hand, tempted to push it away. We weren't strangers but not exactly in a spot where she could show up like this either. "I just..." She drew an invisible little heart on my bicep. "I want to know where we're going."

"Where we're going?"

"Yeah, we've been dating for a few months now."

I didn't think *dating* was the technical term for what we were doing. Friday night booty calls and occasional midweek hookups did not a relationship make, but I let it slide. She skimmed her finger down to my forearm. "I want to know how you feel about me."

I backed away and shoved my fingers through my wet hair so her hand dropped from my arm. "You're a good friend, Bridget."

"Friends?"

"Yes, friends." I checked the time. It was almost seven, and I needed to get rid of her. Gemma was going to be here soon. "I'm going to take a shower." I moved to the door, but she didn't take the hint.

"Jason, we're more than friends. We've been going out for months," she said, curling her fingertips over the waistband of my shorts. "I want you to admit it." When she leaned in to kiss me, I leaped away from her, but my cell rang at the same time, leaving Bridget still by the table with my phone.

"I'll get it." She reached for it, her intent on demonstrating how much we were not *just friends* apparent. Before I could say otherwise, she answered in her syrupy voice. "Jason Mitchell's phone."

The volume was loud enough that I could hear Gemma on the other end. "Hello?"

"Hi, who's this?" Bridget asked.

"It's Gem. Is Jason there?"

I cringed at the waver in her voice.

"Yes, hold on a sec." Bridget passed the phone off. "It's some girl."

I took it, stalking away from Bridget. "Gemma, hey, sorry about—"

"I don't think I'll be able to make it tonight," she said like it was all one word.

"Look, I know this—"

"I'm not really feeling well."

"Gemma, I'm sorry. It's not what—"

On the other end, she huffed. "It's fine. You don't need to apologize. I'll see you around."

Then she ended the call, leaving me staring at my phone.

Bridget teased her hands over my back. "Who was that?"

"The daughter of Frank's fiancée," I said not hiding the frustration lacing my words. No doubt she was the reason Gemma bailed.

Not recognizing the problem she'd inadvertently caused, Bridget massaged my shoulders. "You said you wanted a shower. Can I join?"

I shrugged away from her hands, but she inched closer, snaking her arms around my neck. When she tried to kiss me, I pressed my hands against her shoulders, gently removing her grip on me. "Go home, Bridget."

Put out, she tried one more time to kiss me, though I shook my head and ushered her out of the door before collapsing on my couch.

I fucked up.

And I suspected Gemma didn't give second chances very often.

———

Determined to make it up to Gemma, I headed to Bare Necessities after work on Friday. The small stucco building next to the dry cleaners was drab on the outside, nothing like the colors and smells of the inside. Like before, the bell above my head dinged when I opened the door, and my eyes caught on a sign for vegan brownies and cupcakes. I'd never tried vegan anything, but they actually looked pretty good.

"Hi, welcome to Bare Necessities. How can I help you?"

I spun around at the voice to find a person with pale skin and wavy bleach-blond hair, styled on top of their head with a sparkly lemon pin. "Hey, I'm looking for Gem."

"And you are?"

"Jason."

Their face changed immediately, hands thrusting up in the air. "Jason! Yes, Jason, so nice to meet you. I'm Alex, pronouns are he/they, and I'm owner and manager of this bountiful vegan oasis. I've heard so much about you."

"You have?" I was both surprised and thrilled at that fact. "All good things, I hope."

Alex looked me up and down with a critical eye before pointing to the bag in my hand. "Come bearing gifts?" When I held it up in a silent answer, he patted my arm. "Good man.

Gem, darling," he called over his shoulder. "I need your assistance out front."

My breath caught in my chest when she stepped into view, dressed in a flowing white shirt. Her hair caught the sun streaming through the window, and it highlighted the amber hues waving loose down her shoulders. She looked angelic.

Then her dark eyes narrowed, her face altering into something a lot less heavenly. "Why are you here?"

Finding the closest thing to me, I held up a bottle of liquid smoke. "Shopping."

She huffed and crossed her arms over her chest.

"I came to apologize about the other night." I offered up the take-out bag from a local burger place. "Since we didn't have dinner together, I thought I could make it up to you."

"I'm not eating meat," she said, and Alex let out a sound of horror from where they hid two aisles over, not so subtly watching us.

"It's not meat. I promised you it wouldn't be."

She reluctantly took it from my hand and glanced over to her boss, who gestured to the door. "Go ahead."

Gemma growled out something that sounded like "Fine, come on," so I followed her outside to sit on the steps leading up to the store.

"What is it?" she asked, unwrapping the burger. It didn't have the same mouthwatering scent as beef, but it looked okay.

"Black bean and mushroom. I got you fries too."

She stared at the burger, suspicion lining all her features.

"I had to try three different places," I said, pointing to it. "Not many restaurants make vegan burgers."

"Really?" She turned to me, her eyes sparkling, and if that was all it took to make her happy, I'd personally see she had vegan burgers whenever she wanted them.

I nudged her elbow with mine. "Yeah. Wasn't that big of a deal."

Only took me an hour.

With a hint of a smile, she bit into it, a slice of tomato falling out of the top. She scooped it up and slurped it between her lips, coating them in juice. "How is it?"

"Really good. Here, try." She shoved it at me. "Go ahead."

Sharing her food with me had to be a good sign.

When I accepted it, she dug into the bag for a few fries and ate those too.

"Come on," she cajoled. "I want to witness your face when you try your first animal-free cheeseburger and realize how good it is."

"Eh, I don't know about that," I said, lifting it to my mouth. I took a big bite. It wasn't bad...for cardboard. "It's all right."

"See?" She aimed a fry at my face. "Don't knock it till you try it."

I handed her the burger back. "So, how's your week been?"

"Busy."

"Mine too," I said, brushing my hands off.

"Yeah?" She inclined her head, and I readied myself for what I knew was coming. "With Bridget?"

I cleared my throat and surveyed the strip mall across the street, while the side of my face boiled at what I could only guess was the same temperature as the surface of the sun from her glare. "No, uh, she's..."

It was amazing how I'd never felt guilty about living my life the way I wanted to until now. Until Gemma's eyes sparked with a combination of anger and desire.

We had met only weeks ago, interacted a handful of times. We were barely friends, more enemies than anything, and the friction between us threatened to strike up the kindling we seemed to be stumbling around in. Funny thing was, I'd always had a weird obsession with fire. I'd burned lots of holes in rugs as a kid. And I had trouble keeping my hands off the tiny flame next to me now.

"Bridget's no one. Just a friend."

She clucked her tongue, shoving a couple fries into her mouth in an obvious attempt to stop whatever words were about to come out.

Minefield averted.

"So, are you coming golfing tomorrow?" I asked to change the subject.

"Golfing?" She crinkled her nose in that cute way she always did and took another bite of the burger.

"Frank and Caroline invited me. I figured you too."

She wiped her mouth with a napkin. "You figured wrong. I'm not much for golf."

"Why not?"

"Swinging a stick around, trying to hit a tiny ball, isn't my kind of thing."

"Bigger balls are more your thing?" She glowered at my terrible innuendo, and I inched closer to her, the toe of my Oxfords nudging her instep. "It's relaxing."

"Yoga is relaxing. Golf is boring."

Trying a different tack, I leaned my elbows back on the step behind me. "How's your art class?"

She polished off the burger and stuffed the garbage into the paper bag. "Good. This week, we learned how to use the supplies and started with the basics. Next week, we'll try charcoal drawing."

"How often are the classes?"

"Every Monday and Wednesday."

"And what do the kids call you?"

She perused my lounged position, her eyes trailing down to

my legs and back up to my face as if studying a new species of animal. "Why are you so interested?"

Why was I interested? I doubted she'd sit here while I enumerated the reasons.

"I don't know. I thought maybe big kids might be able to come to this class too."

"Big kids like twelve-year-olds, or big kids like you?" She stood up, her denim shorts revealing so much of her legs. Right there. A few inches from my eyes. Instead of wrapping my hand around her calf and burying my face against her skin, I stood up too.

"Big kids like me."

She almost, *almost* smiled. "I don't think you'd fit in the chairs."

I tilted my head, studying her face—the arch of her dark eyebrows, her high cheekbones, and of course, her mouth. The perfect Cupid's bow on top, the plump and pink lower lip. I itched to push her long bangs away from her eyes, tuck her hair behind her ears, and finally learn the taste of her tongue. "What time do you get off? Can I give you a ride home?"

"We close at six. I don't need a ride."

I searched her eyes, finding no hints as to what was going on in her head, so I tried again, grazing her elbow with my fingertips. From her slightest jolt, I knew she felt the same electricity that I did when we touched. Though she had a damn good poker face.

"Will you come golfing?"

She drew her arm out of my grasp. "I'll pass. See you later, Jason."

I stared after her for a moment, bemused and discouraged. "Call me if you change your mind."

With my keys in hand, I was about to head to my car when I reversed course. *I* needed to know for sure that the tension between us wasn't only because we were complete opposites, and *she* needed to know how I felt about her. Jogging back into the store, I caught Gemma by the waist and tugged her to me, curving my palm against her jaw and softly pressing my lips to hers. At first, she was tentative and still, but when I wrapped my arms around her, taking her weight against me, she relaxed in my hold.

She combed her hands into my hair, her fingernails scraping along my scalp, and it was a straight shot to my dick. I drifted my hand down toward her ass, pressing her against my quickly hardening length, and she let out a tiny moan as she finally parted her lips, allowing me to sweep my tongue into her mouth.

She was my new favorite flavor, and I angled to take the kiss deeper, tongue and breaths melting together. But as suddenly as she gave in was as suddenly as she backed away with a gasp.

She wiped at her mouth with the back of her hand. "What the hell was that?"

Shocked at her reaction, I held my hands up. "What? I thought..." I blinked away the haze of lust to focus on the waves of ire rolling off of her. "Don't you feel anything for me? Because..." I gestured between us with two fingers. "It's driving me crazy."

"So?" She hissed her words at me. "You can't go around just kissing people. You can't grab someone like that without asking. You can't do whatever you want! I'd like a choice too, Jason."

My breath whooshed out of me. "I don't—" I shook my head. "I'm sorry. I thought you were into it."

Squeezing her fists at her sides, she walked in a tight circle then blew out a long exhale aimed at the floor. "That's not..." She huffed out an angry laugh. "Never mind."

She was right. I didn't ask if I could kiss her. It didn't even cross my mind to. I liked her, and I thought she liked me too.

But I was so very, *very* wrong.

Although the fact that she couldn't meet my eyes told me there was something more going on.

"Gemma, I'm sorry. Are you okay?"

"This isn't the place for this conversation," she murmured, her gaze skipping around the store, probably looking for Alex.

I chanced two steps toward her, and when she didn't move away, I took another one so I could whisper, "Talk to me. Tell me what's wrong."

She licked her lips, shaking her head almost imperceptibly.

"I'll leave if you want me to, but please, say something."

At that, she shifted her focus to me, her eyes rimmed red and glassy. I waited, completely motionless, more still than I'd ever been in my life, until she spoke.

"I was at a party in college, like, third week of school. It was my first college party." She let out a pitiful laugh and dragged her hand over her face, clearing her eyes. "I went with my roommate, Bronte, because she'd been flirting with this older guy and wanted to hang out. I don't even really remember much at this point, except for his face."

I closed my eyes, a pit forming in my stomach. There weren't many ways this story could end, and I felt like I might throw up. Which made me feel even more like an asshole. If this was how I felt listening to the story, how did she feel living it?

Fuck. I wanted to punch something.

I opened my eyes to find the corner of Gemma's lip between her teeth, her arms folded like she was cold.

"He was tall and handsome. Wavy blond hair and big arms. He looked kind of like you."

"Jesus, tell me he didn't…"

She lifted her head, meeting my gaze. "He didn't."

I didn't know how I was still standing. How could I be when my chest had collapsed?

"He flirted with me, and I thought he was the hottest guy ever, so when he gave me a drink, I took it. Didn't think anything of it. Next thing I knew, I was in the shower, back in the dorm. My friends saved me, they took care of me. Without them..." She lifted a shoulder, not needing to finish that sentence.

"Gemma, I..." Speechless, I held out my arms. I wanted to comfort her, give her some security, but I needed it too. I had to know she was okay. "Can I give you a hug?"

After a long moment, she sank into my arms, though she kept her own clasped together in front of her chest. I didn't mind. "I'm so sorry," I murmured against her hair. "I don't know what else to say besides it's awful and happens far too often. I'm just so fucking grateful it turned out the way it did, and I'm sorry it happened to you."

She tipped her head up, resting her chin on my chest. "I didn't mean to—"

"No, don't." I was slow to release her, but let her go nonetheless. "If you're about to apologize or rationalize you being upset with me, don't. I get it, and I get why you might think I'm an asshole. We blond-haired, blue-eyed white guys all kinda look alike."

At that, she placed her hand over her mouth, but I could still see the curve of her smile between her fingers. "I don't think you're an asshole for how you look. I think you're an asshole because you're an asshole."

I tossed my head back and laughed. "Okay, whatever you say." Then, because I didn't want to push her anymore, I turned around and walked out of the store. "See you round, Gemma."

CHAPTER ELEVEN

After Jason left Bare Necessities, I was pretty much done and spent the rest of the shift in the back room, texting the girls, filling them in on Bridget. His friend.

Bronte wanted to give him the benefit of the doubt.

Sam told me to forget about him.

Laney suggested I go home, open up a bottle of wine, and put my feet up. Which was exactly what I planned on doing.

I closed my apartment door and leaned against it, sinking down to the floor, emotionally and physically wrung out. It had been a long day, and I was exhausted. Exhausted from working all day, exhausted from my confession to Jason, exhausted from riding my bike home.

I seriously needed to scrounge up some money to buy a new car.

Tap. Tap. Tap.

"What?" I groaned, forcing myself to stand after a few moments in which I contemplated ignoring the knocking completely and hiding under the blanket on the sofa until whoever it was left. I unlocked the door and was greeted by my mom and Frank.

"That's how you answer the door?" She let herself in. "*What?*"

"Yes, I'm good. How are you? Please, come in." I motioned to the couch my mom had already taken a seat on. Frank patted my shoulder on the way in. "So," I said, collecting a few pieces of dirty laundry and a used plate with a bit of peanut butter still on it. "What brings you two over to my neck of the woods?"

"We wanted to talk to you," Mom said, reaching for my hand.

"Oh." I sat on the coffee table in front of her. "'Kay."

"Frank and I were talking. Now, don't get mad."

Which, of course, immediately put me on edge, though at this point I didn't have much gas left in the tank. "I don't have the energy to get mad."

"Good." She squeezed my hand then looked to her future husband.

"How long does it take you to get from here to your store?" Frank asked, his elbows on his knees with his hands folded between them.

"About half an hour, why?"

He tugged on his checkered shirt. "And most nights, you're riding your bike home after dark?"

"Yeah."

Mom chimed in. "You know I worry about you. We both worry about you on that death trap you call a bicycle. And it'll be winter soon."

Frank shifted to dig into his pocket. "I wanted to buy your mother a wedding present, but she had a better idea." He held a small key fob aloft. "We decided to buy you a car."

My jaw dropped as my mom bounded up. "Come one! Let's go see."

She dragged me outside and fluttered her arms like Vanna White to a small green car.

"It's a Ford Mustang. And electric." Frank pressed the key into my hand. "Go sit in it. If you don't like it, you don't have to keep it."

I did what I was told and sat in the car, gingerly placing my hands on the steering wheel.

No one had ever bought me a car before. No one had ever bought me much of anything.

But this was a brand new car. I blinked back the stinging in my eyes.

"You look good, Gemmie," Mom gushed, folding her fingers under her chin. "Do you love it?"

Still stunned into silence, I couldn't answer, so Frank dropped into the passenger seat and explained all the controls and how to charge it. "Say something. Do you like it?" When I nodded like a marionette, his big laugh practically shook the small car, and he slapped his knee. "Good. You'll keep it!"

After I offered them grateful hugs and kisses, my mom and Frank left me sitting in my new car and got into their own.

Frank stuck his head out of the driver's side window. "We're golfing tomorrow. Why don't you come? Show off your new wheels."

In a cloud of happiness and appreciation for a man who'd only ever treated me like his own daughter, I snapped out of my trance and nodded in agreement. "Yeah, all right. I'll be there."

Mom might have sprouted wings and flown away if not for her seat belt. "Oh, Gemmie, I'm so happy you're happy."

Frank winked. "Tee time is ten o'clock. We'll see you there."

Afraid to move, in case my gift would disappear if I got out, I stayed for a while, running my hands over the seats and dash.

I snapped a few photos and sent them to the girls. This little electric dream didn't solve all my problems, but it would save my thighs from continuing to chafe.

And that was something.

87

CHAPTER TWELVE

Jason

It was a beautiful Saturday, sunny without a cloud in the sky. The smell of fresh-cut grass floated on the breeze. A perfect day for a round of golf, if you liked that sort of thing, and I loved exactly that sort of thing.

What I didn't love was having to feign interest in the country club gossip Frank and Caroline exchanged with their friends, but then Gemma strolled up. Much to my chagrin. After our kiss and the conversation that followed yesterday, I wasn't sure where we stood: friends, mortal enemies, or otherwise. Although, she didn't seem bothered by anything, her hair down and completely untamed with waves in every direction, T-shirt hanging off one shoulder, Aztec print shorts, and red Converse.

She waved to the group of mostly middle-aged golfers. "Hey. Where can I get an Arnold Palmer around here?"

I sucked my lips between my teeth to hide a growing grin as Caroline eased away from her friends, towing Gemma off to the side. "What're you wearing? That is not proper golf attire."

From under the shade of my baseball cap, I watched as Gemma shrugged. "I have a bra on."

This time, I covered my laugh with a cough. "Excuse me," I

said when Frank paused mid-sentence to glance at me. "Swallowed the wrong way."

"There's a dress code here," Caroline said, flapping her hand. "You can't stroll in here like a farmer."

"I doubt a farmer would wear this, Mom."

"You need to get a new outfit." Caroline pressed her hand to her temple, peeking over her shoulder, distress written all over her face as she spotted me. She waved me over. "Can you *please* help Gemma? She'll need clothes and clubs. Put it on Frank's tab." Before I could answer one way or another, she pointed a warning finger at Gemma. "My friends are over there, and I don't want them to see you dressed like that." She motioned her thumb to the pro shop. "Go."

Not wanting to rock the boat any further, I followed Gemma inside.

"That happen a lot?" I asked.

She fiddled through some shirts. "What?"

"Arguing over how you dress?"

"Since I was a kid. You'd think she'd be used to it by now, but I guess since she owns her own boutique, she assumes what I wear will reflect on her."

I shoved my hands into my pockets. "She's right, though."

Gemma shot her eyes up to me, a hanger in her hands like a weapon. "Excuse me?"

With the way her gaze narrowed and her tongue darted out to wet her lips, she reminded me of a snake. She could probably taste my fear on her tongue. And, damn it all to hell, it made my dick twitch.

"There is a dress code," I said, earning a quaint little sneer out of her. I lifted a shoulder. Even if there weren't rules about proper attire, I still liked getting a rise out of her.

"Well, seeing as how you are neither a mother nor a daughter, I think you should be quiet about this particular argument."

Glad to be off shaky ground with her—even if this ground was largely covered in mines—I leaned against a clothing rack, checking out the gloves displayed on the table next to it. "I heard you got a new car." I found a glove I liked and put it on. "I didn't think you knew how to drive."

"I know how to drive. I choose not to." She ripped a skirt and shirt off their hangers and gave me the evil eye on her way to the dressing room as I practiced my swing with an imaginary club.

On my second swing, I noticed she'd left the door to the dressing room slightly ajar, lending me an accidental view of her as she pulled her T-shirt over her head to reveal a blue bra. With her lithe curves and hair, she was like some kind of forest nymph, natural, almost ethereal, a breath of fresh air. And I inhaled as deeply as I could.

Which made me sneeze and Gemma's head shot over to me. She frowned at me, slamming the door. "Get enough of the show?"

I slapped my palm over my forehead and dragged it down my cheek with a groan. "Actually, no," I said, loud enough that she would hear. "It was an accident. You were the one who left the door open."

A few mumbled words came from the other side before the door opened again, and she strutted out in her new attire.

"You look nice."

"Shut up."

I waved for her to lead the way toward the counter, where I settled the tab and rented a bag of clubs. I offered to carry it for her, but she insisted she could do it—yet stumbled under the weight when she threw the strap over her shoulder.

Outside, Caroline formally introduced Gemma to her

friends and was met with a chorus of how she looked so much like her mom. Caroline wrapped her arm around her daughter, eating up the compliments while I tried to push the picture of Gem in her bra out of my mind.

I thought of how much a new pair of cleats would cost, how the trees had started to turn orange. How the wind picked up and would affect my swing, and how Gemma's bangs might settle in front of her eyes with each gust of air and how her nipples might pebble in the cool air.

Goddamn it.

I stalked away from the group, waiting until the caddies arrived with our golf carts. Frank and Caroline hopped in the first one, leaving Gemma and me to the second. When I got behind the wheel, she plopped down next to me with a sigh. "You're going to be insufferably good at this, aren't you?"

I only grinned as I drove us away.

At the first hole, Caroline started the round off, followed by Frank in his traditional argyle socks and cap. Next, Gemma stepped up to the tee, swung, and missed.

Frank coached her from a few feet away. "That's okay, try again. Keep your eye on the ball and follow through with your swing."

She tried again, digging up some earth.

"Don't worry about that." Frank pushed it back in with his toe. "Take another crack at it."

Caroline agreed. "Nobody's keeping score."

"I am," I volunteered with a raised hand.

Gemma pursed her lips at me before taking a third and fourth swing. Then she hauled off and threw the ball down the fairway. Even then, it didn't get very far.

"That's okay, that's okay," Frank said with a clap. "We'll work on it. Jay, you're up."

I set up and swung with a near-perfect follow-through, the ball sailing high into the sky.

"Attaboy," Frank cheered, and we all piled into the carts to move on, not even stopping for Gemma's ball.

When we closed in on the green, Frank tossed another ball down for Gemma after we easily sank our putts, but she kept missing by a few inches. Five tries later, it finally sank, and Frank patted her on the back. "Don't worry, you'll get the hang of it."

The thought had crossed my mind to offer my help, but I imagined the scowl she'd give me and thought better of it. Instead, I enjoyed watching her swing and miss in her short cream-colored skirt.

The next few holes followed the same pattern, Gemma taking a few mulligans and chunking up dirt. After the seventh fairway, she plunked down in the cart with a huff. "Besides doing a one-handed cartwheel on a Slip 'N Slide when I was twelve, this might possibly be the worst decision I've ever made."

"You may want to rethink your criteria for the worst decision ever. Save that honor for something really big like going on a hunger strike to save squirrels," I quipped, stepping on the gas, and Gemma jammed her Converse up on the dash of the cart to keep from falling forward.

"Can you not do that? And I've already been on a hunger strike. It wasn't that bad."

"You're kidding," I said, eyes wide.

"Of course I'm kidding. People go on hunger strikes when no other forms of protest are available. Come on, read a book every once in a while."

With a shake of my head, I maneuvered us behind Frank and Caroline's cart, idly wondering why her insults kind of turned me on. Was it the way her voice took on that edge of venom? Or was it the way her eyes sharpened, all predator-like? I didn't mind being her prey.

Next to me, Gemma hung her head back, allowing me a second to admire her throat as she said, "I can't believe people call this the greatest game ever played. This is the worst game ever played." She lolled her head to the side. "How much longer do we have?"

"It depends."

She rubbed her eyes. "On what."

"There are eleven more holes, and the more strokes that are taken, the longer it goes." I deliberately raised my brows at her. "Since you're the worst golfer I've ever played with, I figure another four hours."

"You are quite the charmer."

"I try."

The carts stopped at the next hole, and we all shuffled out except Gemma, who lounged along the bench, her feet on my seat. "I'm going to sit this one out."

"Are you sure?" Frank asked, readjusting his hat.

"Yeah, I need a little break."

I supposed she meant she needed to speed up the game a bit. Not that I disagreed with her, but I still checked in every once in a while. At the ninth hole, she braided her hair, asking me to grab the hair tie she dropped. At the tenth, she twisted her hair into Princess Leia buns and pretended to cut me in half with her lightsaber golf club. And on the eleventh, she sprawled out horizontally for a catnap.

After sinking my putt, I walked back to the cart and watched her for a moment. Her hair was spread out all over, while my aviators shielded her eyes from the sun. The collar of her shirt gaped open enough to allow a centimeter of blue to be seen, and that was all it took for my mind to race. That blue would star in my fantasies tonight, or rather, in a warm shower.

As if she could hear my thoughts—maybe she could, they were screaming in my head—she stirred awake.

"Is it over yet?"

"Nope." I swatted at her leg so she'd move over, allowing me to sit down. "Seven more holes to go."

"Ack."

At the next hole, Frank prodded Gemma to try again, and she halfheartedly agreed, yanking a club out of her bag without looking. She wound up and swung. *Whiff.*

"Go help her, Jay," Frank ordered, and I was nothing if not a dutiful son.

As she lined up to try again, I gripped the club in mid-swing. "First of all, you're using the wrong one. Here." I handed her a different club. "That was a wedge. This is a 3-iron."

Her face was blank. "Uh-huh."

"May I?" I asked, alluding to my forthcoming instruction, and she silently nodded. I guided her to the tee, where I engulfed her with my arms, showing her how to properly hold the club.

When her muscles stiffened, I began to back away, but she stopped me. "It's okay."

Relenting, I stepped closer, my chest flush against her back. "You're too tense. You need to loosen up. Breathe," I told her like it was so easy for me, her hair smelling of vanilla as it tickled my cheek. "That's good. Now, you want to keep your grip relaxed and a slight bend in your knees. Rotate from your hips and keep this elbow straight. Ready?"

I led her movements, lifting our arms up behind us, and in one fell swoop, the club struck the ball high into the air. We faced each other, and the sight of a blush creeping into her cheeks had me smiling.

"I did it," she said.

"*We* did it," I corrected.

She rolled her eyes, but the corner of her mouth tipped up.

"Good job, Gemmie," Caroline cheered.

"Yeah." I readjusted my hat. "Who's next?"

We moved down the fairway, and when it came to Gemma's turn again, she lined up behind the ball. This time, I didn't have to be told. I wrapped my arms around her, and she glanced back at me.

"Keep your eye on the ball," I directed, and those fiery brown eyes refocused. Together, we hit the ball all the way to the green, and I offered her a congratulatory little shoulder rub.

When we arrived to putt, I followed Gemma to her ball and placed my hand on top of hers to tap the ball into the hole. "You made par this time."

"That's good?"

"Yeah."

She twirled her club like a baton. "Getting pretty good."

I held my hand up for a high five, and when she slapped my palm, I curled my fingers around hers, tugging her close. "With my help. I don't think you could get that ball into the air without me."

She wrinkled her nose all adorable like an angry kitten. "We'll see."

At the next tee, she lined up solo and missed.

I slow-clapped. "I told you to loosen up." When she shot me a look, I strolled up behind her and put one hand on her hip, the other on her forearm. She connected with the ball and sent it flying. "God, I'm good."

She shouldered me, and it took all my self-control not to toss her over my shoulder in retribution. Maybe press her up against one of the trees lining the fairway.

At the next spot, I attempted to help her putt, but she pushed me away, saying, "I can do it. I can do it."

And she did. She sank the putt and danced past me, using her club like a cane. Obviously feeling her mojo now, she stepped up to the next tee, leveling her club at me. "I get this one into the air, I'm driving."

I bowed to her. "You don't, you buy me dinner."

"You're on." She stuck her tongue out of the corner of her mouth and wiggled her ass in quite possibly the cutest bout of concentration I'd ever witnessed. She swung, and after the ball rose into the air, she jumped up, whooping. "Get in, loser." She hopped in the driver's seat. "We're going shopping."

"Huh?"

"*Mean Girls*? No? Okay." She shook her head when I sat down next to her. "Never mind."

"Double or nothing?" I asked before she promptly took off, flinging me over a few inches, her laughter ringing in my ears.

CHAPTER THIRTEEN

I was woman enough to admit when I was wrong. Golf was fun...or, really, more than bearable. Because of Jason, that gorgeous jerk.

I liked the way he kept his arm up along the back of our bench seat in the cart, and how he gently coached me without a hint of superiority in his voice. The snug fit of his polo shirt didn't hurt either.

Yesterday, he was right when he'd said he thought I'd been into kissing him. I was *very* much into kissing him, and if it weren't for the way he'd gone about it, who knows what might have happened. Maybe I would've thrown my legs around his waist and pointed him to the back room, where we could have defiled the stock cabinets.

I liked a firm kiss and to be manhandled every once in a while, but I needed a say in the matter, particularly for the first time a guy touched me. Not that I ever felt in danger with Jason. He'd always been gentle—his verbal sparring notwithstanding—but I hadn't expected him to kiss me, and I was thrown off-balance.

I couldn't help the reaction I'd had, my mind spiraling backward. Though, I was glad to have my college experience out in the open, and happy he took it all in stride. He even seemed really emotional about it. The fact that he so easily understood my response confirmed he was a good guy and nothing like the one who still lingered at the back of my memories to pop up at the worst times.

And after our time together today, I could say I liked Jason.

When he parked the cart back at the clubhouse, I pouted. "That's it?"

He laughed. "We played eighteen holes."

"We did?"

"Well, *we* did. You slept through some." He nodded toward the restaurant deck, where my mom and Frank were finding a table. "Come on."

Then I *really* liked his hand on my lower back, palm pressing along my spine and his long fingers extending toward my hip possessively. I tended to prefer shorter guys, ones who had goofy smiles and played Scrabble, but there was something to be said about a tall man. One whose smile threatened a good time. I'm sure Jason would play Scrabble with me, though it might end with the pieces on the floor and me in his lap while we argued over a point score.

Once seated, he plucked something from my hair.

"I picked this just for you," he drawled, handing me a tiny leaf. I twirled it between my fingers, biting back a smile. How could I keep him at arm's length when he could be so cute?

"Oh my god, Jason!"

Oh, right. That's why.

Without seeing where the squeal came from, I could guess who it belonged to.

The statuesque woman strutted right up to our table, placing her hand on Jason's back. "I didn't know you'd be here," she said, massaging his shoulder in a demonstration of familiarity. "You never returned my texts from the other day."

With a fleeting look at me, Jason sat forward so that the woman's hand slipped off him.

"Aren't you going to introduce me?" She smiled, her teeth gleaming white against her honey-brown skin. She wore a pink-and-green sports dress and matching visor. Her straight black hair framed the petite features on her pretty face.

I didn't need an introduction. I already knew who she was.

Jason's shoulders rose when he took a deep breath, and I had to hand it to him. He had me fooled.

"Bridget, this is Frank Santos, my godfather, and his fiancée, Caroline, and her daughter, Gemma. Everyone, this is Bridget Pozo."

The infamous Bridget. Well, she was beautiful in that blindingly perfect way. If you liked that sort of thing. Jason apparently did.

"It's a pleasure," Bridget said.

"Pozo? As in Nelson Pozo?"

Bridget beamed. "Yes, that's my father."

Frank slapped his knee. "How about that! You tell him I said hello. I owe him a drink one of these days. Caroline, Nelson's the one who hosts once-a-month poker. He's married to Eileen Simpson."

"Oh. Oh!" My mother flicked her manicured hand at Bridget. "Yes, of course! Eileen and I have had a few drinks together. She's so wonderful. And, Bridget, doesn't your smile look just like hers. I wish I had her genes. She could pass for your sister."

Bridget lifted a slender shoulder, so put together I felt like a bridge troll next to her. "I think it's that lifetime's worth of skincare products she won from becoming Miss Illinois way back when."

"Well, whatever it is she's using, I'd like some."

My mother wasn't even fifty years old yet and already worried about becoming mummified. I flagged down a waiter, attempting to reign in my agitation. "Something with alcohol, please."

Bridget turned to Jason. "What dumb luck that you're here today, huh?"

"Dumb luck," I repeated, tapping the table with my index finger.

"Isn't it perfect weather for golfing?" Bridget asked no one in particular.

Frank nodded. "Did you play already?"

"No, we're about to. I love it. In fact, I'm in a tournament next week."

Caroline pinched Bridget's watermelon ensemble. "Aren't you the cutest thing? Would you like to have a seat?"

"I'd love to. Thank you."

Not able to take it anymore, I leapt up. "Here. Take mine."

Mom frowned. "But we didn't even eat yet."

"I'm not really all that hungry."

When she moved to stand, I stopped her. "No, don't get up. Sit and eat. I'll talk to you later." Then I gave a quick wave to the table and sped toward the parking lot.

Jason followed. Of fucking course. "Hey, Gemma, wait up a sec."

I didn't slow down, but he and his long legs caught up as I reached the car. "What's wrong?"

"Nothing."

He wrapped his fingers around my elbow. "You're upset."

"No, I'm not." I was spent. It was too draining to continue this pinball game. The up and down, back and forth, love and hate. It had to stop. He'd claimed Bridget was only a friend when I had asked him about her, but that wasn't the truth.

The facts were that Bridget called him at the Labor Day picnic, she'd picked up his phone when I had called the other night, and now, here she was, in the flesh, preening under his attention. Three strikes. I was done.

"I'm really sorry about all that," he said.

I slid on his sunglasses, having no intention of giving them back. After this fiasco, he deserved to lose something to me. Besides, I looked good in them. "You don't need to apologize. You don't owe me anything."

"I feel like after yesterday—"

"I don't care." I attempted to open my car door, but he leaned against it, hands in his pockets.

"But—"

"It's fine. Really. Hang out with whoever you want. I'm a big girl, I can handle it."

He pushed his hands through his hair. "I don't think you understand."

My shoulders caved in, tired of the conversation. "I do understand. I may not be an engineer or have my MBA, but I do understand."

"See," he growled, straightening to his full height. "Right away, you take it to this place it doesn't need to go. You get an idea in that pretty little head of yours and jump off the rails. You need to stop putting words in my mouth."

This situation was unmistakable. Whether he wanted to admit it or not, Jason and Bridget had some kind of relationship, and I had no desire to get in the middle of it.

"I jump off the rails?" I huffed. "Jason, that girl is in love with you. I'm not going to sit there and have it thrown in my face after you kissed me yesterday."

"It's not my fault she randomly showed up here."

"No, but it is your fault for leading me on."

He fisted his hands in his hair then tugged at the hem of his shirt. Once again, I took pleasure in his discomfort because my insides were so knotted up, I didn't know if I'd ever be able to eat again.

"I'm not leading you on!" he finally shouted, his words one big gust of air like he'd been holding it in.

I planted my feet wide so as not to be blown away. "Whatever you're doing, you need to figure it out. Because I'm not going to sit around like an idiot, waiting for any crumb of attention from you. Believe it or not, not everyone is impressed by your pretty-boy act. I'm certainly not."

With that, I got into my car and sped away, leaving him in my rearview mirror.

Jason

While pouring myself a coffee in the break room, my cell phone vibrated with another text from Bridget. Yet another I didn't bother to read. She had been nothing if not persistent over this last week.

After Gemma had skipped out on lunch at the golf course, I definitively ended things with Bridget, earning some tears from her. I'd been surprised she'd felt so deeply about me since my feelings were strictly surface level, but I couldn't keep acting as if what we had was anything close to real. Not since I'd discovered what real felt like.

I had hoped Gemma would have cooled off after a few days, and I could plead my case, but every time I tried to call her, I couldn't seem to find the right words. I didn't know how to explain that my entire world shifted when I met her, and that I didn't care about Bridget, not in the same way I cared about her.

I propped myself against the counter, rubbing at the back of my neck while wisps of my coffee's steam made their way toward me.

"Everything all right?"

I lifted my attention from my mug to Frank, at the door.

"Yeah, fine."

"All your hard work is finally paying off," he said, referring to the contract we signed this morning.

"Yep."

His brow crimped. "Are you worried about the project?"

"Nope." I thrust my hands into my pockets.

"Well, hell, Jay, you don't seem too excited."

"No, I am. I am. It's just..." I paused, attempting to gather my words and feelings together about his soon-to-be daughter-in-law. It would open up a can of worms, and I didn't know how to broach the subject.

Frank snapped his fingers. "Of course. I should have seen this before. My focus has been elsewhere lately."

"Huh?"

"You know I consider you my son, right?" he said, placing both of his hands on my shoulders, digging his thumbs into the soft spot below my collarbone, like he'd been doing for the last fifteen years, thinking it constituted a massage. In reality, it felt like two blunt dowels being shoved into my clavicle.

"When I agreed to be your godfather, I never dreamed in a million years you'd ever actually be placed in my care, but that was the best thing that ever happened to me. You are the best thing that ever happened to me. I'm getting married, but nothing will change the fact that you are my kid."

Frank's eyes teared, and I didn't have the heart to tell this man, who was my father in all ways but name, that I wasn't upset over his impending marriage. Instead, I smiled and let him continue.

"We'll still hang out, play golf. Whatever you want, whenever you want, I'm here for you." He hugged me, and I couldn't hide it anymore, my shoulders shaking. "It's okay, buddy," he said, patting my back. "Let it out."

I snorted out a laugh, and Frank froze. "Was that...?" He

stepped back. "What is wrong with you? I thought you were crying. Here you are laughing at me."

I doubled over, my eyes tearing. "I'm crying laughing." I stretched an arm out to him. "You're the best. Really. The best."

He towed me up to my full height. "And you're an ungrateful little shit."

"I thought I was your child, whom you so adore." I wiped my eyes then patted his shoulder. "In all seriousness, you've done a pretty good job being my dad."

He gently smacked my cheek before hugging me with a clap on the back. When we finally separated, he asked, "So, what's the real problem?"

I took a deep breath, combed my hand through my hair, and then told the truth. "Gemma."

Frank hit his fist on the counter. "I knew it! I knew it."

"You did not."

"Yes, I did." He aimed his finger at me. "I told you from the beginning. What did I say? I said she was good for you."

I bowed dramatically. "Yes. You are the master, the all-knowing."

"Uh-huh." Frank rocked back on his heels. "What about the other one? What's her name? Pozo's daughter?"

"Bridget."

"Yeah, Bridget. She seems like a nice girl."

"We broke up."

He ran a finger under his bottom lip. "You broke up? Thought you said she wasn't your girlfriend."

"You can't remember her name, but you remember I said that?"

Frank winked, his grin open wide, as open and wide as his heart. "What can I say? I only remember what I'm interested in."

I grunted into the cup of my coffee, almost spilling it over the rim when he slapped my shoulder.

"Either way, I'm rooting for you with Gemmie. But, listen, I need your help."

"With that?"

"I gotta get a tux."

Hours later, we were lost in a sea of formalwear.

"Oh hell, why are there so many to choose from? When I got married the first time, it was in a suit the color of shit."

"Nice." I slid my finger along the brim of the top hat on my head and swung a cane under my arm. "Are you going for the same look this time around?"

"That's why you're here. I'm not any good at this stuff. You're young. You're hip." Frank pulled me around the store. "What do you think?"

I pointed to a big poster hanging on one of the walls, male models all grinning. I assumed they were a groom and his groomsmen. "I think you're supposed to match. Like prom."

"Match?"

I nodded resolutely and flipped my cane in the air, catching it deftly as the door at the front of the store blew open. Gemma strutted in, her attention on her cell phone, a smile gracing her lips as she typed something and then laughed with a little shake of her head.

"What are you doing here?" Frank asked, peering out from behind a mannequin wearing a suede suit.

"Mom sent me to make sure you don't screw it up."

"Oh, thank god. Get over here." He moved to greet her with a hug, and she smiled but smothered it as soon as she spied me over Frank's shoulder.

Taking my top hat in hand, I offered her a low bow. She only rolled her eyes and then focused back on her phone as soon as Frank let go of her.

"So, let me get this straight," I said, sidling up next to her. "I saw your mom *scold* you for not following the dress code, and yet she sends you to pick out a wedding tuxedo."

She answered with gaze on her phone. "I know what's appropriate to wear to places, I just like to wear what I want. Rules or no rules."

"I'd expect nothing less." I tried to get a glimpse of her screen. "Who are you texting?"

"My best friends," she responded, head still down.

"Must be important."

She lifted her face and angled a brow—I loved that brow—then, without any warning, snapped a picture of me. She sent the picture to her text thread, her thumbs racing over the letters in some message I couldn't make out.

"What's that about?"

"My friend Sam is having a stressful day, so we're trying to make her feel better."

"And you thought a picture of me would help?" I didn't know whether to be proud or embarrassed.

She dropped her phone into her purse and smiled at the young man headed our way, speaking out of the corner of her mouth to me. "In that getup, yeah."

So, in that case, definitely embarrassed.

"Hi, my name is Remy," the kid said, pointing at his name tag. "What can I help you with today?"

"I'm Gem," she said then motioned to Frank. "And this is my future stepfather, Frank. We need a classic dinner jacket, no satin. Let's stick with one or two buttons."

Remy laced his hands together and nodded. "I like a girl who knows what she wants. You must've done this before."

She shrugged. "I've picked out a few tuxedos, yes. My personal marriage, no."

He inched closer to her. "That's good news for all us out there. We still have a chance."

I flung my top hat onto the head of a mannequin and set the cane in its hand, not bothering to tamp down my audible guffaw at the lines this kid was throwing down. He looked barely legal, a few hairs on his chin in a poor attempt at a beard. I didn't think Gemma would actually go for Remy, but she smiled sweetly at him as he led her to the back of the store, his hands gesticulating in the air as he spoke to her...about what, I didn't know. Maybe the white suit Gemma pointed to, or the fact that Remy could pass for the guy who played Harry Potter in the movies, glasses, bowl haircut, and all.

After a few minutes, the two returned with a tux. Frank nodded in appreciation and took it to the dressing room.

I held my hands up, waiting for one as well. "Do I get one too or...?"

Gemma seemed less than pleased to also have to help me, and she tossed her thumb back in my direction, saying to Remy, "Could you find one for him? He's the best man."

I expected her to have some sort of direction, like she had with Frank. Buttons and colors and whatever, but she just perched herself on a chair next to the dressing rooms and pulled her cell phone back out of her purse.

Remy wasted no time in picking out a few pieces for me to try on then led me back to the dressing room, where Gemma continued to ignore me.

Though, she had a pleasant discussion with Remy when he complimented her sweater.

Christ. This guy was like a puppy jumping at her feet for attention. He needed to cool it. Go lie down in the corner.

Frank sauntered out of the changing room in his tuxedo and spun around in front of Gemma, who rose to her feet. "You look fantastic. Really, really handsome."

"Yeah?" He grabbed her hand and twirled her under his arm. "I haven't worn a tux in years, not since..." He pointed to his gut with a chuckle. "I feel like James Bond, though, eh? What do you think?" He tugged on the lapels of the jacket.

"I guess you could pass for Sean Connery, if I squint."

He ruffled her hair. "Sean Connery wishes he was as handsome as me. Okay," he said with a clap of his hands. "You're up, Jay."

The latch on the dressing room door was broken, and I tried my best to close it before hanging the suit on the rack. Outside, I could hear Frank, Remy, and Gemma chatting about the wedding, and how soon alterations could be done. I stripped down to my black boxer-briefs and socks, and turned, reaching for the white shirt. That was when I noticed the door ajar.

And Gemma staring.

How ironic.

She dragged her eyes up from where they were settled somewhere below my hips. Frank's and Remy's voices had faded as if they'd walked away, so I pushed the door all the way open. "Fair is fair, I guess."

I gestured to my nearly naked body, allowing her a better view. She cleared her throat, stood up, and casually scanned me up and down as if she were window-shopping. I smiled gamely. She did not return it. Only walked away.

"It seems like you have everything under control here," I heard Gemma say as I stepped into the pants. "I'm going to head out." I rushed to get dressed, stumbling into the wall during the process.

"Gemmie, there's no other girl I'd want as my daughter," Frank said to her.

"You aren't so bad yourself."

"Shit." I sucked in a sharp breath when I pinched my middle finger in the zipper.

"I'll see you later," Gemma said, and then presumably to Remy, "Thanks for your help."

His chipper response had me rolling his eyes as I fumbled with the buttons of the shirt. "It was no problem at all. It was a pleasure meeting you. So...uh..."

Their voices started to fade, and I ripped the suit jacket off the hanger, the edge of the hard wood socking me in the eye. I hissed in pain and shoved the heel of my palm against it. "For fuck's sake!"

"What do you think about giving me your number? Maybe I could take you out this weekend?" Remy said, almost inaudibly to my ears.

I hurriedly shoved my arms through the tuxedo jacket, but by the time I got myself together and barreled out of the dressing room, Remy stood at the door, waving at Gemma. She was already in the parking lot.

CHAPTER FIFTEEN

Gem

The following Friday morning, my mom stopped by Bare Necessities, an unusual occurrence. I tossed down my phone, where I'd been reading an article about the Brazilian rainforest and sat up behind the counter. "What are you doing here?"

"I wanted to tell you we're going to Jason's house tonight."

"Okay."

She inspected the products next to the register, picking up each one. "You should be there around six."

"What? I'm not going."

"Why not?" She held a short, round tub. "What's this?"

"I have a date tonight, and it's lavender body butter. One hundred percent organic and vegan."

"Gemma Rose, why didn't you tell me you had a date?" She lit up in delight while digging out a dollop of lotion to smell. "With whom?"

"A guy I met when I was helping Frank at the tuxedo place."

"What's his name?"

"Remy."

"Is he cute?"

"Yes."

She rubbed the butter over her hands. "Well, I think you should come to the party first. A lot of Frank's coworkers will be there. Jason finalized that development project he's been working on. It's a big deal for the company, and they're celebrating."

I perked up. Despite his terrible track record with me, I was interested in his work. "Really?"

Mom found a lipstick and drew a small line of it on the back of her hand. "You have to come."

"I wasn't invited."

"Of course you were. We're all family now." When I chewed my lip in thought, she swatted at me. "Don't bite your lips. It's not—"

"Not ladylike."

Eyeing me, she snagged her wallet. "Exactly. And you need to come tonight to support Jason, for a little while, at least. He's important to Frank, and Frank's important to me."

"Fine. But only for a few minutes."

"Good, and I'll take the lipstick and lotion."

I pulled up to Jason's block a little after six. He lived in a townhouse which boasted a two-car garage, basketball hoop, and perfectly groomed landscaping. A few familiar faces greeted me as I entered the front door, and with a quick glimpse around, I noted the house was bigger than it appeared from the outside, with a huge flat-screen in the living room along with every piece of technology and gaming system imaginable in the entertainment unit. Surround sound music echoed in every room, over the din of all the chatter.

I found my mom sipping red wine in the kitchen. She kissed my cheek.

"Honey, you look so sweet. Where'd you find that dress?"

"Thrift store."

"Looks like something from Nordstrom." She touched the straps crisscrossing over my back. "It gives you a nice shape."

"Thanks." I tugged on the blue and gray dress with cutouts at my waist.

She lifted her glass, motioning in a circle. "So, what do you think of the house?"

"It's very...beige."

"I know, right?" she whispered. "He's been here for a few years now, but it's so...blah." She poked my hand. "Frank's on the deck smoking a cigar, but I don't know where Jason ducked off to. Why don't you see if you can find him?"

When she physically shoved me away, I begrudgingly went on the hunt, starting with a self-guided tour of the second floor. The first room held an ironing board, a few cardboard boxes, and a desk. The room next to it had only a twin bed, along with a nightstand in the corner. There was a bathroom and laundry room and, at the end of the hallway, double doors. Nosy, I opened them and tiptoed into the master bedroom, like a spy crossing enemy lines. On the right, Jason's clothes filled up less than half the space of the huge walk-in closet. I inspected the attached bathroom, a herringbone-tiled floor with a shower in the corner. The clear glass doors spread from floor to ceiling, and it had more than enough room for two people. Circling back around, I settled my attention on the king-size bed held up on a plain black bed frame, bookended by night tables on each side. An overstuffed gray chair sat in the corner beside one small chest of drawers.

An unbidden scene unfolded before me, and I closed my eyes to it, hoping to drive it away. But my mind had other ideas. My blood heated, envisioning Jason carrying me through the double doors. I recalled the taste of him when he kissed me, the warmth of his tongue, the pressure of his hands in my hair, tenderly pushing it back from my face.

My heart tripped over itself as I imagined that same pressure all over my body. His fingers on my hips, stomach, breasts, between my legs. My spine tingled as I pictured us in the shower. I could almost smell the now-familiar scent of his skin and wondered what it might feel like soaped up with bubbles. Soft and hot as water sluiced over his muscles, the planes of his back, the ridges of his abdomen, that length of him which I'd gotten a glimpse of in the tux shop.

I ached for it to be real, for some relief. My nipples pebbled and my thighs clenched together, every part of me aware of how close I was to Jason now. Here, in his bedroom, in his innermost sanctum. If only—

"Hey, you."

I jumped, clutching at my chest, and whirled around. Jason knocked the breath right out of me, and I couldn't speak as he stood, leaning against the doorjamb, hands in his pockets. "Sorry, didn't mean to scare you."

Sudden cottonmouth made anything more than one syllable impossible. "Hi."

He tilted his head to the side, regarding me with his careful, cool gaze. "Are you okay?"

I nodded, fidgeting with my dress as his eyes roved over me. I wasn't often this dolled up. I'd pulled my hair back in a sleek ponytail and wore dark makeup, and he seemed to appreciate it.

"You look beautiful."

The compliment, though simple, had my heart racing at its honesty. "Thank you."

His lips turned up in an easy smile. "I like that dress on you."

Here he was, totally calm and casual, having absolutely no idea that I'd been fantasizing about how many places we could have sex in this room. I felt the blush creeping up my cheeks and excused myself with a mumbled apology then hightailed it downstairs as fast as my feet would carry me in the cursed wedge sandals my mother had given me for my birthday.

Back in the kitchen, I found Frank and my mother cuddled up together in the corner. He immediately drew me in for a hug. "How are you? Want something to drink?"

"No. I've actually got to leave. I have a date."

"Who has a date?" Jason asked, joining us.

"I do," I said, scratching at a cut in the wood of the butcher block island. "With Remy."

"You're kidding. The tuxedo guy?"

He didn't have to sound so shocked. "Yes."

"The Harry Potter guy? Seriously?"

"Yes." I reminded myself to unclench my jaw. "Why? You don't think anyone would want to take me out?"

He heaved out a long breath like I was such a chore. "No. I didn't say that."

"That's what it sounds like you're saying."

"Maybe you need to get your hearing checked," he said, over enunciating each word like he was itching for a fight.

Well, he got one.

"I don't see Bridget anywhere."

"She wasn't invited."

"No? That's too bad." I crossed my arms. "Guess it's on to the next one."

"You are—"

"All right." My mom stuck her hand out, tapping her watch. "Gemmie, don't you have to go? It's almost seven."

I tucked my little black purse into the crook of my elbow, kissed Mom and Frank, and pivoted.

I should've known Jason would follow me outside.

"Gemma, wait."

"Nope. I'm late."

The door slammed shut. "You are exasperating, you know that?" He caught me around the waist, spinning me to face him. "Utterly exasperating."

"I'm not interested in what you think about me," I said, slipping out of his grasp to fix my dress from where the cut-out slanted out of place. His gaze lingered there for a few moments before trekking up to meet mine, but not without spending time at my breasts, neck, and lips.

His brows narrowed over his eyes, somehow both freezing blue and burning hot. "I'm sorry, Gemma."

"Okay." I nodded then went off on my merry way to meet Remy.

"Gem—"

I held my hand up behind my head. "Bye, Jason."

He didn't tail me to my car. Thank god. I didn't know how much fight I had left in me until I finally gave in.

CHAPTER SIXTEEN

With mere days until the wedding, I rode my bike to yoga for some extra relaxation. I needed time to enjoy the quiet of nature to center myself for class. Mom had called no fewer than three times every day for the past three days with a number of emergencies. First with her hair not being dyed the right color, then the wedding singer coming down with a sinus infection, and as of yesterday, a meltdown about a thirty-percent chance of rain. I'd invited her and Frank to come to my class then immediately turned my phone off, hiding it in her closet for good measure. One more frantic phone call and it might have gone down the toilet.

"Hello! Hello!" My mom chirped

I got up from my position on the floor. "You actually came."

"You said it would help." She dropped her bag in the corner of the room. "I tried calling you last night and this morning."

"Sorry," I mumbled as I high-fived Frank, who wore sweat-pants and a T-shirt a tad too tight around his belly.

He halfheartedly stretched side to side. "Is this going to be hard?"

I grabbed a yoga mat from one of the extras in the back and tossed it to him. "You'll be fine."

"Why do I not believe you?"

I laughed as a few more people filed in. After greeting my regulars, I stepped in front of the room, taking my usual spot at the top of my orange mat. That was when I spotted Jason, his tall form ducking in while I began my introduction.

"Good evening and welcome. This is an all-levels Vinyasa flow class." I raised my brow at Jason in question. "I'm surprised to see so many new faces."

He replied silently by tipping his chin toward my mom and quietly removed his sneakers then found an open space in the back with one of the extra mats.

I refocused and brought my hands to my heart, determined not to give him any more attention than necessary. If he wanted to waste an hour trying to impress my mother, that was his prerogative. "I invite you all to start by planting your feet firmly on the earth, breathing deeply, in through your nose and out through your mouth."

I began the class with some cleansing breaths then moved through sun salutations. In the front row, my mom easily transitioned from one pose to the next, while Frank grunted with every exhale. During the more advanced moves, I took some time with each student for support or gentle correction, although it took a minute to get Frank unstuck from reverse warrior.

"I thought you said this would be easy," he rasped, finally standing upright.

I'd never laugh at any of my students, but I needed to bite my lip to keep a straight face. "I never said easy."

He wiped sweat away from his forehead. "I don't think I'm going to make it to Saturday. I may have a heart attack before then."

"Don't worry. I'm first aid certified," I whispered, patting his back, then continued instruction on to the next pose. "Nice long inhale, and on your exhale, slowly transition into side angle pose."

Everyone followed the direction except for Frank, who bent to touch his toes, only getting halfway there.

"If you're feeling good today, you can always extend out into half-moon pose."

A few of the students moved onto one leg and hand, and I readjusted some before approaching Jason, who attempted the pose, though it was all wrong. "Turn out from your center."

"I have no idea what that means." His usually smooth voice was ragged, but I hesitated to help him. His head hung upside down, his face red and pinched together. "I'm feeling a little light-headed down here."

After everything—the constant arguing, the kiss, the whole Bridget situation—I didn't want to be nice to him, but this was my yoga class. I *had* to be nice. "Then pick your head up. Your neck is an extension of your spine. Keep it straight." I placed one hand on his back. "And open up from your hips."

"They are open," he groaned.

I pushed on his hip. "Like this."

His right leg swung higher into the air, and then he came tumbling down, taking me with him. His long legs pinned me to the floor as he grinned, hair flopped over his forehead. He leaned up on one elbow. "Like this?"

A laugh escaped before I could stop it, and everyone in the studio paused to see what the kerfuffle was.

"Sorry," Jason said to the class. "My bad." He untangled himself from me and stood, offering his hand down to help me up off the floor. "You okay?" When I nodded, he slanted his head, playful alarm in his crinkled brow. "Is the drop-in fee extra if I break the instructor?"

"No." I tucked loose hair that had fallen out of my ponytail behind my ear. "I'm fine."

He hit me with his steely gaze full on, silently mouthing *Good*, his pinkie finger brushing my forearm as he stepped forward on his mat. The dimmed lights, slightly heated temperature, and soothing chime music were all meant to be comforting, but with that tiny touch, it all whirled together like a hurricane, and Jason and I were in the eye of the storm. I'd already been so aware of my body, so connected with the energy flowing in and out of every person, the charge between us was a heavy, pulsating thing. In that moment, everything became sharper.

The sweat dotting his upper lip.

The soft fiber of his T-shirt, clinging to his chest.

The burn of his eyes on me.

I wanted more, wanted to stay in this bubble, but someone coughed, and Jason blinked away.

I folded my fingers into my palms, bringing awareness back to my body. I was in the middle of teaching class; I couldn't go all gooey-eyed now. Pivoting away from Jason, I shook out my arms. "When you're ready," I said, clearing my mind as much as possible, "slowly bring your right foot to meet your left, forward fold."

A few minutes later, with everyone stretched out on their backs, I couldn't quite shake the tension away, even as I directed the class to breathe, reading my daily affirmation in a low voice. I should have been quieting my own thoughts, yet my mind constantly drifted back to Jason and his soft smile and the feel of his fingers around mine. When I opened my eyes to check on the class, I found him staring straight at me.

You feel this too?

"Thank you for sharing your practice with me, and I look forward to seeing you all next week," I said, bowing slightly toward the class before turning the lights all the way up.

Frank stayed on the floor. "This was torture."

"I thought it was wonderful." Mom wrapped an arm around me. "Frank, sweetheart, come on. While I'm feeling energetic, I want to go home and go over the seating arrangement one last time."

"Sorry, I can't. I live here now. On this mat. Gemmie, you'll need to bring me some food every once in a while."

Jason shook his head with a chuckle, and the sound tickled my skin. His laugh would haunt my dreams.

"Come on, big guy," he said and hoisted Frank up.

I escorted them all outside into the cool night air, a shock to my overheated body, then locked the door to the studio. From the car, Mom waved out of her window. "Rehearsal is at five o'clock. Don't be late, Gemma. Jason, you're a peach." Frank beeped the horn once, and Mom blew a few kisses. "Love you both!"

"I'm not always late," I muttered, grabbing my bike from the rack, and Jason stopped in his tracks.

"Where's your car?"

"At home."

He dropped his head back to his shoulders, letting out a growl. "Wasn't it bought for you so you don't have to ride that thing?"

"I guess."

He threw his arm out to the side, scolding me like it was his favorite thing to do. "Then why are you still using your bike?"

I glared at him. "Because I like it."

"Get in." He opened the door to his truck.

"I'm good, thanks."

He tilted his head toward it. "Get in."

"Nope." I threw one leg over the bicycle and settled my feet on the pedals.

"Don't be so stubborn." He stalked over to me, trapping the front wheel between his legs. "We've done this before." He shrugged, and I hated it. "You know I win this one. Get in my truck, Gemmie," he said with a smirk.

And I hated that too. All he did was shrug and smirk. Smirk and shrug.

"You're the worst." I hopped off the bike, making sure to shove the handle bar into his stomach on the way. But if I wasn't mistaken, his eyes flared in a challenge.

He enjoyed fighting with me.

Once we were inside his truck and buckled in, he took off down the street, the last vestiges of the sunset leaving traces of deep purple on the horizon while the navy night sky twinkled with stars above us.

"It's really not safe for you to be riding a bike when it's so dark," he told me.

"I have reflectors." I picked at my long-sleeved bright-white zip-up, evidence that people could see me on the bike.

"But you never know who's on the road. I know you'll be fine, it's the other people I don't trust."

In all of our conversations, I'd never heard him like this before. Jason's voice was always full of certainty, laced with a little humor. Even when we were picking fights with each other, I'd come to expect and sort of look forward to the hint of arrogance.

But this, this voice, was something I had never heard.

It sounded like...like he actually cared for me.

That possibility was a little too suffocating, so instead of pursuing that line of thinking, I changed the subject. "Class was a bit of a struggle for you, huh?"

He kept his eyes on the road, left hand on the steering wheel, his right elbow on the console between us. "The human body isn't supposed to bend like that."

I bit back a smile.

"At least I didn't fall asleep," he said, referring to Frank letting out a rumbling snore during Shavasana.

I didn't hide my laugh as I tugged my hair tie out, my hair blowing around my face from the window opened halfway. But I did ignore Jason's double take from the other side of the truck.

"How was your date?" he asked after a minute, and I bent closer to the open window for more air.

"Fine."

"Going on a second?"

When I didn't answer, he hummed inquisitively. "I knew it wouldn't work out. He's what? Fifteen?"

"Twenty-two," I corrected, not sure how I felt about Jason being so positive the date would be a flop.

"Probably majoring in something ridiculous like philosophy."

"He's a political science major."

Jason snorted. "He's a child."

"He is not a child," I said defensively. The date wasn't terrible, but we also had nothing in common. "He's planning on moving to DC after he graduates and is working to put himself through school."

He harrumphed. A literal harrumph. "What could you possibly have talked about? Double-breasted jackets? The subtle differences between white and ivory?"

It almost sounded like he was jealous, and my spine tingled at the possibility. "We didn't talk about jackets."

"Colors, then?"

I huffed. "I'm sure I had as much fun with Remy as you have with Bridget."

He stopped at a red light and fixed his eyes on me. "So you didn't have any fun?"

I could lie, but what would be the point? He'd already

sniffed out the truth. "I wanted to stab a fork in my ear so I didn't have to listen to him." When he snickered, I jabbed a finger in his direction. "Why are you laughing? You just admitted you don't have any fun with your girlfriend."

"Yep," he said without any preamble then drove on when the light turned green.

I bobbed my chin, unsure what to say. "Well...what... Why are you with her?"

He parked in front of my apartment building and let out a loud exhale, his hand raking through his hair. "I'm not with her."

I didn't know what to believe at this point. Bridget, like a ghost, showed up at the most inopportune times, spoiling any momentum Jason and I had gained. "Whatever you say."

He paused mid-step out of the truck and glanced over his shoulder, his face softening from frustration into something that appeared an awful lot like regret. "Gemma, I'm not with her. She isn't the one I have feelings for."

My breath caught, and I had trouble moving, my hand frozen on the door handle.

"Come on," he said, "let's get you upstairs." He hopped out of the truck, pulled down my bike, and was halfway to the door before I remembered how to walk again.

After setting my bicycle against the living room wall, Jason glanced around the room, his hand on the back of his neck. "I, uh, guess I'll see you tomorrow." He stepped to the door. "Bye, Gem."

I had felt stifled by him and this *thing* between us all night, but now that his back was to me, I couldn't stand to see him leave. "Wait!"

He whirled back around, eyebrows raised, hair drooping toward his right eye.

"You called me Gem."

His smile was endearingly confused. "That is your name, isn't it?"

"You've only ever called me Gemma, like I'm some naughty child."

He let out a deliciously horse laugh. "Well, if the shoe fits."

We stood staring at each other for a while, my heartbeat in my ears. "Do you—" I cleared my throat. "Do you want a snack or something? I'm kind of hungry."

His gaze roved over me, and I picked at the hem of my jacket, my bare feet rubbing against each other after I'd kicked off my shoes. As if he really liked my chipped toenail polish, he grinned. "Yeah, me too."

He was an absurd man, and I don't know why I liked him so much.

I pulled out hummus and chips, while he sat down on one of my mismatched chairs, scooting it away from Mr. Clooney, who lounged on his back on top of the table. His silver eye followed Jason's actions.

"Your cat's freaking me out."

"George, off the table." I snapped, and he vaulted from the table to a cabinet by the doorway to the couch in the living room.

"That's pretty impressive to do with one eyeball."

"He's missing an eye, not a leg," I said, pouring us drinks into mason jars.

"What is that?" His lip curled up slightly at the sight of the whitish liquid.

"Coconut water."

He lifted one of the glasses. "If it's water, why isn't it clear?"

I sipped some from my own glass. "Because it comes from a coconut." When he held it aloft, examining it from side to side as if he'd find a bug or something in it, I jostled his shoulder.

"It's full of nutrients and replenishes electrolytes after a work-out. Try it, it's good."

"I highly doubt that," he said with a skeptical eyebrow raise.

"You liked the vegan burger." I pushed the glass toward his mouth with one finger on the bottom. "Don't be such a baby."

He grumbled something unintelligible then took a big gulp.

"So?"

He wagged his tongue. "Gross. Tastes like a mix of feet and cereal milk that was left out overnight."

"How many toes have you been sucking on that you know what feet taste like?"

"Hey, don't kink shame," he said with a cringe. "And I'm assuming that's what feet taste like." He wiped at his mouth. "It's offensive to call that water. How do you drink that?"

"I have to change. Help yourself to whatever." I poured him a glass of regular old tap water then ambled down the hall, smiling to myself. At least he tried it. Most people didn't even taste my vegan offerings. I shucked off my jacket and lifted my oversized T-shirt over my head before I discovered it.

The monster in the corner.

I screeched reflexively, my phobia in control of my body. "Jason!"

"What? What's wrong?" He bounded down the hall instantly, running into me as I sprinted from my bedroom. We collided with an *oof*, and he seized my shoulders, a half-eaten chip still in his hand, as his eyes scanned my body in panic. "Are you hurt?"

My palms were already wet with sweat. "Spider."

"What?"

"In my room." I shivered. "There's a gigantic spider in my room. You have to kill it."

"You're kidding."

When I shook my head, he shoved the rest of his chip into his mouth and pressed his lips together, suppressing his stupid smile, and I bounced on my toes, covering my eyes. "Please, Jason, don't laugh at me. Please."

He skimmed his fingers back and forth over my shoulders. "All right. Okay. It's okay. I'll take care of it."

As I followed close behind, he walked down the hall to my bedroom, his head on a swivel, probably taking in the hand-drawn pictures everywhere, the clothes piled up on my unmade bed.

"Where is it?"

"There." I pointed over his shoulder.

"Where?"

"Right there." I grimaced. How could he miss it? It was enormous. "By the bed, on the wall."

"Oh, that little thing?"

"Little?" I nearly shouted. "It's huge! Like a half-dollar!"

He grabbed a tissue and promptly killed it. "A half-dollar? I don't think I've ever seen that coin in real life, and this thing was, like, a dime at most."

"Is it dead?"

He held the tissue open to me, with black legs mangled in every direction. I threw my arms up, squirming and sputtering.

"Coming from the girl who doesn't eat things with mothers," he mocked, tossing the arachnid corpse away in the trash before turning back to me. His cocky grin dropped, and he paused in the middle of whatever he was about to say. His attention leisurely tracked down my body, in contradiction to how he'd studied me in alarm mere moments ago.

This time, his eyes blazed, pupils widening, and I suddenly realized—two seconds after Jason did—that I only had my leggings and sports bra on. My skin dotted with goose bumps, and I crossed my arms over my chest, hiding my hard nipples.

"Are you cold?" he asked, stepping closer.

"No, spiders make my skin crawl."

But it was too late. He knew the truth, the sound rough when he let out a low, "Mm-hmm."

Slowly, he reached up and skimmed his thumb and index finger down a wave of my hair. "You amaze me sometimes."

"In a good or bad way?" Between his concentrated stare and gentle touch, he was dragging me into him like some gravitational force, and I had to hold on to his forearm for balance.

"In a very good way." He dropped his head a fraction of an inch, so close yet so far away.

"You think I'm some naughty child." My words were barely a whisper.

His tongue traced his bottom lip, his teeth scraping over it, and I wanted that to be me. Pressing up onto my toes, I weaved away from him slightly, and he caught me with a hand on my waist. I felt each of his fingertips press into my side.

"You have no idea," he rasped, my skin prickling almost to the point of pain, desperate to be soothed.

"About what?" I asked, so close I could smell the hint of salt on his breath from the chips.

He swallowed thickly, his throat working hard. "What I would do to you."

Oh god. My nipples ached with every passing second, my core throbbed with arousal, eager for relief, and yet he held back. Waiting for permission.

What an absurdly perfect man.

"Kiss me, Jason."

And that was it. His mouth met mine in an explosion of *finally*.

Finally, I gave up the battle I'd fought against him.

Finally, I felt the plushness of his lips and the scrape of his teeth.

Finally, I could let go of the anxieties holding me back.

I wrapped my arms around his neck, bringing my body flush with his. I could feel his hard cock against my stomach, and I *needed* to be closer. At my whimper, he picked me up, urging my legs around his waist to walk me backwards until I was pressed up against the wall.

"Fuck, Gem," he breathed, his lips brushing along my jaw as he thrust one hand into my hair, the other tight on the outside of my thigh. He ground his length against me as he adjusted the angle of his lips, coaxing my tongue out to meet his. He kissed like he fought, to win, to bend me to his will.

This time I was going willingly.

He released his hold on my hair to trail his hand down to my chest, his thumb brushing over my nipple. The elastic didn't make it easy on him, but he finagled my strap down low enough so he could put his mouth on the top of my breast, his tongue hot and wet. Then his teeth were on me, and I yelped.

"You bit me!"

He raised his head, a lazy, lust-filled smile crawling across his face. "I wanted to for a long time."

"Jesus, you're going to kill me." I slumped my head back against the wall, and he dragged his hand up past my collarbone to my throat, where his fingers rested against my hammering pulse.

"I should go."

"What? No."

He situated the strap of my sports bra in place then gently dropped my feet to the floor before not so surreptitiously adjusting his pants. "Yeah."

I shook my head. "You don't have to. We didn't even get to eat anything."

"I'm not hungry right now." He curled his hand around my neck and bent to nip at my collarbone. "At least not for food."

"But—"

"Let me be a gentleman tonight, huh?" He placed a lingering kiss below my ear then rested his forehead against mine. "We gotta big couple of days coming up."

I couldn't argue with that, but also...he could stay a little bit longer.

He straightened up to his full height and plucked at my pouty bottom lip with his thumb, grinning my favorite crooked smile. I was no match for that smile. All his smiles, really, but especially that one. My body drooped against his, my head on his chest so I could hear the rumble under my ear when he said, "I won't be so gentlemanly next time."

"Promise?"

He caught my chin between his fingers, forcing me to look at him. "I promise." He kissed me once more. "You need a ride tomorrow?"

"In the red Transformer out there?"

He squinted one eye thoughtfully in an attempt at being cute. It worked. "I was thinking the Mercedes."

"That's worse than the truck. How about I pick you up in my new electric car?"

"Am I even allowed in it with red meat and gasoline in my veins?" He toggled his eyes between my own as if he were memorizing the exact color of them.

"I'll permit it this one time," I said, and he nodded, sliding his fingertips down my cheek, blazing a trail of fire.

"Good." Then he kissed me once more, so sweet and tender, my heart fluttered, endeavoring to fly out of my chest. "Have a good night."

Before I could snap myself out of my daze, he'd walked out

of my bedroom and down the hall, calling back, "Pick me up at four thirty."

Then he was gone with a quiet snick of the front door. I flung myself onto the bed, one arm over my feverish forehead. I was in trouble.

CHAPTER SEVENTEEN

Jason

By the time Gemma arrived at my house, I was already waiting by the curb. Coming to a stop, she rolled down her window, and I ducked my head to see her. "You know what time it is?"

She pursed her lips, glancing at the clock on her dash. "Uh...4:37. Why?"

"Do you genuinely not realize you're late, or do you not care?"

"Oh." She let out a carefree little laugh.

"Oh?" I opened the passenger side door and dropped into the seat, adjusting it so my legs had more room. It was only marginally better. "That's all?"

"What? I'm seven minutes late, big deal."

"Gemma."

Her teeth sawed into her lower lip, doing nothing to contain her amusement. "Jason."

I tugged at my hair, my stress about being late ratcheting up. "It takes, like, twenty minutes to get to the country club from here on a good day."

"Yeah." She nodded and pulled into the street. "We'll get there right on time."

I wiped my hands down my face in irritation, and when

she giggled, I leveled her with an annoyed gaze, "I can't with you right now."

"Relax. We'll be there in plenty of time."

"I can't relax when traffic will add at least ten minutes to the drive time." If there was one thing she had to know about me, it was that I was *always* on time. "I'm buying you a watch."

"A watch? Who wears watches anymore?"

I stuck out my left arm. "I do."

Briefly taking her eyes off the road, she held on to my wrist, twisting the brown leather strap back and forth. "Yes, you do."

She sounded all squeaky and very un-Gem-like. "What's the voice for?"

"You have nice hands, is all." She let go of me, and I settled my hand in her lap, gripping her cotton-covered thigh. She wore some kind of adult onesie pants thing. I didn't understand it, but she looked damn good in it.

"You have nice everything," I said in possibly the least suave compliment I'd ever given. She glanced my way, her dark eyes sparkling with mirth, and my mouth was a runaway train. "You're gorgeous, but I hate that you're so tardy all the time."

"Tardy," she repeated, laughing again, and the fact that I could put that look on her face, tease that unabashed sound from her, made me feel ten feet tall. "Sorry, Principal Mitchell," she said seriously, "it won't happen again."

"Already on to role-playing, huh?" I sucked in a breath, tightening my grip on her thigh. "I could get down with that."

She flicked at the collar of the white button-down I wore under a camel-colored sweater. "You look very academic."

I rubbed my palm up and down the length of her thigh, and she pressed her legs together, trapping my fingers so I couldn't continue toward the triangle of heat there. I leaned closer to her. "You like it?"

She lifted one shoulder, a few strands of hair falling out of her loose braid, and she tucked them behind her ear, her cheeks blooming red, goosebumps breaking out across the skin of her arm. "I'm not feeling super well-behaved, if that's what you're asking."

"Are you ever?" My mind reeled with possibilities of what I could do to this misbehaving girl, starting with stripping her of that black one-piece suit and bending her over the nearest hard surface.

"I don't like being told what to do," she said as if I didn't know.

"Yeah, I got that."

"And you can't help but follow directions."

I nodded. We were polar opposites, two hemispheres with completely different seasons, and I didn't know if we could ever meet in the middle, but I was damn sure interested. I'd always wanted to visit the equator. Being with Gemma felt like that, blistering heat. Burning sensations everywhere. Hell, that kiss yesterday was enough to consume me late into the night. The early birds had begun to chirp before I'd finally gotten the taste of her lips and feel of her legs wrapped around me out of my mind.

That's what she did. Made me feel out of myself, a little out of control, and I liked it.

But I didn't like arriving ten minutes after five. Caroline frowned up at me as if it'd been my fault, and I pointed at Gemma with one hand, holding the other up in innocence.

"Snitch," she hissed, batting at my stomach.

"Let's get this rehearsal started, then," Caroline said, gesturing to a woman in a light-pink pantsuit, although rehearsal was a loose term.

The real ceremony was slated to last only thirty minutes or so, but they spent over an hour staging the entire thing, poring over every word, line for line, and each tiny movement, before practicing the kiss a few times to make sure it wasn't "too showy." As Caroline and Frank spoke with the officiant, Gemma and I were banished to the corner to fold programs.

I creased the corners at exact angles while she gave up after one minute and found a pen to play tic-tac-toe, poking me every few seconds to make my X mark.

"These look great," Caroline said, finally finished up. "Thank you both."

"No problem." Gemma smiled up at her mother, and I yanked on her hair. She fluttered her eyelashes at me.

She thought she was cute.

"Oh, but look at this," Caroline said, motioning to the table settings which had already been put up for the following day. "These napkins are all wrong."

Frank stepped in, struggling to release the taupe cloth napkin from Caroline's death grip. "I know you want everything to be perfect, but you have to let the people here do their job. I don't want you stressed out."

"These ugly folded napkins are stressing me out. They're supposed to look like a rosebud, not a cone."

"I think they look okay," Gemma said, but her mother was determined.

"Honey, honey." With one last hard tug on the cloth, Frank wrestled the napkin from Caroline's death grip and tossed it me. "We'll be late for dinner." He kissed her temple. "I love you and I respect your wishes for a napkin to be folded like a rose, but if you want a groom with both of his arms, you better leave now because I am ready to chew one off."

"Oh, you." She rolled her eyes in a rare display of impatience, but one I'd seen her daughter wear on multiple occasions. "Let's go. Where did you make the reservations?"

"Somewhere real nice. Very lively."

We found ourselves in front of a massive stone building with a neon orange-and-blue sign.

Caroline scrunched up her face. "Who are Dave and Buster? I thought we were going to hibachi."

Gemma slapped a hand over her mouth and tucked her face into my shoulder, hiding her snort-laugh. I dragged a knuckle over my top lip, much smoother about it.

"I think we could all use some old-fashioned amusement, especially you, *mi vida*," Frank said, opening the door. "Let's eat some greasy food."

Caroline stepped cautiously inside. "I don't know about the grease. Oil and satin gowns do not go well together."

We were shown to our table, where the bride-to-be decided on a liquid diet. One-and-a-half fruity drinks later, she joined an air hockey game with a middle school kid. She tugged up her skirt, trying and failing to bend far enough over the table, balancing on one foot, her other shoe somewhere under the game table.

When she scored, she whirled around, waving. "Gemmie! Gemmie, look, I made it!"

I elbowed Gemma. "She looks like you."

"Like me?"

"Messy hair, shoes off, tipsy. That's you."

She feigned anger, wielding a piece of edamame—one of the few vegan options—at me. "Are you accusing me of being a bad influence?"

I stole the pod from her. "You were the one who convinced her to order the second drink."

"And," she started, motioning to her mother, "she no longer cares about rosebud napkins. Ergo, we don't have to care about rosebud napkins. You're welcome." Then she flicked another stalk at me and got up from the table to meet Caroline.

I squeezed the beans out with my teeth and tossed the

empty pod down into the basket, watching as Gemma slung her arm around her mom's shoulders. Even though they argued a lot, the bond they had was strong. Anyone could see it.

Across from me, Frank chomped on a big bite of his burger. "Things are going good."

"Is that a question?"

He shook his head, chewing, and motioned toward Gemma with a ketchup-covered thumb.

I smiled, watching as she bent down, trying to put her mom's heel back on. "Yeah, things are good."

Swallowing, Frank wiped off his hands. "I like her for you."

I turned away from the mother and daughter pair, now laughing about something. "You trying to make us into some kind of Brady Bunch?"

"No, I'm serious."

And that was exactly what scared me.

Only a few weeks ago, Frank had spouted off about Gemma being fun and how I needed more fun in my life, but it wasn't that simple. In less than twenty-four hours, Frank would marry Caroline. I wasn't related to Frank biologically, but we were family, nevertheless, meaning Caroline would also become family, and I couldn't take this blossoming thing between Gemma and me lightly. The repercussions of it going wrong would ripple, not only for the two of us, but also for Frank and Caroline.

If I was going to do this, I had to go all in. Or not at all.

Gemma reappeared next to me, her eyes bright with joy, Caroline's hand in hers. "I think the clock has struck midnight for this Cinderella."

Caroline's smile drooped to the side. "Gemmie told me about a potato remedy for dark circles. Do we have potatoes at home?"

Frank tossed his balled-up napkin down onto his plate. "I think so. If not, I'll stop at the store."

"You're too good to me," she said, having trouble with her cardigan, and Gemma held one sleeve out to help. Once she was put back to rights, Caroline kissed my cheek. "You take care of my girl for me, okay?"

"Yes," I said instantly and wholeheartedly.

Then Caroline towed Gemma in and rubbed their noses together. "Don't stay up too late. I don't want you to have dark circles either." She patted her daughter's cheek. "Potatoes, who would've thought?"

Frank led Caroline out of the restaurant, and I held up the gaming card to Gemma. "You feel like seeing what Ms. Pac-Man is up to?"

She shot me two finger guns. "Winner with the most tickets gets to pick out the prizes?"

"What?" I huffed out a laugh. "You going to force a stuffed animal on me?"

She spun away from me, her braid swishing with the movement. "We'll see."

If I won, my prize would have nothing to do with light-up toys and everything to do with wrapping her hair around my hand and feeling those pliable lips on mine again. I caught up to her, bending down to her ear, almost missing her tiny shiver when I said, "We will see."

We played some classic arcade games, a few rounds of Skee-Ball, and one intense motorcycle race. There was some name-calling, a couple arguments, and a lot of not-quite-accidental touches to her shoulders and back.

"I do believe it has come time to pay up," I said, leading the way to the prize corner, plastic baubles and knickknacks in neat rows.

Gemma grabbed a small Styrofoam football and tossed it in the air as I held up a shot glass.

"No, no shot glasses."

"That's not the game, Gemmie. I won, I get to pick out your stupid prize."

She put the football back and picked up a slap bracelet. "Well, contrary to what you think about me, I don't do shots."

"What I think about you?" I frowned. "What do *I* think about you?"

She flicked her wrist, curling the bracelet around her other arm with a crack. "That I'm completely irresponsible."

"Gem, I don't think that at all." I set the shot glasses down and walked back to her, unfurling the neon-colored bracelet from her arm and slapping it on my own wrist above my watch. "You have multiple jobs, two of which are teaching—that's pretty much the height of responsibility."

"They're not full time, though. No benefits, no insurance." She held up my arm, examining the two adornments on my wrist. One simple and brown and worth a lot more than the plastic bracelet covered in swirls of pink and green and purple glitter, although at the moment, I wasn't sure which one I liked better.

"So? That doesn't matter," I said. "It has nothing to do with the type of person you are."

She considered me with a guarded gaze. "What type of person do you think I am?"

"I think you're caring, in a real, tangible way. You care about people and the consequences of the choices we all make. You care about the environment and..." I circled my hand not currently in Gemma's grasp behind her, as if I could encompass everything. "You care about what happens in the world, and you care very much for your mom. You might annoy the hell out of me, but I think you're smart and funny and exactly what this planet needs more of."

Her attention fell back to my wrist, and she skimmed her index finger over the face of my watch and the slap bracelet. "You thought I was rude when we first met, and I was. I made a snap judgment about you, and I shouldn't have. I'm sorry."

I gulped back my words to placate her because I knew—somehow felt it—that she needed to get whatever this was off her chest.

She turned her palm flat against mine. "I think you're attentive and considerate and so damn perfect with your dumb shiny loafers and ironed shirts." She moved her fingers in line with mine, her skin warm and slightly clammy as if she was nervous. I wanted to tell her there was no reason to be nervous, but she continued, "I've always been confident in who I was. I didn't care that people thought I was a slacker or—"

"You're not a slacker."

She tossed me a reprimanding look for interrupting. "I've always gone where the wind's taken me, and that's how I like it. But lately, it's felt... It feels like I've been falling further and further away from the pack. My friends are all gorgeous gazelles, leaping and running, and I'm the one with the broken leg about to be eaten by a lion."

This time, I couldn't help it; I needed to understand why she felt like she was living in the wild as opposed to standing in this crazy-loud Dave & Buster's. "Just because you don't have a full-time job doesn't mean you're going to be eaten."

Lacing her fingers with mine, she nibbled on the corner of her mouth, and I'd lose the last of my patience if she didn't spit it out soon.

"It feels like you're the lion."

I clenched my jaw, momentarily stunned into silence by

her confession, but when she offered me a small, tight smile, the knot in my chest unwound a little.

"I think part of the reason I've been so defensive with you is because I always felt some kind of, I don't know, pull or something. I didn't want to believe it." Her little smile widened to show her teeth. "I didn't want to believe I could like someone so…" She waved her hand down my body.

"Flawless?"

"Exactly," she said, shaking her head in faux scorn. "I don't know if you've noticed, but you and I are completely opposite. I'm not exactly the sweater-set Barbie type, and my credit score is horrible."

I sniffed, tugging her close with our joined hands, guiding her toward the counter with her prize in hand. "I don't care that you don't have a 401(k) or whatever it is you think you're missing or self-conscious about. And you don't care that I am, much like Mary Poppins, practically perfect in every way."

"I'd like to stuff you in Mary Poppins's bag if I could."

"That's my girl," I said and handed over the gaming card to the guy behind the counter before slapping the temporary tattoo down. "Where do you want it?"

"I'm not putting that on."

"Yes—" I drew her arm toward me, flipping the inside of her forearm up "—you are. Them's the rules."

She began to argue, but I laid the sticker on the soft skin above the inside of her wrist and bent over it. I heard her suck in a quick breath when my tongue glided over the thin paper, and I took extra care to massage the wet sticker onto her flesh. Our gazes met, and she licked her lips, leaving them wet and so damn tempting.

And I gave in.

Right there in the middle of Dave and Buster's, I wound her braid around my hand and brought her mouth to mine. She tasted tart like her drink, and I lapped up the flavor, wrapping my other arm around her waist, taking her weight against me so her feet barely touched the floor.

A throat cleared next to us, and I blinked back into reality as Gemma blew out a breath, her neck and cheeks blooming red.

If she thought she'd be eaten, she was right. My baser instincts were slowly surfacing, and the more she opened up to me, the closer I got, the more I wanted. Like an insatiable animal.

I held my hand up to the guy behind the counter in silent apology then peeled back the paper on her arm to reveal a two-inch, black, fire-breathing dragon. I skimmed my index finger over it. "This, Gemma, is art."

"My mother's going to kill me. I hope you're satisfied when you're sitting in the police station, being questioned about my whereabouts."

"It's not that bad."

"You have met my mother, haven't you? You think she'll be fine with this on my arm at her wedding?"

I clucked my tongue. I hadn't thought of that. "Sorry."

"No, you're not."

I laughed and threw my arm around her shoulders, my new slap bracelet shining under the fluorescent lights above. "You're right, I'm not."

Back at my house, Gemma parked her car and twisted in her seat. "So, what do you think of my little battery-powered car?"

"Not bad. It's faster than my Hot Wheels."

She pinned me with one of her you're-about-to-be-lectured stares. "Electric cars emit fifty-percent less carbon dioxide in their lifetimes than those that run on gas."

"Yeah, but electric cars still operate on lithium batteries, which account for something like thirty percent of emissions when they're made."

She tossed her hand in the air. "It still comes out in the negative column if you think about how much less carbon would be produced if every automaker switched over."

"It's negligible."

"You're an engineer," she said accusatorially. "Come up with a new way of powering my car!"

I hated to state the obvious, but… "Even if I did, it still wouldn't do anything to change the handful of companies responsible for the majority of emissions."

"It's little changes, but if everyone made these little changes, we could come together to push for bigger ones." When she swiped her palm over her forehead, I caught sight of her tattoo. "You can't be so nihilistic. Why are you smiling?"

I took hold of her arm and smoothed my thumb over the dragon. "This."

"I hate you for it."

"I know," I said, closing the gap between us, gliding my fingers up her cheek and into her hair. She closed her eyes and nuzzled into my palm, breathing evenly through open, inviting lips. "So pretty," I said, then kissed her.

She grabbed at my sweater, her fingers groping for purchase at my shoulders, and when I teased her with nibbles of her exquisite lower lip, she chased my mouth. She craved this as much as I did, her tongue searching for mine. When I finally gave it to her, she moaned, and I wanted to gobble up all her little noises.

In the beginning, kisses were usually about finding a rhythm and learning what each other liked, but with Gemma, each kiss was as if we'd done it hundreds of times before. Like my whole life was only practice for this moment, for these kisses with this woman.

Curling my palm around the bottom of her throat, I kissed down her chin and across her jaw, her mouth close to my ear so I could hear her panting breaths. I smiled against her cheek then backed away. "I have to go to this big wedding tomorrow, and I don't have a date. You wouldn't know anyone who might be interested, would you?"

A slow smile etched across her face. "Maybe."

"Maybe I'll see you tomorrow?"

"I won't be the one in white," she said coyly, and I kissed her one more time before exiting the car. I swept my thumb over my mouth, savoring the feel and taste of her lips on mine.

Yes, I was in. I was all in.

CHAPTER EIGHTEEN

It was unseasonably warm for being the last day of September. The sun had not yet set but was low enough to provide shade over the lawn. The surrounding trees of green, brown, and yellow formed an enclave for the wedding ceremony.

I peeked out from where my mom and I were hidden behind a wall to spy Frank and Jason stationed under a canopy of cream linen next to the officiant. Frank swiped at his forehead with a handkerchief then fidgeted with his calla lily boutonnière, while Jason stood with his hands casually tucked in his pockets, saying something that earned a laugh and back pat from Frank.

"Are we ready?" The wedding planner asked, interrupting my ogling of perfection in a tux.

Mom turned to me, a huge smile on her face. "What do you think, Gemmie?"

I didn't think I'd ever seen her so full of joy. "You're glowing."

Her cheeks pinked, eyes slightly wet, and she grabbed hold of my hand, towing me closer to her. "I know you and I don't always see eye to eye, and you haven't always understood the decisions I've made, but you have to know, I did everything with you in mind."

"Mom, I—"

She shook her head. "I always thought you deserved better than me."

"What? No, that's not—"

She smiled, and held our clasped hands between our chests. "I was so young when I had you, and after your dad left, I didn't think I could do it on my own. I never felt good enough."

"Mom—"

She shushed me with a fingertip to her own lips. "This is important. I know I didn't set a good example for you in that way. I settled for men who weren't good for me—and certainly not good enough for you—and I'm sorry. It took me a long time to realize I was strong enough on my own and that I didn't have to force a man into our lives just because I was afraid of failing you as a parent. I was afraid of being alone."

My eyes burned with tears. Sure, I'd argued with my mother a lot, but I'd never blamed her for the choices the men in our lives had made. "You are strong, Mom," I croaked, and the wedding planner, who I'd forgotten about, stuffed a tissue in my free hand. "I always thought you were. And you did raise me on your own. Those other men..." I huffed. "You thought you weren't a good enough mom or wife, but they weren't good enough for *you*."

Mom pulled me in for a hug, careful not to smudge our make-up. "I love you. Have I told you that lately?"

"Not today."

"You're the most amazing girl." She kissed my cheek. "You're everything I'm not and everything I wished you would be. Smart, independent, and so damn stubborn."

"You like that I'm stubborn?"

She held my face between her hands. "It's one of my favorite things about you."

We were minutes away from her wedding ceremony, and yet here I was swelling with pride at her compliments. We might as well have been the only two there, even though one hundred guests sat mere feet away while a trio of musicians played a waltz. "I love you, Mom."

"But I need one more favor," she added with a sheepish smile.

I snorted. "What?"

"Could you house-sit while we go away?"

I laughed and nodded my answer. Then my mom kissed me one more time before signaling to the wedding planner that we were ready. The music changed, we were handed bouquets, and suddenly I was walking my mom down the aisle one more time.

This time, though, I knew it was going to stick.

Mom's eyes welled with tears when she saw Frank, who couldn't control his broad smile.

"You look beautiful," he said softly, when we reached the canopy, and I handed her off to him. I stood off to the side, catching Jason's playful gaze over their heads.

Hey you, he mouthed.

The officiant began the service by welcoming everyone and read a few passages before introducing me. I stepped up to the mic, unraveling a small piece of paper.

"This poem is titled *Maybe,* but the author is anonymous," I said and glanced over to Mom and Frank, staring into each other's eyes, and then to Jason. He smiled at me, my attention momentarily drifting to how damn good he looked, until he covertly motioned to my paper. With a blink, I got back on track, though I didn't miss his smug smirk.

"*Maybe we are supposed to meet the wrong people before*

meeting the right one so that, when we finally meet the right person, we will know how to be grateful for that gift.

Maybe it is true that we don't know what we have got until we lose it, but it is also true that we don't know what we have been missing until it arrives.

Maybe the happiest of people don't necessarily have the best of everything; they just make the most of everything that comes along their way.

Maybe the best kind of love is the kind you can sit on a sofa together and never say a word, and then walk away feeling like it was the best conversation you've ever had.

Maybe you shouldn't go for looks; they can deceive. Don't go for wealth; even that fades away. Go for someone who makes you smile, because it takes only a smile to make a dark day seem bright.

Maybe you should hope for enough happiness to make you sweet, enough trials to make you strong, enough sorrow to keep you human, and enough hope to make you happy.

Maybe love is not about finding the perfect person, it's about learning to see an imperfect person perfectly."

When I finished the poem, I took my place back on the side of the make-shift alter, so the bride and groom could exchange vows and rings, which got me unexpectedly emotional, and I had to hide my sniffling behind the flowers. After they lit a candle, the officiant introduced everyone to the new Mr. and Mrs. Santos. Frank picked up my mom, swinging her in a circle, entirely disregarding the kiss protocol, and the guests went wild as they made their way back down the aisle.

Jason stuck out his arm to escort me. "Hey, you."

"Hey, you," I echoed, wrapping my hand around his bicep.

He slanted his chin down to my distinctly naked forearm. "How long was it before she noticed the dragon?"

"A few hours, longer than I thought it would take."

"She was probably preoccupied," he said, waving at a few people, "being her wedding day and all."

"Though she had enough time to supervise the alcohol scrubbing."

"The next one will have to be permanent, I guess," he replied, moving his arm so he could hold my hand.

I laced my fingers with his and tipped my head back. "I would have to lose an awfully big bet for that."

He arched an eyebrow. "I'll see what I can do."

Inside, there was a short photo session with the bridal party on the carved white staircase, and I molded myself to Jason's side, smiling at the camera. A few weeks ago, I never would have guessed I'd be attending another one of my mother's weddings. Especially next to this blond and blue-eyed rascal of a man, yet in this moment, tucked up against him with his fingertips drawing circles against my spine, there was nowhere else I wanted to be.

Inside the reception, Mr. and Mrs. Santos had an intricately choreographed number for their first dance to "This Will Be" by Natalie Cole, and Jason bowed his head down to my ear, whispering, "He's surprisingly light on his feet."

"It must be all the flexibility he gained in yoga class."

"If that's true, call me Fred Astaire."

I elbowed his side. In return, he wrapped an arm around my waist, holding me tight so I couldn't do it again then placed a kiss behind my ear.

When the dance ended, everyone took their seats except for Jason, who picked up his water glass as the MC passed him the microphone. "Many of you know me, but a few of you may not. I'm Jason, the best man, and I'm grateful you could all be here to celebrate this special day with Frank and Caroline. I have put up with this..." He motioned toward Frank, who smiled in delight.

"Put up with that son of a bitch!" someone shouted from the back, and the guests all laughed at the suggestion, but Jason continued with a shake of his head.

"No. I've put up with this guy for over fifteen years now, talking about the great love of his life." He took a few seconds to scan the room, dazzling the guests with his smile. Me included. "Sandy was Frank's first wife, as most of you know, and sadly passed away too early. But fortunately for me, I was taken into his care a few months later and became the great love of his life." He waited until the cheers subsided to go on. "Gemma read a poem about hoping for enough trials to make you strong and sorrow to make you human. Frank, you have had enough of both."

His voice broke as he gestured to his friend and adopted father, and I reached out, hanging on to his suit jacket. It wasn't enough comfort, but it was some, at least.

I'd never lost anyone I was close to but recognized how he struggled—still—with the reverberations of it. I pictured Jason as a young boy with his parents, and I wondered if his father was the first one to teach him how to play basketball, if his mother sang to him at night. And I imagined what it might feel like to have all that gone in an instant. How easy it might have been for a young teenage boy to cling to the things he could control and create a perfect image of himself to hide the raw, broken bits inside.

Everybody protected themselves in different ways. I did it by pushing people away before they could get too close. Jason did it by showing the world how *fine* he was.

So, I offered him the only thing I could in that moment —myself.

"I'm so grateful for everything you've given me," Jason said. "You deserve to have all the happiness in the world, and I'm so glad you have found the woman who knows how perfectly imperfect life can be. I hope that one day I will be as in love as you two are." He lifted his glass. "To Mr. and Mrs. Santos."

Frank strode over to him, throwing his big arms around Jason's neck, saying something only they could hear. Jason nodded a few times and swiped at his eyes with his index fingers before sitting back down at the table. I wiped uselessly at my own cheeks, and he unfolded a napkin to dry my tears.

"I never thought you'd be the type to cry at weddings," he said, and I let out a blubbery giggle.

"I never thought *you'd* be the type to cry at weddings. Your speech was really good."

"I said what I felt." His winter-snow eyes pinned me, stealing my breath. "You and that poem inspired me."

I fiddled with the napkin, finding a few mascara marks on it. "Do I look a mess?"

"Absolutely not. In fact—" he grabbed my hands and steered me to the dance floor "—I think you look—" he spun me under his arm before placing his left hand on my back "—like a sun goddess."

I laughed as he led me into a simple two-step. "Where'd you learn to dance so well, Fred?"

"I'm not usually. Must be my partner."

He dipped me backward, and I lifted my leg like in an old movie musical. "Call me Ginger."

By the time we took our seats, the first course had been served, and a woman with salt-and-pepper hair patted my hand. "You two make a sweet couple."

"Thank you, but we're not—" I glanced over my shoulder at Jason. We hadn't had any explicit conversations about what was unfolding between us, but if I were honest with myself and this random woman in front of me, I wanted a relationship with Jason. Much to my own astonishment.

The man in question smiled at me, crooked and mind-shattering, his arm draped over the back of my chair. "Do you want a drink?"

For the seventy-eighth time today, I had to blink out of his stunning orbit when he traced a finger down my shoulder. Then I blinked again. And he grinned as if he knew exactly what he was doing to me.

He brought the back of my hand up to his mouth for a kiss that lingered a little longer than socially acceptable. "Gemma. Drink?"

I nodded, marionette-style. "Wine."

"Preference?"

"White," I said, even though the gerbil, straining to get the wheel of my brain back on track, reminded me that white wine would give me a headache tomorrow.

"I'll be right back."

"You're not what?" the woman across me from asked, dragging my attention back to her when she tapped the table.

"I'm sorry?"

"You and Jason." She moved forward in her seat. "You're not a couple? You could have fooled me with the way you two look at each other." She introduced herself. "I'm Joann, Frank's administrative assistant."

I shook her hand. "Oh, hi. Nice to meet you. I'm Caroline's daughter, Gemma."

Joann smiled, poking at her salad. "I could tell. You look just like her." She speared a cherry tomato. "I never thought I'd see this day. Frank married again. Jason smiling and happy with a girl."

I paused with my water glass midair. "What do you mean?"

Joann held the tomato aloft. "Well, after Sandy passed, Frank was crushed."

"I mean about Jason. What do you mean, happy?" He had never struck me as being *unhappy*. Was he unhappy?

"Jason is… He was always so broody," Joann said, munching on the tomato. "Even as a teenager, he was always so serious. And girls would fawn all over him."

"Brooding? Really?" I scoffed. From the moment we met, Jason had been constantly laughing. At me. And then, of course, there was that ever-present arrogant smile.

"Speak of the devil." Joann pointed to Jason's chair.

He arrived with three drinks held between his hands. "Chardonnay for Gem, Kahlúa and cream for Joann, and ginger ale for me."

"You know me so well." Joann winked at him. "Gemma and I were just talking about you," she said casually, sipping her cocktail, as if she hadn't broken rule number eight of girl code.

"You were?" He crossed his right ankle over his left knee. "Anything interesting?"

I flicked my hand in the air. "Oh, you know, only how she knew you when you were awkward and geeky."

He bent his head to me. "Those two words are not in my repertoire. Try super masculine and cool."

"Yes, the bow tie is very cool and masculine," I teased.

He patted it down. "I think it's fetching."

I did too, but I wasn't about to tell him that. His head was big enough as it was. I inched closer to him but spoke to Joann. "Do you have any good stories? Maybe an unfortunate haircut or prom incident? Did Mr. Perfect here flip out like Carrie?"

"No, no pig's blood." She leaned her temple on her index finger. "But he was homecoming king, if I remember correctly."

"Of course he was." I rolled my eyes when Jason jutted his chin out, extra peacocky.

"You're sitting next to royalty, Gemmie."

CHAPTER NINETEEN

Jason

After the cake had been cut and the china cleared away, the dance party commenced. Caroline immediately stole Gemma away, and I watched from the table, unable to control the stupid grin on my face, as she twisted and twirled around to "I Got You Babe" with her mom. Her gold dress was long and silky, cut low, almost down to her lower back, with thin straps that had tempted me all night. One little slip, and I could have my mouth on her breast.

I had big plans for her later.

Tonight, I would not be a gentleman.

"Well, what do you say, Jason, take me for a spin on the floor?"

I stood up, and offered my hand to Joann. "Of course."

After one dance with Joann, I caught up with a couple of coworkers, and then took Sylvia, Frank's sister, out for a dance. By the time Van Morrison's "Brown Eyed Girl" played over the speakers, I'd lost sight of Gemma.

But I couldn't look for her because Frank cut me off, going wild on the parquet floor. He danced his jacket and tie off at some point, and was now pulling at his suspenders, jumping in circles to "Shout." I joined in, barking out a laugh that was the opposite of cool when Frank tried to get me on his back for a piggyback.

I honestly didn't think he had anything to drink.

He was just high on life.

It was in the middle of my hysterical laugh that Gem caught me by surprise, fitting her arm around my waist. Before I could pull her into me for a dance, the DJ changed the song and called all the single ladies to the middle of the floor.

It was time for the bouquet toss.

She shook her head, refusing to play along—and I certainly wasn't going to make her—but a family friend yanked her out to the front of the giggling group of women, and Caroline threw the flowers over her head right to Gemma, who sidestepped it. Frank's cousin, Mimi, picked it up and held it over her head like a trophy.

Next up was the garter. Frank, sweaty and sans suspenders, disappeared under Caroline's dress to reemerge with blue lace in hand. I tried to hide, but Gemma didn't let me saying, "Oh no, if I had to, so do you." Then shoved me out to the center of the floor.

Frank twirled the garter around his finger as the men around me hooted and hollered. I glared at Gemma, who covered her smile with her hand. And when Frank finally threw the balled up lace into the center of the rowdy crew, I easily caught it. Gemma lifted a glass of champagne to me in salute.

The band played some cheesy burlesque music, and someone brought a chair out to the center of the dance floor, so I could push the garter up Mimi's leg. I made a production out of it, pretending to peek up her dress and then pass out. She loved every second of the attention and laid a big kiss on me at the end of it.

When I strolled up to Gemma a few minutes later, she

wiped lipstick from my mouth. "Do you need a minute to yourself?"

"Got me hot under the collar." I unknotted my tie, leaving it hanging around my neck, receiving an appreciative once-over from her in return.

"You're lethal in a tux. Like, it's a real problem."

"Is it?"

She nodded, and I held my hand up by my chest. "I think I've lost my date. 'Bout yay high, eyes that can murder a man. Sharp tongue but soft lips. Have you seen her?"

"See? Real problem," she said, even as she took my hand.

I led her in a slow dance, luxuriating in the feel of her fingers toying with the ends of my hair at the nape of my neck.

"I must admit, I'm a little jealous," she murmured after a minute.

I splayed my hands wide against her spine. "Of who?"

"That little old lady."

"Of cousin Mimi? Yeah. She's been pinching my ass for years."

"She's your cousin?"

I nodded. "Frank's eighty-four-year-old cousin, who was left a ton of money by her multimillionaire husband. She spends most of her time in Florida, but I get ten dollars in my birthday card every year."

"I wish I'd have known that earlier. You know I like a big bank account." Her coy smile faded as she tipped her head up, sliding one of her hands from around my neck to press her palm over my heart. Those dark eyes of hers, usually full of fire, were all soft and round, urging me to open up my chest and allow her a peek inside.

"You asked how I learned to dance. It was from my parents. They danced around the house all the time."

"It sounds like they had a lovely relationship. I'd like to hear more about them one day, if you're willing."

I swallowed the lump in my throat and nodded, wrapping my hands along her jaw, my thumbs skating along her cheekbones. I angled my head down, close enough to smell her breath, sweet like cake icing, and she stretched up to meet me halfway.

"Jason, hi!"

And we froze.

That voice belonged to Bridget and she was headed our way.

"You've got to be fucking kidding me," Gemma mumbled, stepping away from me, although I loathed to let go of her.

"What are you doing here?" I said to Bridget, sure she wasn't on the guest list.

"I was having dinner with my parents on the patio, and we wanted to congratulate the happy couple." She held out her hand to Gemma. "Hi, I'm Bridget."

"I know. We've met."

"Oh." Bridget smiled ruefully. "Sorry. Um, Jason, could I talk to you?"

Gemma's head toggled between Bridget and me, and I wanted to show her there was nothing between us anymore. "Yeah. Sure."

Bridget's normally bright eyes dimmed, her hands uncharacteristically restless by her waist. "In private. Please, Jase?"

It was unlike her to ask for anything. Bridget was a go-getter—in work, in romance, she took. She didn't ask. I got a weird feeling about it and looked to Gemma to gauge her reaction.

She huffed, throwing her hands up. "Whatever, *Jase*. I'll be at the bar."

I watched her walk away, the material of her dress clinging to her hips and ass, and I ran a rough hand over my face.

"Did I interrupt something?" Bridget asked, raising her shoulder.

I sighed and pointed to a couple of empty chairs at a table. "Yeah. What's up?"

She smiled, although it didn't reach her eyes. "That tuxedo fits you really well."

"Bridget, what do you want?"

"To say hi."

My attention fell to the bar, where a dark-haired guy had crept up next to Gemma. He worked at the firm...Matt or Mark or something. I started to stand, needing to go to her. "Come on, Bridge, this isn't—"

She stopped me with her hand on my wrist. "Where are you going?"

"I have a date."

"Don't go." She added her other hand. "I need you."

"I told you. I can't be with you," I said, frowning as Matt or Mark touched Gemma's elbow, sliding a drink of something dark in front of her. I ground my molars at the audacity of this guy, although she pushed it away and accepted a new drink from the bartender.

"Please, Jason," Bridget pleaded, her voice rising in what sounded like alarm. "My mom's sick. That's why we're out to dinner tonight. My dad thought it might take her mind off it. She got the results back a few days ago, ovarian cancer."

I sank back down into the chair, briefly forgetting about Gemma and Matt.

"Bridge, I'm so sorry." I draped my arm around her and handed a napkin over when her eyes turned glassy. Letting her cry on my shoulder for a few minutes, I found my focus floating back to Gemma every once in a while, her actions becoming looser, her laugh a little louder with every sip of her drink. She'd told me she didn't do shots, but from the lime she sucked on, it seemed like she was downing tequila.

"She's starting treatment next week," Bridget told me, redirecting my attention.

"That's good. How's she feeling? How are you feeling?" We'd broken up, and even though I would rather be with Gemma at the moment, I also didn't want to leave this woman who needed support right now.

"She's trying to be strong, she's putting up a good front, but I'm so scared. They only found it because my mom had been having pain for a while. She tried to ignore it, thinking it would go away, but..." Bridget held the napkin against her eyes, and it darkened with a mix of tears and makeup. "I'm sorry to dump this on you, but I saw you here and you look so handsome, and I felt, I don't know..." She lifted her face to me, her pretty features marred with streaks of mascara. "I miss you, and I needed to tell you."

"Bridget, if you need someone to talk to, I'll be there for you. But only as a friend, okay?"

She nodded, a wave of fresh tears springing to her eyes, and lunged forward, hugging me.

Back at the bar, Mark slid his hand up Gemma's shoulder, and she shifted as if to nudge him off. That was when my eyes met hers, and I exhaled harshly. "Bridge, I hate to—"

She stopped me with a kiss on the mouth, and I startled, immediately taking my hands off her, lurching my head back. "Bridget, no."

I pushed away from the table, panic flooding my chest at the way Gemma's face morphed to stone. She'd seen the kiss.

She tossed back her drink in one gulp then gestured for another. *Fuck.*

Bridget stared up at me, crestfallen, and I tried to let her down as easy and fast as possible. "You're going through a really hard time right now, I get it. You need someone to be there for you, but I'm not that guy, Bridget. I'm sorry. You deserve someone who will give you his full attention. I meant it when I said I'll be there if you want to talk, but that's it."

She covered her face with the napkin again, and I offered her one more apology before heading straight to the bar, where Gemma teetered on the edge of her stool, laughing with Mark, who didn't seem at all concerned.

I righted her so she didn't fall over. "Come on, I think you've had enough to drink."

Matt raised his glass in her direction. "She's all right."

"Yeah, I'm all right."

I motioned to the door, tugging on her hand. "Gemma, let's go."

"No," she snapped and pulled away from me. "I'm having a good time with…"

"Martin," the other guy supplied. "Don't worry, I got her. I'll take her home."

I hated him. Hated everything about him. His goatee, his stupid drunk laugh, and his complete disregard for Gemma's safety.

"Seriously, Gem. It's not funny anymore. Let's go."

He put a hand on my shoulder. "Buddy, don't worry—"

I scowled at his hand then back at his dopey face. "Listen, Mark."

"Martin."

"I've seen you around, so I know you work for Santos and Mitchell. That means you know I'm Jason Mitchell, head of the development department." I knocked Matt's hand from my shoulder. "I don't give a shit what your name is."

His face dropped, his ears tinged pink, a kid caught with his hand in the cookie jar.

"You know damn well Gemma is not fine, so you can put your dick away because she's sure as shit not going home with you." I stepped up, literally, toe to toe with him, lowering my voice to drive the point home. "And if you continue to disrespect the CEO's new stepdaughter, I will make sure somebody else has your job. I'm positive there is a college intern somewhere who could do it."

He stuttered a response as I hauled Gemma off the stool to the closest exit. Rage took over. Rage at that motherfucker, at Bridget's bad timing, and at Gemma's own senselessness. After everything she'd experienced, she was going to let it go down like that?

Yet she dug her feet into the floor, twisting her arms. "Let go of me."

I managed to get her out of the reception area and into a hallway, where I crowded her against the wall. I meant to shield her, but when she glared at me, I backed away two inches.

"You were making a fool of yourself in there," I said, my anger picking the worst words I could have chosen. But I couldn't do anything now. They were out there.

She jutted her chin out. "Fuck you and your high horse."

With my control slipping through my fingers, I yanked at my hair. "How could you do that?" I waved toward the reception hall. "You're drunk, and that guy was all over you. Why would you—"

"Why would I drink and flirt with a man paying me attention? Oh, I don't know, Jason, because it feels good. Because I like it. Because I can and I want to. Don't think I'm some damsel in distress because I told you something from my past, and now, you're a white knight saving me from any random guy. I don't need that from anyone, including you."

I didn't think she needed saving all the time, but that guy

didn't strike me as the most upstanding citizen. Besides, she'd come as *my* date. But as usual, it was two steps forward and one step back. Here we were, fighting. Again.

I jammed the heels of my palms against my eyes then shot my arms out to the sides. I was crawling out of my skin. Meanwhile, she stood there, arms crossed, face completely rigid, save for one angry eyebrow.

"You can't go around doing whatever you want," I said, grasping at straws.

"So, you can go around kissing any woman you want, but I can't have a drink with someone?"

"That's why you got drunk and hung all over him? Because you're mad at me?" I wanted to punch something—preferably Matt—but more than anything, I wanted to go one goddamn day without having words with Gemma. I curled his fist against the wall, barricading her in. "I'm tired of this tit for tat game."

She needled her index finger into my chest. "Don't blame this on me. You kissed her. Right there, in front of everyone."

"I didn't kiss her. She kissed me."

"Semantics." She ducked under my arm.

"Her mom is sick and—"

Scooping up the side of her dress, Gemma kicked off her heels, dropping down two or three inches, but she set her shoulders back, her gaze unrelenting. She aimed straight for my heart. "I didn't make a fool of myself, Jason. *You* made a fool of me."

Direct hit.

Then she grabbed her shoes and walked away.

CHAPTER TWENTY

I woke up, still in my dress, with one leg hanging off the bed and George Clooney asleep next to my head. Groaning, I rolled to the floor. The pounding in my temples recalled the bottle of white and that musty Uber ride home. Not exactly how I'd expected the night to go.

An old-school clock on my nightstand flipped numbers, 10:23, and I wiped my eyes, rubbing makeup off onto the back of my hand. My mother and Frank were leaving on their honeymoon this afternoon, and I needed to get up and shower. But at the moment, everything was a tad blurry.

I grabbed my cell phone from the floor, my home screen flooded with well-wishes and questions about the wedding from the girls, begging for photos. I hadn't plugged it in to charge last night and the battery life was at four percent, enough to text them a selfie and a short message.

long story.

I let out a pitiful laugh, remember how my hopes for a future with Jason went down the drain, along with my dignity. What a waste of a perfectly beautiful dress.

It was the exact reason why I never planned more than a week in advance. I was a fly-by-night kind of girl, remaining unattached and uninjured. Yet here I was, on the floor of my apartment. Disappointment settled in my bones like cement, keeping me there, as a physical ache bloomed in my chest.

Jason and I were on the cusp of something amazing, and to have it wither in my hands like the brown leaves of a plant that never really had a chance to grow made me want to throw the whole thing in the compost bin. Forget it ever happened.

Fortunately, now that the wedding was over, I could.

The pads of my feet throbbed as I toddled to the shower, where I turned on the cold water. Each drop pricked my skin like a needle, erasing the feeling of Jason's searing touch. If only I could somehow bleach my brain of the memories. Of the emotion weaving over his features as he gave his toast and then talked about his parents while we danced. Of feeling his heartbeat under my hand against his heart, of the small glimpse I had of his insides.

Then his reaction of me drinking with...Mark? And, of course, Bridget.

I wanted—needed—to forget it all.

When I pulled up into the Santos's driveway, Mom and Frank were in the midst of loading matching suitcases into a limo. I found sunglasses and, goddamn it, they were the ones Jason had given me—I couldn't escape him—but put them on anyway to cover the dark circles, before stepping out of my car.

"You're just in time." Frank beamed, bear-hugging me. "Did you have a good time last night? I did." He chunked my chin. "Looks like somebody had a little too much fun."

With rosy cheeks and her hair unusually loose around her shoulders, Mom grabbed my hands. "We're going to Thailand! Can you believe it?"

"Thailand. Nice," I croaked.

"What should we bring you home?" she asked as she double-checked her purse, presumably for her passport.

Frank raised his index finger. "How about a monkey? I hear they hang out anywhere, in houses and restaurants."

I had to clear my throat before answering. It cracked anyway. "No thanks, Frank. No wild animals."

"All right, then." He clapped. "Asia awaits, Mrs. Santos. Let's get going." He held the door open.

Mom kissed my cheek. "Make sure you turn the alarm on before you go to bed."

"Okay."

"And water the plants in the foyer."

"I will. Have a good time."

"I left some cash in front of the coffeepot."

"Honey, she can handle it," Frank said, laughing as he drew her into the limo and shut the door. Mom blew kisses from the window when they drove off, and as soon as they were out of sight, I made my way into the house.

I headed to Frank's den, decorated with leather recliners and a sectional. Long shelves were stacked with hundreds of movies, and a projector screen hung down from the ceiling. I took a running leap onto the couch, pulled a knit blanket around me, and drifted off to sleep for a long winter's nap.

CHAPTER TWENTY-ONE

Jason

Wednesday afternoon, I drummed my fingers on my desk. A cold cup of coffee sat untouched next to the phone as I read the report in front of me for the hundredth time. I cursed and sank down in my chair as my mind wandered to Gemma. Also for the hundredth time.

I'd texted her once every day since the wedding, and even though I understood why she was upset, I still half expected her to respond. The scent of vanilla followed me everywhere. I couldn't get it out of my head. I dreamed of her pink lips, her fingers in my hair, and her naked back under my palm. Even those minor physical remembrances of her had me waking up every morning painfully hard.

I had to see her, convince her of the truth. I felt nothing for Bridget because Gemma had stolen my heart from the moment we met, no matter how hard we both fought against it. I'd briefly toyed with the idea of going to her apartment, but I knew she'd hate that—find it wholly presumptuous—and probably not let me in anyway. So, there wasn't much left for me to do. Maybe tomorrow I would go to her yoga studio. It was public, and she couldn't very well throw me out of the class.

Or could she? I wouldn't put it past her.

Setting aside that particular debate, I laser focused back on the report, and by the time I checked the time again, it was after eight o'clock. The floor had emptied except for the maintenance workers. I still needed to send out a contract Frank had signed, but after scouring his desk and Joann's office, the papers were nowhere to be found. The only other place I knew to look was Frank's home office.

Everything was dark when I opened Frank's front door. I shut the alarm off, flipped a few light switches, then went upstairs, where I rustled through desk drawers and a filing cabinet before finally locating the folder I needed. Sudden movement caught my eye, and I reared back. Gemma was there, a flip-flop raised over her head as if she were about to pummel me with it.

"Oh my god, Jason." She heaved out a breath and slumped backward. "What are you doing here?"

"What am I doing here? What are *you* doing here? And did you really think you could do actual damage with a flip-flop?"

"It's the only weapon I had." When she tossed the shoe at me, I batted it away. "And I asked you first."

"I need to send this contract out." I held up the papers as evidence and watched the fear drain from her eyes, replaced by fire, apparently remembering herself.

"How'd you get in?"

"I know the alarm code and have keys." I held up said keys. "I did live here. What's your excuse?"

"House-sitting." She brushed her hair back from her face, the movement calling focus to her body. I'd been too preoccupied before to notice she wore only underwear and a thin white shirt. I could see right through it.

I forced my eyes up from her nipples, and for fuck's sake, I deserved an award for that. "Did you get my text messages?"

"Yeah." She threw a hand on her hip, an annoyed scowl slanting her lips, her fingers lifting her shirt enough to display a two-inch-wide strip of skin above her purple boy shorts.

They were my new favorite thing, and I shut my eyes to them, losing my train of thought. "You don't, uh, wear clothes anymore?"

"I was in bed. Sorry I don't meet your pajama standards. I'm sure you sleep fully dressed."

The mental picture of her in bed had me shooting my eyes back open, and I felt the papers fold under my tightening grip before throwing them down. "You always do this. You blame me for this high-and-mighty bullshit. I'm not like that."

Gemma muttered an argument under her breath, and between the stress at work and the direction this conversation was headed, my temper exploded. "I don't have standards! In fact, if I had my way, I'd prefer you completely naked. All the time."

She huffed, her lip curling in anger. "Do you think I'm dumb? You must."

"What?"

"You think I'm going to fall for that? You come in here and toss around a few ridiculous lines about getting naked and think I'll come crawling back?" She took two steps closer to me, hissing, "You get to do whatever you want, thinking you can pick me up and put me down at your leisure? You're wrong. I'm not going to wait around for you. I am not anyone's second choice!" She had risen up on her toes, shouting the last word at me.

I held my hand up to quiet her. "Believe it or not, Gemma, but you don't exactly give off that weepy kind of woe-is-me vibe, and, quite frankly, I wouldn't be here, in this never-ending cage match with you, if you did. You don't have to tell me how fucking tough you are. I already know. So, can you, for once, shut up and give me a chance to explain?"

"There's nothing to explain. You left me at the reception to go play nice with another woman."

"I know, and I was wrong," I said, but my irritation got the best of me. "Something else to add to the list. Along with the car I drive, what I eat, what I wear, everything I say. It's all wrong."

"Because you are wrong. You can't talk to me the way you do. You can't—"

"You think this is all my fault? Everything we've ever said or done to each other since we've met? It's all my fault?" I stood right in front of her, my breath ragged as if I'd run a marathon—being with Gemma sometimes felt like that—as I stared down at her. With our bodies mere centimeters from each other, her indignation started to wilt, and something close to tears took its place.

"You can't look at me the way you do and then choose some other girl," she said in a barely audible voice, and if I could have ripped my heart out of my chest to show it to her, I would have.

"I can't help it. I can't help looking at you." I dared to touch her, tracing my fingertips over her jaw. "I can't stop this. What do you want me to say?"

"I want you to tell me the truth," she said hoarsely.

I ventured lower, curving my hand around her neck. "The truth is I've never felt like this before. I know you don't believe me, but I don't fight with people, Gemma. I don't argue with people every day like I do with you. But that's why it's different. I want to be here with you. For some godforsaken reason, I would rather fight with you than be with anyone else."

"You're right. I don't believe you." Her voice was small, and her eyes, usually so bright and full of spirit, dulled.

And it was my fault.

My blood coursed with primal desire to show her how it could be between us, how good we could be together, but I needed her to come to me. I had to prove I wasn't the guy she thought I was.

I wrapped my fingers tight around her biceps. "Believe me. I'm here, and I'm not letting you go."

When her forehead pressed to my sternum, she mumbled words into my chest that I couldn't understand, and I lifted her chin. "What?"

"You make me feel stupid," she said.

I bent my knees, getting closer to her eye level. "Why?"

"For wanting to be with you."

My heart galloped away, and I couldn't help my smile. "That's not stupid," I said, molding my hand to her jaw.

"It is when you grow up with a mother who only ever concerned herself with jumping into relationships. I never thought I would be like that, but that's what it feels like with you. Like I'm jumping without looking."

I breathed out a sigh, drawing the tip of my nose along hers. "But you're not jumping alone. I am too."

She swallowed, taking a moment to digest my words, and I held steady, although my eyebrows rose slightly in question. "Gem?"

She answered by stretching up on her toes, tangling her fingers in my hair to pull me close, and, Christ, I'd follow wherever she wanted me to. When her lips touched mine, I forgot about everything else. Gemma and her perfect, smart mouth and her fearless yet sensitive spirit had ruined me. Past Jason no longer existed. Future Jason had yet to be shaped. As long as it was by her hands, I didn't care what it looked like.

I slid my hands under her T-shirt, sinking my fingertips into her waist, and I parted her lips with my tongue as I backed her up against the doorframe. Lifting her slightly, I dragged her leg to my hip and left openmouthed kisses across her throat, nipping at her ear. She arched against me, sweet and soft and *mine*, and I couldn't get enough of her, couldn't touch or kiss or breathe in enough.

Gemma roamed her hands down my shoulders, chest, and stomach before unbuttoning my fly and slipping her fingers between my pants and underwear. I bit into the soft skin at the curve of her shoulder to keep from howling in pleasure as she familiarized herself with the feel of me. It wasn't until she slid her thumb under the elastic, scraping against the root of my cock, that I froze. "Stop."

She paused, her fingers wrapped around me. "What?"

I hung my head, exhaling roughly. "I don't have any condoms."

"I do."

As her words resonated through my fog of lust, I slowly raised my head, defeat rallying to anticipation. "You do?"

She tossed me the sexiest smile I'd ever seen over her shoulder and towed me down the hall to the guest bedroom. She rummaged through her knit bag and held up what appeared to be a tiny tin can.

"What's that?"

"A condom."

When she pitched it to me, I caught it in one hand and flipped the packet in my palm.

"It's vegan." She pointed to it. "With recyclable packaging." Then she pointed to me. "Now, take your clothes off."

I laughed, grabbed her hips and tossed her on the bed, before peeling my shirt off. Gemma propped herself up on her elbows, shamelessly gaping at me, and I stripped down to black boxer-briefs, allowing her to look her fill. I'd never lacked confidence, but under her wanton gaze, I felt enough strength to scoop her up and fly her out into the universe.

As it was, though, I had better things to do and crawled onto the bed next to her. "Now you."

She raised her arms so I could lift the shirt over her head, then it was my turn to stare. I'd seen her before, at the pool in her bikini, in the golf shop's changing room, in her goddess dress at the wedding. I'd had a hint of what her lithe form felt like under my palm, but with her laid out before me like a feast, I didn't know where to start. I trailed kisses from her chin to her belly button and back, leaving goose bumps in my wake. I smoothed my hand over one of her breasts and then the other, sucked at the pink tips until she writhed beneath me, her hips rising off the mattress. Still, I took my time, kissing the small birthmark on one of her upper ribs, then stroked down her sides, plucking at those hip-hugging panties of hers.

She grabbed at my neck, trying to drag my mouth back to hers, but I only lowered myself down her body, tucking my nose into the apex of her thighs. She smelled like heaven, and I kissed her there, over the cotton.

"Please, Jason, please, please," she panted, tugging at my head, her heels digging into the bed on either side of me.

"Don't worry. I'm here, and I'm not letting you go." I reminded her of my promise, dragging her underwear down and off her legs, then sat back, admiring her. "You're beautiful."

She let out a rough breath and sat up, wrapping her hand around my hard length. "I'm already naked. You don't have to sweet-talk me."

It took every ounce of restraint, but I gently removed her hand and kissed her palm before pressing the back of it into the bed, holding her still as I moved back down between her legs.

My first taste of her pussy had me groaning, her flavor and heat filling my mouth, and I was like a starving man at a buffet, all tongue and teeth. I couldn't eat fast enough, no nuance or technique to be found. Only want and need and desire.

The more Gemma writhed, the more unhinged I became for her. But I had to calm down. We had all night.

And that thought was the one to placate me. With my eyes on her, I folded my arms around her thighs, holding her open to me, and I watched how her skin flushed, how her mouth opened on a moan, learning what made her muscles tense under my fingers.

She liked when I followed a long suck on her clit with a little flick of my tongue. It made her body jerk, and I did it so many times, she finally knocked her knee into me with a whine. I merely laughed into her glistening pink skin.

Then I really got to work, reveling in her noises, obsessed with how she unconsciously fought against me, attempting to squeeze her legs against my ears. My dick was so hard, I could feel it leaking, but I wasn't about to stop. Not until I had her falling apart.

"Right there, right there, right there," she cried, and I slid one finger inside her while I sucked and nibbled and tongued her. She tried to buck away from me, incoherent words tumbling from her mouth, but I only pressed another finger into her, finding the soft spot against her front wall. "Oh, oh, oh fuck."

I kept my eyes focused on her as she fisted the comforter in her hands and growled out her pleasure in complete abandon, her climax rippling over my tongue. My hips thrust against the mattress of their own accord, my need bubbling up until it was almost impossible to think of anything but being inside her now.

Now.

Now.

"You look fucking incredible when you're wild like that," I said, grabbing the tin and struggling to open it in my haste. She laughed and stole it from my grasp, flicking her dark eyes up at me from under heavy lids. She removed the condom and carefully slid it down my cock, giving it a playful tug before pushing me down on the bed.

"I want to see it again." I yanked her leg over me, holding her steady as I lined myself up at her entrance and she lowered onto me inch by delicious inch. "Fuck," I ground out, closing my eyes. I knew it would be good, but this, this was *so good*. I feared if I dared to look at her, I might spontaneously combust.

But then she made the choice for me, dragging my hands up her body to place them over her breasts. "Touch me," she ordered, and I snapped my eyes open, her fingers demonstrating how she wanted to be pinched and pulled. "Make me wild."

I did as she asked and played with her nipples, rocking my hips up against hers, and she licked her lips, staring down at where our bodies met, where my cock disappeared inside of her with every movement. She was soaking wet, I slipped out of her, and she whimpered before I held her hip, pumping back into her with such force, my teeth snapped together.

"Yes, like that," she rasped, tilting her weight forward, finding the angle she needed. "Jason."

I loved the sound of my name on her lips. Loved how she moaned it. Loved how I could feel her pulse quickening around me.

"You're close, I can feel it." I pulled her body down toward me so I could suck one of her nipples into my mouth, holding on to her hips to piston up into her harder, faster. Some desperate part of me hoped to leave bruises on her skin, showing the world she was mine.

This one? She picked me. I'm giving her this pleasure.

The familiar burn sparked deep within me, my spine stiffening, my skin going hot all over. "You look so good riding me like this, Gemma. I need to feel you come on my cock."

She tossed her head back and forth, lost in her pleasure.

"One more. Come on, Gem. Give it to me." When I plucked at her nipple with my teeth, she was coming again, and I gave in too, stuttering my thrusts, my mouth finding any part of her to suck and hold on to as I left this earthly plane.

It was so good. Too good. Died and gone to heaven good.

"Hey," she wheezed out, pushing off me with her hands against my chest to settle against my side. "You'll leave a mark."

I wrapped one arm around her, the other flopping over my forehead. "Sorry, not sorry."

We were both slightly clammy but cuddled together for a few moments before she walked to the bathroom. I needed a few minutes to myself anyway to get my scrambled brain back into functioning order.

Once she finished, I took her place, cleaning myself up, planning on having some more naked time, but when I reopened the door to the bedroom, she was poking her head and arms through her T-shirt. "Hey, whoa, what are you doing?"

She raised an eyebrow at me as she covered up all her good bits.

"I set one rule, and already, you're breaking it." I settled back on the bed. "I said if I had my way, I'd want you naked all the time."

"When do I ever let you have your way without a fight?"

"Never." I grinned, looping a finger around the collar of her shirt to tug her in for a kiss. "But I'm okay wrestling it off you."

"Don't stretch it out!" she whined, bobbing away from my hold. "This is one of my favorite shirts. Perfectly worn-in."

"Yes," I agreed. "My favorite too. But, really..." I tipped my head off to the side, in the same direction all our other clothes lay on the floor. "Off, please."

After a few seconds, when I really wasn't sure if she'd comply or not, she stripped it off. "Only because you said please."

I immediately pressed a kiss to her breastbone then her throat and curled her into my side. I buried my nose in her hair, inhaling the intoxicating vanilla scent.

"I like you," I said in the understatement of the century, and she snuggled in closer to my chest.

"I like you too."

Not too long later, with this wild woman firmly held in my arms and my breaths matching hers, I drifted off to sleep. All as it should be.

CHAPTER TWENTY-TWO

I rolled over onto my stomach, arms and legs starfishing to the corners of the bed. My eyelids fluttered open to find a note on the pillow next to me, scribbled in permanent marker.

I had to go in to work early. You're too cute to wake up when you sleep. —J

A nervous energy started in my toes, spread up through my fingers, and before I could stop myself, I texted the girls.

Guess where I am right now??

When they didn't immediately message back, I snapped a picture of Jason's note and sent it. Still, no response.

Don't make me squee on my ooooooown

SAM

Tell me that is the Boy Scout's handwriting?!
That means you forgave him?

I had, of course, kept the girls up-to-date on every high and low between me and Jason for the last month and a half. Bronte, ever the optimist, thought it would all turn out fine. Laney had told me to follow my gut. Sam, though, was warier.

She'd been through the wringer with her parents' relationships and didn't fully trust Jason after so many run-ins with Bridget.

We have to talk more about that situation, but I know and trust he was never stringing me along.

SAM

If you say so.

I like him.

SAM

Then I'm happy for you. I'll save my judgment for when I meet him. We are going to meet him, right?

You know I'm not a long-term planner.

Sam's reply was only a side eye emoji.

After throwing on some clothes, I headed to work, avoiding Alex's eagle eye for what they said was "morning-after face," and set up shop in the back room, sorting through new merchandise.

During Bronte's lunch break, she FaceTimed me. "You look different today."

"I would hope so. I saw God last night."

She tossed her head back in laughter. "It's good?"

I widened my eyes and nodded once sluggishly.

"Ugh. Okay." She waved her hand, swatting at an imaginary fly. "Don't brag," she said with a smile, although I didn't need to know Bronte and Hunter's history to see the longing in the slight downturn of her mouth. "So, now what?"

I stacked a few face toners on the floor then flattened the box they'd arrived in. "I don't know."

"Are you guys together or...?"

"I don't know. It only happened last night. We didn't do too much talking."

She set her chin on her fist, dipping a small piece of broccoli in what looked like ranch dressing. "I figured, but did you think about it at all?"

"Think about what?" I ripped open another box.

"The future," she said, as if she were telling me it was Thursday.

Thinking about the future. Easy for Bronte, the ultimate planner, to say. Sam had her next few years mapped out with her schoolwork. And Laney, she didn't need a plan with all her luck; good things simply fell into her lap.

I was the odd one out. A lifetime of men disappointing me didn't exactly bode well for making future plans. I'd rather stay loose, focus on today instead of worrying about tomorrow. Making plans led to expectations, and unmet expectations led to worlds of hurt. I'd rather avoid that, if possible.

After hanging up with Bronte, I finished my work, eager to head to the yoga studio. It was a welcome change from Alex's relentless questions all day.

What does Jason do for a living?

How much does he make?

Does he own a house?

Is his hair really as soft as it looks?

I began the class with my eyes closed, as usual. "Clear your mind." I inhaled through my nose. "Relax your mouth." And exhaled through my lips. "Let the tension from today roll away with every breath." Another inhale. "Arms up." And exhale. "Swan dive to forward bend."

The class followed as I folded in half, taking more deep breaths. "Back up to mountain pose."

I rose back up, opening my eyes, and there was Jason in the back of the room, hands pressed together in front of his chest.

Heat flushed my neck, and I bit my lip, covering the idiotic smile I knew I'd been sporting all day.

Continuing the class, I felt his eyes on me the whole time. Attempting to keep my back to him as I helped students adjust their movements, I made my way past him, but he stretched out his long arm and flicked my thigh.

I whipped my head around to find a grin plastered across his face.

I hated that I loved that face so much. I'd forgive a lot for that stupid grin.

At the end of the hour, everyone left except for Jason, who stayed seated on his mat as I went about the room, picking up my supplies.

"I was thinking we could have pizza tonight," he said, and I piled up a few blocks in the corner of the room.

"It's weird I have to keep reminding you I'm vegan, when the night we met, that's, like, all you talked about."

"Patently false," he said, towing me down to his lap as I approached him, and positioned my legs on either side of his hips. "I did my research. I grabbed a few frozen vegan pizzas from the store after work."

"Really?" I played with his hair—because, yes, it was incredibly soft—feeling my cheeks stretch wide. I didn't think I'd ever smiled so much as I had in the last twenty-four hours.

He nodded, moving his hands to my thighs, where he plucked at the material covering them. "I love these pants on you."

"Does that mean you're coming over to my parents' house tonight?"

"Well, when you put it like that…"

I gasped. "This is weirdly incestuous, isn't it? We're basically step siblings."

"Like *Game of Thrones* up in here." He laughed then kissed

my chin. "Back to the issue at hand. Is it okay with you if I come over tonight?"

When I made a show of thinking about it, he skated his hands under my shirt. "I'm coming over. With pizza. The cardboard kind for you, the real kind for me."

I smacked his wandering fingers away and stood, lugging him up with me. He walked me out after I locked up and opened the car door for me, leaning inside to kiss my cheek. "I'll be over in an hour."

After stopping at my apartment to feed all my animals and give Mr. Clooney a scratch behind his ears, I was off again to Mom and Frank's house. By the time I'd showered and changed, I heard Jason thumping around in the kitchen.

His back was to me as he grabbed plates from the cabinet, the muscles in his back visible beneath his tight gray T-shirt.

"Smells good," I said, and he whirled around, his eyes alight as he took me in.

"Those pants look familiar."

I pinched the long flannel pajama pants that I'd rolled up around my hips. "You said I never wear real clothes."

He pulled out a stool for me at the kitchen island. "Where'd you find them?"

"I went on a little tour of your room when I got home." I watched him slide on a mitt to remove the pizzas from the oven and placing them on hot pads on the counter. So domesticated.

"These pants were hiding a few *Playboys* in one of your drawers." I held up my right hand like I was in a court room. "But I won't tell. I didn't even know they still printed physical copies anymore."

"Hey, when you're thirteen and your friend's older brother offers you pictures of naked ladies, you don't turn it down, no matter the format." He offered me a plate with a slice of my pizza on it. "Your cardboard, madam."

When I bit into it, he paused with his slice halfway to his mouth, a piece of pepperoni sliding off with a glob of cheese.

"What?" I asked mid-chew, and he shook his head, bemused.

There was something about his enigmatic smile, the same one he'd worn the first night we met when he'd insinuated he had caught me changing from my shorts to a skirt in Frank's driveway, that told me had another secret.

"Nothing." He bit into his own animal-product junk. "How was your day?"

Maybe it was the comfortable way he spoke about Bare Necessities and laughed about Alex, but the effortlessness of our conversation scared me. An everyday, home from work, kiss on the cheek kind of conversation. It was scary because it was so easy. Ease that allowed minutes to slip into hours, days into weeks, years into decades, and suddenly—as Jason waxed poetic about the science behind the eco-friendly renovations to the Empire State Building, and how he was trying to use those same principles on new developments—I could see it all.

Dinners after work.

Quick kisses over coffee in the morning.

Texts about items we needed from the grocery store.

The future.

"You okay?" he asked after a while, wiping off his fingers on a napkin, almost his entire pizza devoured. I had barely gotten more than one piece down before I gave up, a slightly woozy feeling in my belly like I'd drunk too much.

"Yeah, yeah. I'm fine. I was...wondering if you brought dessert with you too."

To answer, he hopped over to the gym bag he'd packed and pulled out a box of condoms.

"First of all, those are made with casein, and second of all, it's really presumptuous of you to think I'd let you stay over."

"Is it, though?" He closed the gap between us. "Technically, this is my home too." He linked his arms around my middle, inching his mouth closer to mine. "And in that case, I don't need your permission. You're only babysitting this little sardine can, after all."

"Good point," I said into a kiss.

"I don't know what casein is."

"Those condoms aren't vegan. Casein is a milk protein that the latex is—"

He shushed me with another kiss, his tongue teasing into my mouth. "We don't have to use them if you don't want to. I have a lot of ideas about what else we can do."

My body practically hummed in anticipation, and he backed away two inches, raising a challenging eyebrow. "First one upstairs gets the first orgasm."

I pushed off his chest and bounded out of the kitchen. Jason's laughter reverberated off the walls as he chased after me. I had lots of ideas too.

CHAPTER TWENTY-THREE

Jason

The next few days were a blur of sex, Gemma's homemade blueberry-and-banana pancakes, my favorite superhero movies, and more sex. We woke up Sunday morning in my old bedroom. A few posters still clung to the gray-painted walls, along with one framed photo of me in a cap and gown next to Frank.

I yawned and rolled onto my back, blinking awake in Gemma's direction. She stretched like a cat, languid and soft, and I ran my hand along her stomach, saying, "Morning."

Refusing to open her eyes, she draped one arm over my torso. "I couldn't sleep last night. You were squirming all over the place."

"Really? Sorry. Must've been my dreams. Have you been awake long?"

"No." This time, she crooked her neck back to look at me, her bangs falling in front of her eyes. I opened my mouth to let her know how pretty she was in the morning, but she cut me off, asking, "What were you dreaming about?"

"My parents."

"Do you dream about them a lot?"

I shrugged. "Sometimes."

"Do you want to talk about it?" She stacked her hands on top of each other on my chest, elevating her chin on them, and I was once again struck by how simple it was to tell her the truth. I'd always been private, particularly when it came to my family, but I wanted to tell Gemma what happened. I wanted to tell her everything.

Mistaking my pause for something else, she backtracked. "You don't have to tell me if you don't want to."

"I do." I wound a lock of her hair around my index finger. "When I dream about them, they're alive. They're talking and laughing and dancing, sometimes with me. It's like I'm ten again or something. My friend is really into psychics and stuff, and he said when I have those dreams, it's them trying to communicate with me." I huffed out an incredulous laugh. "I don't know about that."

She drew lazy figure eights on my sternum. "What were they like?"

Memories inundated my mind, and I sighed in contentment. It had taken me almost a decade to be able to think of my parents without getting choked up. "My mom's name was Jane, and she was the quintessential mom, cooking and baking. She was the mom who brought the orange slices to basketball games. You know that kind of mom?"

"I've heard of her," Gemma said, giving me a half smile. "What about your dad?"

"Everybody called him Bill, except for her. She called him Billy. That's what I remember most about him. The way he perked up when he heard her say his name. I was just a kid, but I knew they loved each other a lot."

"What happened?"

Even though she could ask any and all questions she wanted, that one was still tough to answer. I wasn't there that night, and when I was younger, my imagination often spiraled out of control, inventing terrible images of what it might have looked like. Anchoring myself to the present and Gemma's deep brown eyes, I told her, "They were on their way home from dinner when a drunk driver hit them from behind."

She eyes closed tight, wincing at the information.

"Their car spun out of control and flipped. My parents weren't wearing their seat belts. They were dead before the ambulance arrived."

I had been through enough therapy to be able to relay that information with some detachment. As a thirteen-year-old kid, I didn't know how to process my grief, though as I got older, it had been to have every detail in my life in order. No surprises, good or bad. It was better for me to take the straight and narrow; I could see exactly what was coming and where I was going.

As if Gemma could read my thoughts, she leaned up on her elbows. "That's why you're so straitlaced."

"Hmm?" I tipped my chin down, brushing her hair off her shoulder. "Why I'm what?"

She counted off with her fingers. "You're super smart, good at everything you do, your house is spotless. I mean, you even make your bed. What single guy does that? You like everything perfect."

I rolled onto my side, supporting my head with my hand, thinking back to those middle school years. "I wasn't always like that. I went through a rebellious period. I was having trouble dealing with everything, and I got into trouble. I was drinking, smoking a lot of pot, staying out late."

She wrinkled her nose. "I can't picture it."

"The last straw was this party the summer before I started high school. Frank found me at this kid's house at one in the morning or something, and right there, he laid into me. Verbally kicked my ass into the next county, screamed at me about how acting that way wasn't going to change anything." I shook my head. A shadow of guilt still followed me around, even all these years later. "He had his own stuff to deal with too, and it made me understand what an extra burden I was to him by acting the way I was. He needed me as much as I needed him, but I was too high to notice. It took him finding me at that party, yelling and crying at me in the front yard, for me to finally see it."

"And look at you now," Gemma said, sitting up with a playful tilt of her lips, "you're as uptight as they come."

I scooped her up, wrestling her back down to the mattress. "I'll show you uptight."

She shrieked with laughter, trying uselessly to push me away as I blew raspberries down her stomach. I wiggled her legs apart with my own and laced our fingers together as my tickling turned into kisses. "Every day with you, I feel like I'm being unraveled."

"Yeah?" She writhed under me. "Feels like you're the one doing the unraveling right now."

"You said it yourself. I like to be good at everything I do, and practice makes perfect." I licked at the crease of each thigh and came to hover over the soft pink skin between them, prepared to stay down there for hours and then, "Gemmie! We're home!"

I froze with my mouth barely touching her pussy, and Gemma let out a frustrated moan, echoing my internal one. "Unbelievable."

The honeymooners were home three days early. She rolled away from me and grabbed the first articles of clothing she could get her hands on. "You owe me one orgasm."

I held my hand out for a high five. "As many as you want, Gemmie."

"Ugh. God, don't call me that *now*." She gestured to me,

naked and half hard, then let out one more groan before heading downstairs. I threw on jeans and a long-sleeved thermal T-shirt, interrupting Caroline, in a gold sarong dress and appearing tanned and refreshed, mid-conversation with Gemma. Frank, on the other hand, hunched over a chair, his face drawn and pale.

"Oh, Jason, I didn't know you were here," Caroline said, landing a kiss on my cheek. "It's so nice you were here to keep Gemmie company."

Gemma's eyes snagged on me, and I sewed my lips together to keep from grinning. "*So* nice."

She rolled her eyes.

"Frank got food poisoning, so we decided to cut the trip short," Caroline informed me.

"Oh, man. That sucks. How was it besides that?"

Frank grunted while Caroline rubbed his back. "It was wonderful. The resort was so peaceful, and the spa was out of this world. I had the best hot stone massage of my life. Frank even tried acupuncture. Everything was great up until..." She frowned, motioning her thumb to Frank then inspected her daughter. "What're you wearing?"

Gemma held out her arms as if only realizing now what she'd put on. My red boxer-briefs and white undershirt sagged off her body. "I, uh, must have gotten the laundry mixed up."

I clapped. "So, anyone want coffee?"

Caroline helped Frank up. "Actually, hon, I'm going to put him to bed, but help yourself."

They trudged upstairs, leaving Gemma and me alone, and I smiled down at her. "You hungry?"

"How are you so casual about this?" she said, following me into the kitchen.

The past few days, we'd been eating at the island, but I

pointed to the table in the sun-room next to the kitchen. "People have gotten food poisoning before. No big deal."

"I mean…" She clenched her jaw tight, her words muffled through her teeth. "My mother and Frank."

I kissed her jaw and scrunched up my underwear at her hip. "You're killing me in this."

"Don't change the subject."

I opened the refrigerator for orange juice and the mixture of berries and gross vegan yogurt she had stored in there then set it all on the table. "You worried about being caught?"

"Like we're fourteen-year-old kids, yes, it's a little awkward."

I grabbed a pan to fry myself some eggs. "What's so awkward about it?"

"I don't even—we don't…" She gestured between us and sank down in a chair. "What are we supposed to say to them when we haven't even talked about it ourselves?"

I cracked two eggs in the pan. "Then let's talk about it."

She picked up a spoon and dished out her yogurt and berries into a bowl. "Okay."

"Okay."

Then we stared at each other for a minute, waiting for the other to start.

"You first," I said, concentrating on my scrambled eggs as I scraped the pan with a spatula.

"Okay, well." She dragged that word out into three syllables. "I don't want to sound like an annoying girlfriend or anything, but…"

I looked up from my food to find her staring daggers at me.

"What was the situation with you and Bridget?"

"She wanted a boyfriend. I wanted to be friends."

"With benefits," Gemma corrected. "How long were you —" she bent her fingers up in quotation marks "—friends?"

"A couple of months." I spooned out my eggs and sat down at the table with her, silence descending between us. I poured myself orange juice and played with the glass, rolling it back and forth between my palms. "Since you asked that question, does it make you my annoying girlfriend?"

"Annoying?" she repeated, pausing with a berry halfway to her mouth.

"You're the one who said it first."

She aimed her spoon at me. "But you don't have to agree."

"But I do." I snapped my mouth around her bite of breakfast then stuck out my tongue. "Nope, still gross."

She threw a balled-up napkin at me.

"You never answered my question," I pointed out, lifting my juice to take a gulp.

She dipped her spoon back into her yogurt mixture, swirling it around. "I liked playing house with you for a couple of days. What do you think?"

"I think," I started, swallowing the last bite of my eggs. "I kind of like the idea of you being my annoying girlfriend."

She scraped her bowl with the spoon, the noise like nails on a chalkboard.

"You don't like that idea?" I asked, my voice sounding squeaky in my ears.

Setting her spoon down, she sat up, breathing deeply. "You aren't the only one afraid of commitment."

"I am not afraid of commitment. I'm afraid of losing..." I trailed off as my gaze drifted to the window, my words suddenly dust in my mouth as my terrible imagination got the best of me.

But there was Gemma, wrapping her fingers around my hand, her lips curling up into a promising smile. "I'm not letting you go."

CHAPTER TWENTY-FOUR

Monday afternoon, I was in the middle of explaining how to make a pumpkin with a three-dimensional face using of variety of materials, but as usual, I heard Cole talking behind me.

"I'm going over the directions, so I don't know why I hear so much chitchat." I pivoted, ready to redirect Cole when I spotted Jason sitting at the table, his long legs barely fitting under it. "Ah, we have two troublemakers today."

"He started it." Jason pointed to Cole, who shook his head in denial.

I tried and failed to hide my laugh, as I handed out the rest of the supplies to the class, including Jason. Once the kids started the project, I bent over his shoulder. "What are you doing here?"

"Art." He sorted through scraps of newspaper, felt, and cardboard before finding a piece of green tissue paper he apparently liked. He tugged on my ponytail. "You smell good."

"Thank you. You know you're in a class of ten-year-olds, right?"

"Yep."

"Okay then, have fun," I said and proceeded with the art

lesson, which Jason fully participated in, to all the kids' amusement.

At the end of class, Cole gave his new friend a dap and ran out of the room. "Bye!"

Jason waved. "See ya, buddy."

I crossed my arms.

"What?"

"You and Cole are best buddies now. Going for pizza and beer later?"

Jason stalked over to me, hands in his pockets. "Apple juice and peanut butter sandwiches."

I yanked on his tie, lowering his face to mine, and nipped at his bottom lip. "You finished work for today?"

He nodded, giving me a little pat on the ass, as I started to clean up, wandering from table to table and back to the closet in the corner. "Want to give me a ride home?"

"That's why I'm here," he replied, dropping a pair scissors back in their bucket before escorting me out of the classroom and the building. He carried my bicycle to his truck, his annoyance plain. "Isn't it getting a little cold out to still be riding this?"

"It's not snowing yet," I said and ignored his grumbly mumble. When he made a left out of the parking lot, I held up his art project to assess it. "You did a pretty good job."

"Pretty good job? That's an awesome mixed-media pumpkin," he said, wiggling his eyebrows like I should be proud of him for remembering the terminology I had gone over during class. I was.

"Maybe we could sell it at the auction," I said, sliding his aviators on.

He regarded me with a sinful smirk. "You look so good in those. You know that, right?" When I shrugged one shoulder, he clucked his tongue with a stiff shake of his head as he refocused on the road. "What auction?"

"Every year, the museum has a fundraiser for Artist Point, which is the program that employs me. They auction off stuff by local artists—paintings, sculptures, even some of the projects from the kids. We actually raise quite a bit of money. And since you're…" I paused, comprehending the importance of what I was about to say out loud, "…my boyfriend, that makes you obligated to go, right?"

"I suppose I could pencil it in. Anything for the kids."

"Truly magnanimous of you." I poked his side before taking a look out of the window. "Where're you going?"

"Home."

"This isn't the way to my apartment."

"I know. I'm kidnapping you."

"Damn it." I banged my fist on the door. "I didn't pack my weapons in my purse tonight."

"Eh, I don't know that you need much more than your mouth. Cut somebody to the quick with that." I ran my tongue over my teeth, and he brought my hand to his mouth, kissing my palm. "Don't tease."

Inside his kitchen, I stuck the pumpkin on the refrigerator with a magnet then studied the picture of Jason with his parents. He stood behind me, crisscrossing his arms over my chest, tugging me back against him. I angled my head to ask him, "How old were you there?"

"I don't know. Maybe five or six."

He looked so young and happy in that moment with his parents, my heart broke all over again for him and his family. Of all the time and memories he lost out on. Not knowing what to say, or if I even could say anything, I turned in his arms, and laid my hand over his heart.

He rested his forehead against mine, his voice barely audible. "Thank you."

"For what?"

He didn't answer for a long time, his breath mingling with mine, his fingers cupping my jaw, but eventually he let out a quiet, "Being you." Then he lifted his head and slowly quirked his mouth to the side. "Let's go."

In one swift motion, he threw me over his shoulder and carried me upstairs to his room. I yelped in laughter when he tossed me on the bed. "I had fantasies about being carried through those double doors," I said breathlessly, fixing the hair that had fallen over my face. "But not like that."

"I couldn't wait any longer. I owe you from yesterday." Wasting no time, he tugged off my pants and made himself at home between my legs, humming like a man hungry. He nibbled on the tender skin of my upper thigh before moving to my pubic bone, scraping his teeth over me. In our short time together, I'd learned he liked to mark me.

But I didn't mind. For once, I wanted to be claimed. I was his.

"I love that you don't wear underwear," he murmured against my skin before dragging the flat of his tongue up my slit.

I gasped his name, digging my fingers into his hair, and he held my hips down so I couldn't wiggle away under his onslaught. All of my muscles clenched as he alternated fluttering the tip of his tongue and sucking at my clit, and I could hardly fill my lungs with a breath before he was robbing me of it with another lush kiss or bite to my tender flesh.

Digging my heels into the mattress, I canted my hips, circling and seeking more, and he groaned, his mouth open on me like he couldn't get enough. He pushed his hand down on my lower stomach, keeping me in place, even though he whispered words about loving how wild I was, and slipped his thumb over my clit until I was muttering incomprehensible words. Tension coiled through me, but as I felt the first spark of an orgasm, he lifted his head.

"Wh-what…what are you doing?"

"Enjoying myself."

I whined as his thumb and index finger held me open so the cool air of the room washed over my soaked skin.

It was lewd, how hot and wet I was.

Yet with Jason's filthy grin, I couldn't help but let out a delirious laugh.

Then his mouth was on me again. His tongue plunging into me, his fingers working over the sensitive bud at the top of my sex. And once again, I was shuddering with pleasure, completely unable to control the shaking in my legs or ragged exhales.

"Oh god, Jason."

He broke away from me, brow raised in question, as if I was actually calling him for a reason other than him breaking my brain with near orgasms.

My jaw flapped open.

"Yes?"

"Are you doing this on purpose?"

"Doing what?" he said, lips brushing over my clit.

I growled and gripped his hair with my hands, forcing him to stay there. And I swear I heard the son of a bitch laugh.

He had perfected kissing and touching me over the last week, and he would be able to get me off in minutes if he wanted to. Instead, he insisted on torturing me.

Each time I was close, he left me hanging on the precipice, raining sloppy kisses up and down my legs or dragging his fingers down my center, like he had all the time in the world to explore. I tried to yank him back to where I wanted him, whin-ing, "Jason, come on."

Instead of giving in, he continued edging me. Finally, I dug my fingers into his scalp. "Jason! Please! I'm dying!"

"I like playing with this pretty pussy. I want to drive you crazy, like you drive me crazy."

"I hate you," I whimpered, covered in a sheen of sweat.

"No, you don't." He slid two fingers into me, and my back bowed off the bed. "But I guess you've earned it." Then he twisted his hand, crooked his fingers and found the spot to set me on fire. I exploded, screaming his name, in quite possibly the hardest orgasm to ever rack my body.

As I trembled with aftershocks, Jason levered himself over, his lips glistening with my arousal. "I love watching you come."

"You love torturing me."

He swiped his palm over his mouth and kissed me, but I could still taste myself on him. "I love to be the one to make you sweat and swear and beg. Normally, you're the one to use your mouth as a weapon, but I like doing it too." Then, as if he didn't stun me into silence, he tweaked my big toe. "So, dinner in, like, half an hour?"

He didn't wait for my answer, just headed toward the bedroom door. With one last sizzling look, he raked his eyes over me and licked his lips, letting out an appreciative sigh before leaving the room. I stayed on the bed, my gaze on the ceiling, my blood still buzzing from the orgasm.

It took a few minutes—or maybe hours, I don't know—until I could move my limbs again. Lured by the sound of pots banging around the kitchen, I eventually stood up to collect my brain and pants. I hadn't known Jason very long, and we'd only solidified our relationship status yesterday, but since he accepted my invitation to the auction and now he was making me dinner, it all hit me at once.

This was real.

This was setting dates and sharing calendars and attending potlucks or whatever it was couples did.

Gem and Jason. Coupled up. We were going to try to make a real go of this.

Wild.

The scent of tomato sauce and garlic bread brought me back to the present, and I was about to leave the bedroom when a picture on his dresser caught my eye. It was framed in popsicle sticks and looked like one that hung on the wall in my living room. The photo, from last year when I had volunteered at a summer camp, showed me and the kids covered in rainbows from finger painting day. I turned it over. A messy note was scrawled on the back, *For Miss Gem, Love, Peyton.*

I brought it to the kitchen, where my newly-minted boyfriend stirred spaghetti. "Jason?"

He set down the spoon, leaning his hip into the counter. "Hmm?"

I remained silent, holding up the picture.

"Oh. About that." He smiled impishly. "I may or may not have stolen it."

"What? When?"

"The night I dropped you off."

"After yoga? The night you killed the spider?"

He laid his palms against my throat as he massaged the nape of my neck, but I wasn't to be deterred. I shrugged him off. "When?"

He didn't answer, but his eyes told the truth, and I gaped. "The night we met? You drove me home. We fought the whole time, and then you took this?"

He nodded and twisted back to the stove, his face redder

than I'd ever seen. Behind his back, I stared at the frame in my hands. "I thought you couldn't stand me."

One then two and three seconds passed.

"Hey. Make me understand," I said, and he suddenly circled around, trapping me in his arms, burying his face in my neck.

"I wanted you the moment I saw you. But you were—are—so...goddamn frustrating. I just needed a piece of you."

"So, you stole a picture of me? Like some creep."

"Yeah." He laughed. "I'm an awful creep. Forgive me for stealing it?"

"I didn't even realize it was gone until now."

"So you don't mind?"

I shook my head, and he picked me up in a bear hug, tilting his head back for a kiss. "Hungry?"

"Starving."

Setting me down, he pushed me against the counter, my spine arching over the cool marble, a contrast to the skin of my stomach growing warm when his hands moved underneath my shirt. I moaned when he traced the shell of my ear with his tongue, and I found his belt loops, tugging his hips closer to my own. Which was exactly when the pot of water boiled over with a noisy hiss. Steam swamped the kitchen.

I brushed my bangs back from my damp forehead, the heat from dinner nothing compared to this near-constant fever. No matter how many times he kissed me, how often he had his hands on me, it was never enough.

I was full of want and need and wasn't ready for the fever to break yet. I hoped it never would.

Jason opened up a window, waving away the last of the steam. He still hadn't changed out of his work clothes, making the show of him finishing dinner all that much more enticing. He wore dark, fitted pants that showcased his long legs and tapered waist. His white shirt flaunted the muscles in his broad shoulders, and when he emptied the pot into a colander in the sink, his forearms flexed from under sleeves that were rolled up to his elbow.

"It's ready," he told me, dipping his head toward my chair. I loved that move, the tiny head nod directing me where he wanted, always right next to him.

I didn't have a whole lot of experience with boyfriends, but this one seemed to be pretty perfect.

After dinner, I stood to take the dishes to the sink, but he snatched hold of my waist. "Leave 'em. Let's go upstairs."

"I can't. I need to go home." When he attempted to sit me on his lap, I dug my heels in and he put on a pained face. "I'm opening the store tomorrow," I told him, drawing my finger across his narrowed eyebrows. "What do you want me to do? I don't have any clothes here." He didn't move, so I yanked him up out of his chair. "Give me a ride home?"

He looked none too pleased but grabbed his keys from the counter to drive me home anyway. Like the perfect boyfriend he was. He carried my bike upstairs to my apartment, where George Clooney lunged at him from behind the sofa. "Jesus!"

"What are you, six-three, six-four and you're afraid of a cat?" He ignored me, setting down the bike, and I suppressed my giggle, placing my hands on his chest. "You're funny."

"And you're not." He kissed my nose. "Can't I sleep over?"

"No."

He dropped his forehead to my shoulder petulantly, so I stumbled under his weight. "Why not?"

"Because," I said, forcing his head up. It weighed fifty pounds. All that ego. "You need to go to work tomorrow. You left all the lights on in your house. You have to—"

He stifled my words with his mouth, his fingers weaving into my hair, holding me in place. Little by little, my body unconsciously gave in to him, first with my arms around his middle, then my tongue tangling with his, then arching against him as he stepped me backward to the couch. The flames that rose in my veins had become so much a part of me when he touched me that I almost didn't feel it anymore.

Almost.

In one quick motion, I was out of his arms, my hands moving up in defense.

"Fine," he grouched.

I offered him a chaste peck on the cheek, careful to avoid getting too close. One more kiss like that, and it'd be all over. "Another time."

CHAPTER TWENTY-FIVE

Jason

The next day, I slunk down at my desk after lunch and opened my email to find one from Gemma. I clicked on the attachment, and my jaw dropped.

Her naked body covered my screen. Her long hair was the only form of modesty besides a sheet that hung limply from her left hand. Her pert, pink nipples were right there. That small patch of hair covering her pussy like some Renaissance painting. She was gorgeous, and like a good little soldier readying for deployment, my dick was already stiffening in my pants.

I readjusted myself and picked up my phone, never taking my eyes off the monitor.

"Hey, you," she answered, all smoke and gravel.

"You can't send me stuff like this on my *work* email, Gemma. I'll get in trouble."

"With who? Aren't you basically second-in-command?"

"Yeah, but—"

"You don't like it?"

My response was a sort of guttural sound from somewhere deep in my gut.

She laughed. "Can I come over tonight?"

"Of course. Pack a bag so you can slee—shit. I forgot. I'm meeting my friends after work to watch the game."

"Oh." She deflated, sex voice gone. "Okay."

"You can meet us," I said, scrambling to make it up to her, but she hesitated.

"No, that's okay."

"I want you to come. Please?"

"I'll be all sweaty from yoga."

I sat back in my chair, smiling at the terribly inappropriate picture still up on my computer screen. "Perfect. I like you like that."

She snorted. "How about I meet you at your place later?"

"No. Come to The Grill when you're done with class."

"I don't know."

I pretended not to hear her. "Great. I'll see you later." I hung up before she could argue and downloaded the picture to my phone in order to erase it from my computer. Two could play her game.

> I can't wait to get your beautiful, naked ass in my bed. Smack it for sending such a naughty picture.

GEM

Promise?

I spent the next ten minutes recounting all the sex positions I had yet to try with her before I got back to work.

That evening, my friends and I sat at a high-top table covered in beer and wings, a play-off baseball game showing on every TV screen. A Cubs player slid home, and the place went crazy. Some random guy from the table over even high-fived us. That was when I spotted her.

Gemma sheepishly waved at me from the entrance, and my smile instantly grew bigger at the sight of her bundled up in a plush cardigan and scarf, her cheeks flushed red from the cold air. I motioned her over, introducing her to the guys at the table. "Gem, this is Kevin and Luke." I kissed her temple and ushered her down to a chair next to me. "How was your day?"

"Good." She arched her eyebrow, a mischievous smile on her lips. "How was yours?"

Her hair was knotted on top of her head, but I wound a loose strand of it around my index finger. "Picked up this afternoon."

"Oh yeah? Why?" she asked all innocent-like, and I tugged on her hair before pulling her chair closer to mine.

"Gem," Kevin began, swallowing a bite of his chicken wing, red sauce on his fingers, "you hungry?" She cringed at the sight of the bone in his hand, and he furrowed his bushy eyebrows in return. "What?"

"She's a vegan," I explained.

Luke, a veritable garbage can, shook his head. "That sucks, man. I couldn't live without cheeseburgers."

She shrugged. "You get used to it. Jason's tried some of my food."

I nodded in agreement, glad my friends didn't feel the need to point out how a girl—*my girl*—had invaded our guy night. "Yeah, it's not bad."

"Are you totally disgusted being here?" Kevin asked after polishing off another chicken wing.

Gemma smiled indulgently with a laugh. "No, it's fine."

"Out!" Luke banged his fist on the table at a play on screen. "I gotta piss."

Kevin also stood up, wiping his hands. "Another pitcher?" he asked no one in particular, before heading to the bar.

"They seem sweet," she quipped, and I gripped her thighs, urging her to face me.

"I like them," I said, leaning in close.

"Then I do too. Besides, this is a much easier test than you'll get from my friends."

"Oh yeah? Should I be scared?"

"Scared, no, but prepared, yes. It's a lot of different...energy when we're together."

"I can't wait to meet them," I said sincerely and wrapped her thick sweater around her tighter. "You look cute all bundled up."

Under the table, she snaked her hand up between my legs, cupping my dick like she owned me—but who the fuck was I kidding? I'd been hers since that hot August day—and she whispered, "I thought you wanted my naked ass in bed."

I bent to kiss her, but she crooked her neck, and my lips landed on her cheekbone. She gave me a little squeeze over my pants and stood up. "Can you order me a garden salad with vinaigrette? I'm going to freshen up."

I muttered a sulky agreement as she patted my head and sashayed off. I watched her go, like a dog with its owner.

But it wasn't until a few minutes after Luke and Kevin returned, and her salad was ordered, that I noticed Gemma still hadn't come back. I stalked to the bathroom to find her, although the door opened before I got to it.

She hopped back in surprise. "What are you doing?"

"Looking for you. Thought maybe you fell in."

"Not quite."

The bathrooms were set back in a little hallway, and with no one around, I hauled her to me. My brain had been working in overdrive ever since I opened that attachment, and I had to have her. Immediately.

My lips devoured hers, my tongue licking into her mouth in a way that mirrored what I would much rather be doing. She whimpered, and I backed her up against the wall, the cotton of her cardigan soft against my chest, but I could feel the heat radiating from her body, and I yanked it off.

She curled her tongue around mine, digging her fingers into my hair as I urged her legs apart with my thigh. When I teased the juncture of her hip with my fingertips, a soft curse escaped her lips, her shoulders sinking down.

"What?" I backed away, searching her eyes.

"Your plan to get me naked…"

"Yeah," I breathed, my lips on her neck.

"It's dashed."

I continued nibbling at her throat for a few seconds before her words sank in. Straightening up to my full height, I stared down at her. "Huh?"

"I got my period."

My own shoulders sank. "Well, that's inconvenient." I fixed her sweater back around her shoulders and readjusted myself for what felt like the hundredth time today. "You feeling all right?"

"You want TMI?"

"Yes." I caught her finger and kissed it. "Always, when it comes to you."

"I'm a little crampy, but my second day is always worse than the first. Like a murder scene."

I had nothing to say and assumed it was better to stay silent in this kind of situation, so I kissed her temple then laced my fingers with hers on the way back to the table. Gemma's salad was waiting for her.

Kevin smirked. "That was quick."

I mushed my palm against his face. "Shut up."

Gemma poured herself a beer from the pitcher, and Luke raised his glass to her, openly surprised at how she helped herself. "You drink?"

She answered by taking a few gulps then covered her mouth when she let out a tiny, adorable burp.

All three of the us laughed, and Luke tipped his chin to her. "Didn't expect that to come from a vegan yoga teacher."

She picked at her salad, fumbling over a cherry tomato, probably figuring out that I'd been talking about her. "I told you," I said, speaking to my friends even though my eyes were on her. "She's full of surprises. In the best ways possible."

After dinner, we drove back to my place, and she popped a couple Advil before we cuddled on the couch, watching some nature documentary about climate change. It was so depressing I had to keep myself busy by sucking marks into the undersides of her breasts.

That night, I fell asleep with my hand splayed across her belly since she said the heat of my hand felt good on her stomach, but I woke up to her side of the bed cold when my alarm blared.

I squinted, focusing my bleary morning eyesight around the room until I found her. "Hey, you," I said, all groggy and rough. "You're up early."

She nodded from where she was perched on the big grey chair in the corner, her pencil scratching along a paper. "I had cramps so I made tea and took some more Advil."

I yawned. "What are you doing?"

"Drawing."

"What are you drawing?"

"You."

I sat up on an elbow and wiped sleep from my eyes. "Me? Can I see?"

She stuck the pencil between her teeth while she crawled up onto the bed next to me and turned the paper over in her lead-covered fingers.

I took the paper to study it, blown away even if it was a

rough sketch. She captured me asleep, arms around my pillow, the sheet at my waist, my back on display.

She nudged my shoulder after a while. "Do you like it?"

"Yes, of course, yes. You're so talented." I shook my head ever so slightly, a little embarrassed. "I guess I... It's nice to see me through your eyes. You see me as beautiful."

She tugged the sleeves of one of my sweatshirts over her hands, like she wasn't sure what to say. Like maybe her art spoke for her. That when she couldn't sleep, it was me who kept her company, soothing her mind. Or, at least, that's what I hoped it meant.

I cupped her knee with my hand, my thumb stroking her soft skin. "When I'm with you, I feel like I'm in a different world. Like my whole life, I've been living in black-and-white, and then you came along and gave everything color. You know what I mean?"

She bit her lip, not responding, and maybe I was wrong. Maybe I was way off the mark and this sketch was just that. A sketch. I recoiled my hand. "It's okay if you don't feel like—"

"No. Jason, no." She launched herself into my lap. "You make me so happy it hurts. At the end of the night, my cheeks get sore from smiling so much. You kiss me, and my chest feels like it's going to explode. I miss you when we're not together, and when we are, I wish I never had to leave." She rested her forehead against mine, her voice wavering with emotion. "It scares me that in just a couple of weeks, I feel so attached to you."

"And me to you," I said, holding her hands against my chest.

"But I'm afraid." She tried to pull away, but I held on tighter. "I don't want to drown in this."

"I won't let you. I'm not letting you go, Gemma."

CHAPTER TWENTY-SIX

Jason

A week later, I brought lunch to Gemma at Bare Necessities. With October in full force now, it was way too chilly to eat outside, so we sat down next to each other in an aisle between the all-natural pet supplies and gluten-free cereals.

"Where are we going tonight?" she asked, leaning against a big bag of dog food.

I shoved a piece of sushi into my mouth. "Some steak place."

She picked at her avocado roll. "I'll be eating a cup of soup, I guess."

"It's Frank's birthday, his choice. For your birthday, you can take us to some tofu place if that's what you want." I poked her with chopsticks. "You could always order a New York strip and call it a day."

She snorted. "I'll stick with the breadsticks."

"So, what did your mom say about us?" I asked, dipping a piece of my roll in soy sauce.

Gemma stared at her food like she was dissecting it for a biology assignment.

"Oh, come on. I thought you were going to tell her yesterday."

"I was. I didn't."

"Chicken."

Her mouth snapped open to argue, but she shut it just as fast, and I clacked my chopsticks at her.

"She'll eventually figure it out since we'll continue to go places together, and I'll be...I don't know, holding your hand, kissing you."

She pouted. "She's going to make a big deal out of it."

"I am a pretty big deal." I shrugged, and Gemma grumbled.

"Isn't your neck tired from holding up that big head?"

I leaned toward her as if to kiss her cheek but instead grabbed the last piece of her roll. "Kinda."

She swatted at me, our usual game. Me stealing her food, her pretending she was actually going to eat it. "Pick me up at six?"

I nodded, swallowing the roll in one bite. "Make sure you bring some slippers or something. I have no socks left since you keep taking all of mine." When she sighed, I raised my brow. "What?"

"I'm always staying over at your house," she said, and I stared at her blandly because, yes, that was true. She went on. "It's a little one-sided, don't you think? Me always having to pack a bag. Why don't you like staying at my apartment?"

"It's not that I don't like staying there. It's that—" I engulfed her in my arms, pulling her close "—I need a big old bed to sleep in. Your bed is too small, Goldilocks, but my bed is just right."

"I'm serious, Jason." She shoved away from me. "I'm always staying at your place. I want you to stay with me tonight."

She pinched my arm when I grimaced. "Ouch!" I grabbed my bicep. "I'm kidding. I don't have a problem packing a bag. No need to come to blows."

"You deserve it. My bed is well worn-in and comfortable."

I threw my arm around her neck. "You're right. Who needs leg room when you've got lumps in the mattress?" She lifted her fingers to pinch me again, but I trapped her hand. "As long as you're next to me, I'd sleep on a rock."

Her glare eventually fizzled to a reluctant smile, and she rested her head on my shoulder. "It's hard to be mad at you when you're so charming."

I kissed the top of her head. "That's the point."

That night, at ten minutes to six, Gemma opened her door, still in sweats. "You're not ready."

"You're early."

"Don't pretend you didn't know I would be."

She raked her gaze over my sweater, brown leather jacket, and fitted jeans. "Does it ever get tiring being so pretty? Like, do you fear the day your looks will fade and wonder if people will still like you?"

"Well, I know you won't so..." I shook off George Clooney, who rubbed his head against my shin, and followed Gemma when she spun on her heel, heading back to her bedroom. I let my duffel bag drop to the floor as she let her sweats do the same, whatever further retort I had dying on my tongue. Her ass called to me as she bent to step into a pair of skinny jeans, and I slid my hand over one cheek, squeezing.

"What are you doing?"

I nuzzled her neck, my fingers trailing down between her legs. "I hate knowing you're bare under your clothes, and I can't do anything about it."

"We're going to be late."

"I'm early," I crooned, dipping my fingers into her wet heat while my other hand roamed under her T-shirt to her breast, plucking at her nipple how I knew she loved. "We do have some time. Besides, I know you're stressed about tonight. Let me help you with that."

She started to argue, but I curled her hair around my fist and angled her head to quiet her mouth. Her tongue tasted like her toothpaste, but I wanted to taste her somewhere else and pushed her toward the bed. "Bend over," I told her with a smack to her ass. "Spread your legs. This is going to be quick."

For once, she stayed quiet, and good god, my cock grew instantly hard when she followed my instructions. I dropped to my knees, licking up her tangy sweetness, and she moaned. "Oh, please."

I smacked her ass again, this time hard enough to leave a mark.

"Fuck, yes, Jason."

"Say my name again." *Smack.*

She threw her head back. "Jason."

"You're dripping." I circled my finger around her clit while I lapped at her juices. "You love being bossed around, huh? Not so tough when I have my hands on you."

She whined, rolling her hips, and she was right on the edge, but I wanted her coming with me inside of her. I snagged one of the vegan condoms I special ordered and tugged my pants and underwear down just low enough to take my cock in hand. "Head down on the bed, Gemma. Let me see that sweet ass up in the air."

Once I was sheathed, I grabbed hold of her hips with what I knew was bruising strength and thrust into her, filling her to the hilt. She grunted as if I pushed all the air out of her lungs. And nothing was as perfect as this.

I was so hard and primed, it only took a few strokes until I was already coming, but so was she. I slowly pulled out, both of us groaning at the loss, and I gave her butt a rub before marching off to the bathroom to take care of the condom. When I returned a minute later, she had her jeans and bra on.

"See?" I said, smug as can be. "Only took six minutes."

"Is that really something you want to brag about?"

I slid my hands around her waist, up to her rib cage. "When I can make my girl come in five minutes? That's absolutely something to brag about."

She threw a thin shirt over her head. "Here, button me up."

I gathered her hair over one shoulder to close the hook and eye. A small oval of skin was left open between her shoulder blades, and I bent down to kiss it. When my lips traveled back up to her neck, she shivered. "So arrogant."

"Confident," I corrected. "I'm confident you've never screamed anyone else's name."

She merely stepped into her boots, which was answer enough.

"Still feeling stressed out?" I asked as we walked out of her apartment building.

"No, but my ass stings."

"I'll kiss it better tonight."

When we arrived at the restaurant, Gemma tried to make a break for it, but I held her to my side as the hostess in all black led us to a table, where Frank and Caroline were seated. Her eyes rounded, pieces clicking into place. "Am I imagining this?" she asked, bobbing her head excitedly. "Are you two...?"

I held up our linked hands and nodded.

"This is wonderful!" Caroline hugged each of us. "I knew it. I knew you two would make a good match. Didn't I say that, Frank?" She whipped her head back and forth from her husband to her daughter. "I did say that. Oh, this is amazing." She settled back into her seat, dragging Gemma to the chair next to her. "Why didn't you tell me? I'm so happy." She clasped her hands together in front of her heart, beaming. "One big happy family."

I handed Frank an envelope as he sat down. "Happy birthday."

"Thanks, Jay."

"It was Gem's idea. I wanted to get you Depends, but she said that would be rude."

Frank opened the birthday card, and a gift certificate fell out. "Hot Sauce of the Month Club!" He grabbed Gemma's hand. "Excellent. Thank you."

A young waitress, probably barely eighteen, in a vest and tie, approached the table. She introduced herself and offered a drink menu along with the specials. Frank ordered a round of appetizers, all of which had some sort of animal in them, and I held up my hand to order something else for Gemma, but she tapped my foot under the table. Even though she had playfully made a big deal about eating at this steakhouse, I knew she wasn't going to say anything about how there were literally only two items she could eat in this whole place. Yet instead of letting me ask the server about options, she glared at me and reached for the bread baskct.

Dinner went relatively smoothly as Frank stayed quiet, sawing his way through the biggest cut of meat they had, and Caroline stuck to basic questions about me and Gemma, no real prying. For dessert, the waitress brought out a round chocolate cake topped with a few tall candles which Frank repeatedly failed to blow out. After his fifth attempt, he wiped his forehead. "Guess you hit sixty, and the lungs are the first thing to go."

"They're trick candles." Caroline giggled behind a napkin.

Frank's gaze transformed to pure adoration as he reached over the table to kiss Caroline, and I wondered what my life would be like at his age. If there would be romance and laughter and love.

I took hold of Gemma's hand under the table, her eyes puddles of some emotion I couldn't read, though from the thoughtful quirk to her lips, maybe it was the same thing I'd been imagining. "Gem, I—"

Before I could finish my sentence, the waitress tripped next to the table, sending a glass pitcher full of water flying high into the air. Its descent to the floor ended with a spectacular smash into a million pieces, but not before most of the liquid made a pit stop all over Gemma.

Every head in the restaurant spun to find the clatter. Her once-loose cream top was soaked through and almost entirely sheer.

"I'm sorry. I'm so sorry." The young girl apologized from her position on the floor. A middle-aged man, who I assumed was the manager, sped toward our table. When the waitress spotted him, she wiped her face with the back of her hand. "I'm sorry. I'll get this cleaned up as soon as—"

"It's okay." Gemma slipped off her chair to the floor and began to pick up some bigger pieces of glass as the man reached the table. "It was an accident."

"Morgan, in the back, please."

The girl nodded but was slow to get up.

"Now!" he barked.

She ventured another glance at her mess, tears trickling down her cheeks before hurrying off toward the kitchen, head down, broken pitcher in hand. The man offered his hand to Gemma. "I am very sorry about this unfortunate incident."

"Don't worry about it." Gemma ignored his help, getting up on her own. Although once she was upright, the manager's eyes glued to her chest and the distinct outlines of her nipples through the thin material of her bra and shirt now stuck to her skin.

I curled my hand into a fist, striving to remain calm, knowing Gemma could handle herself. She wouldn't want me to step in.

He cleared his throat and brought his attention to Gemma's face, which was a good fucking thing because I didn't know how much longer I could sit at this table with his leering. "I would, uh, like to offer a discount on tonight's meal."

Turned out, I didn't even last a few seconds. I got up and wrapped my jacket around Gemma's shoulders, making sure she was covered. She smiled her thanks to me then said to the manager, "It's no big deal."

"I insist." He brought his hand to his chest, inclining his head to Frank and Caroline. "I apologize again for this inconvenience on your birthday. You can be assured I will be taking care of the problem."

Most of the patrons in the place were watching the scene unfold, and I felt Gemma tense next to me. "Morgan was very helpful tonight. She was polite and knowledgeable, and if you fire her over a few drops of spilled water, you can be assured you will lose my business here."

I covered my snicker with a cough, but she elbowed me anyway. There was no need for the manager to know her vegan ass wouldn't be stepping foot back here.

"Morgan was a great server," Caroline stated with a smile, slipping on her coat.

Frank ushered her toward the exit with a, "Food was great!"

Then I signed for the check without a word and guided Gemma to a quick getaway. Inside my car, she shivered beneath the wet material of her top, and I blasted the heat all the way up. "Better?"

She nodded, zipping up my jacket, and I breathed out a quiet laugh.

"Man, you've got no fear whatsoever, huh?"

"What?"

"You told off some guy while wearing a see-through shirt and with everyone staring at you. Incredible."

She held her fingers up to the heater. "I couldn't let her get fired."

"No, I know. I know. It's just that not everybody would have done the same thing."

"It was no real tragedy, just some water. If somebody has to get ice water thrown on them, I suppose why not me?" She rubbed her hands along her thighs, obviously trying to warm up, and I replaced her hands with my own.

"And that's exactly why you're so incredible because you ask why not you."

Her face flushed with color, and I cupped her cheeks between my hands.

"You're thoughtful and smart, and I'm so lucky you picked me."

"I will always pick you," she whispered, kissing me sweetly.

Back at her apartment, we discarded articles of clothing on the floor as we made our way to her room, expressing words not yet spoken until passing out from exhaustion, tangled up in each other's arms.

———

My alarm beeped near my ear, my cell phone stuffed under the pillow. I'd barely gotten a few hours of sleep and dreaded going to work. With Gemma draped over me, I considered taking a sick day.

Last night, being with Caroline and Frank, witnessing their devotion to each other, I couldn't help but visualize my future. I had imagined being sixty and struggling to blow out trick candles while Gemma laughed in amused satisfaction next to me. It was her I wanted next to me in twenty, forty, sixty years. A lifetime with her would never be enough.

Because I loved her.

The truth had struck me like a slap across the face, and I had been close, so close, to telling her at the restaurant until the water fiasco.

Words somehow seemed insignificant and not nearly enough to describe the world I now inhabited with Gemma. It was big and wide, and every day was something new to learn and explore. I couldn't possibly explain all that to her, so when we'd gotten home, I tried with my mouth and hands.

Smiling in contentment, I carefully lifted Gemma's limbs off me and shimmied out of bed to get ready for work. Shuffling into the living room, I retrieved my forgotten clothes from the previous night and spied my jacket clumped on the floor underneath Mr. Clooncy. I shooed the cat away, my eyes almost popping out of my head when I saw the ruined material. Scratches and holes dotted the new brown leather. I gritted my teeth and stomped back to Gemma's bedroom to wake her up. "I'm going to kill that goddamn cat."

"What?" She squinted awake. "What's wrong?"

"My jacket." I held it up. "Look at it. It's brand-new."

She sat up, still rubbing sleep from her eyes, tand assessed the evidence. "It has character now."

"Character," I repeated in a huff.

"What?" Her eyebrows knit together, and the fact that she didn't seem to care that my stuff had been destroyed pissed me off. She bought almost all her clothes at thrift stores, and I totally respected whatever she wanted to do. The favor was not returned.

"This is real leather," I told her. "It cost me a couple hundred dollars."

"I'm sorry," she said, getting up from the bed to take it from me, inspecting it for a few moments before handing it back. "But maybe you shouldn't spend your money on such expensive things. It's only a jacket."

When she brushed past me on her way to the kitchen, I trailed her. "What's wrong with spending money on nice stuff? I earned it. I shouldn't have to come here and watch it get ruined."

"It's not ruined." She flicked on the coffeepot then held her hands up like I was a rabid animal, and that pissed me off too.

I marched down the hall, cursing, and came back with my bag, stepping into my shoes.

"Where are you going?"

"Home." I was tired and going to be late for work.

"Why?"

"Why?" Once I had the butchered jacket on, I threw my arms out. "Because I don't want to be here anymore. Because you're acting as if I'm the jackass for being angry, when it was your cat that ripped holes in my jacket."

"I'm sorry, but I don't understand—"

I cut her off with a growl. Ten minutes ago, I was thinking about staying in bed with the woman I loved, and now we were arguing. Of course.

Fearing I'd lose my temper, more than I already had, I clenched my jaw, measuring my words. "Gemma, I get that you hate capitalism, animal products, or anything nice—" I threw in the last bit for at least one jab "—but just because you don't like it doesn't mean I can't or-or-or..." I stuttered over my words, my anger blocking out rational thought. "If it goes against what you believe, then you don't care about it." I went on in a higher voice, imitating her. "It's only a jacket."

She forced out a laugh that bordered on condescension. "You're being ridiculous."

"It's my jacket, Gem. If we were at my house and something of yours got trashed, I'd at least apologize."

"I'm sorry," she said, although the damage had already been done.

"You want to know why I always want to go to my place? Because your cat claws up everything, you never throw anything out, and you have a turtle, a fish, and a fucking compost heap in your kitchen. Jesus, you might as well live in a tent."

Gemma flinched at my words and took a beat in which I wished I could pluck my words out from the air and shove them back into my mouth.

"I would rather live in a tent with nothing and be happy than spend money on expensive shit just to fill up a closet. So, go ahead. Leave." She jammed her finger toward the door. "If that's what you care about, then go. Go home in your fancy car to your big, empty house, with your big televisions and state-of-the-art everything. I don't need you yelling at me about it." Then she put her hands on her hips for the pièce de résistance, delivered with quiet condemnation. "I hope you're proud of your jacket and all your *stuff* because it'll need to keep you company since I won't."

I deserved her anger. I was angry too, but her words hit their intended target. Air whistled from my lungs, and without anything else to say, I picked my bag and heart up off the floor and left.

In the twenty-four hours since our knock-down, drag-out fight, I hadn't felt much better. Sure, we had argued before, but what had happened between us yesterday was completely different. Maybe because we knew each other so well now, we could take each other out at the knees.

Jason certainly had done that with me. He'd insulted me and my lifestyle choices, and then he'd left. With the slam of my door, the reality of the situation had hit me like a ton of bricks, and I'd sunk to the floor, where I hugged my legs to my chest and cried.

I hadn't meant what I said to him, but like a child, I had wanted to hurt him as badly as he had hurt me. And I'd practically seen him deflate, the fight leaving every part of his body, even his spirit, and guilt had lodged in my gut, making a home there ever since.

The day had crawled by as pain settled in between my ribs, and the urge to call Jason had crossed my mind more than once. But with each passing hour, nothing I sought to say felt like enough. A lackluster yoga class had been followed up by a Tylenol PM and an early bedtime.

I had battled my doubts and fears about Jason, but this

fight which ended with him walking out brought them all back to the surface. And the light of a new day didn't make me feel any better.

Jason had a soft and genuine heart, but he guarded it with a façade built of bravado and tailored perfection, and I both loved and hated that about him. I admired how hard he worked and how he was so open about what he wanted, even though there was no material good in the world that could provide him the stability and security he desired.

But I could.

I didn't know how to do a lot of things. I was crap at remembering birthdays and anniversaries, almost never paid a bill on time, and had lost my driver's license so many times I'd made friends with Bomani, who worked the DMV desk. But I was really good at loving people.

I loved that even though Jason had thrown a fit about George Clooney, he secretly gave him treats and pats when he thought I wasn't looking. I loved the way he protected me, from giving me his jacket at the restaurant to making sure I always felt in control of the decisions about our relationship. I loved him, and I wanted to make him feel as stable and secure as he made me feel.

Normally, I'd FaceTime the girls if I was this upset or needed advice, but I had to figure this out on my own. I needed to work through our first real fight, be an adult about this. Hopefully, there was still something to work through. Deciding on a plan of action, I dressed and headed out the door.

A few hours later, I wound my way through the offices of Santos & Mitchell, speaking briefly to Joann, who pointed me in the direction of Jason's office.

His door was open, his head down in his hands. He looked miserable. Like I felt.

"Hey, you." My voice was hoarse, and I cleared my throat. "Can I come in?"

He jerked like he'd been hit with an electric shock, and he stood up. With his bloodshot eyes, I guessed he hadn't slept much.

"I just called you," he said.

I took a few unsure steps inside. "I forgot my phone at home."

We stared at each other in silence as the seconds ticked on into what felt like years.

"I'm sorry," we said at the same time, then laughed at the awkwardness of it all.

"I'm surprised to see you." He stepped around his desk, muttering a rushed explanation, "Not that I'm not glad you're here. I am. I'm really glad you're here."

My heart fluttered at his unmistakable tension, a sign that maybe things weren't as bad as I anticipated. "You're rambling."

"I know." He shook his head, a sad sort of smile threatening his lips. "I don't know what to say besides I'm sorry." He sat on the front of his desk, his shoulders hanging in defeat, and I positioned myself between his knees.

"I shouldn't have called you materialistic or said I would leave you. It's no excuse, but I was—"

"Angry. I know." He placed his hands on my hips. "I was angry too. You're right. It's ridiculous to get so upset about a jacket. I never want you to think I care more about shit like that than I do about you."

"I am sorry George ruined your jacket, and you're right, if it were something of mine, I would've been upset. We may not hold the same value for certain things, but I want you to know I won't ever judge you for it. It's still strange sometimes," I said, pausing to gather my words together, and he tugged me two inches closer. "It's strange sometimes to remember it's not only me anymore. I'm stubborn and stuck in my ways, and being with you is forcing me to challenge my views and..." I trailed off with a self-conscious shrug.

"Me too, Gem. As soon as I said what I did, I wanted to take it all back. I didn't mean it. I love your place and your habits. They're weird and wonderful, and I wouldn't want you to be anything else than exactly what you are." He dropped his forehead to mine, breathing his words into my mouth. "A little vegan socialist who has a devil cat and sucks at loading the dishwasher."

I tossed my head back and laughed, feeling lighter than I had in years. Stepping backward, I held up the dark jacket from my bag. "I got this for you. It's not real leather, and I bought it from a thrift store."

He swiftly looped his arms inside it.

"I won't be offended if you hate it," I told him, tugging on the well-worn, spotted collar.

"It's perfect. Like you. Thank you." He pulled me into a tight hug, his nose buried deep in my hair. "I'm so sorry, Gem."

"Me too."

He straightened up, taking me with him, kissing away my reservations about us not fitting into each other's lives. True, we were opposites—from our music choices and diets to our bank accounts—but that wasn't what mattered. As long as we stayed true to each other and what we were together, we'd be okay.

"You'll still come to the auction with me tomorrow?" I asked as he tucked a wayward strand of hair behind my ear, his fingers lingering on my neck.

"Of course."

When our lips met, we consumed each other with hurried licks and nips like we'd been apart for months instead of a day.

Needing physical reassurance, I yanked at his tie, loosening it from around his neck, but he cursed and held me at arm's length. "We can't. Not here."

I blinked around the room. I'd almost forgotten we were in his office. Although, it wasn't like we were out in public. We were alone and would remain undisturbed. I locked his door then turned to him, smiling at his frightened rabbit look.

"Gemma, I'm working."

"Well..." I prowled my way back to him. "It seems like you need a break."

He checked his watch. "I have a meeting in ten minutes."

"Perfect." I stood on my toes, sucking and nibbling at his throat as I dragged my hands down his chest and sides until I reached his pants.

"You're a troublemaker," he rasped, his voice thick as I unbuckled his belt and knelt down to the floor.

"Maybe you need a little more trouble in your life." I dropped his pants and underwear to his knees, and he let out a deep, throaty groan when I kissed his hip bone.

"That's why I keep you around."

I agreed with a hum as I took his cock between my lips. Above me, he leaned his hands back on his desk.

"If this is your way of apologizing, I think I might pick a fight more often."

I swirled my tongue around the tip before taking over with my hand so I could stare up at him. When he traced his thumb along my bottom lip, I nipped at it. "This is my way of saying I know how hard it is for you to move out of your rigid comfort zone. Thank you for bending for me."

He let out a mix of a choked laugh and a moan as I licked back up his length before sliding him into my mouth.

"You look so pretty on your knees like this," he murmured, and I preened at the praise.

I didn't like to give up my power, obviously, and Jason knew that, which was why I felt so emboldened even in this position, because he gazed down at me with such respect and emotion. I wanted to show him in whatever way I could that he meant the world to me.

As if he could read my mind, he said, "I'd bend over backward if it made you happy." Then I wrapped my hands around the backs of his legs, and he let his head drop to his shoulders. "Christ...Gem..." With a few long pulls and a little scrape of my teeth, I soon felt his thighs bunching under my fingers. He breathed harshly, biting out, "I'm gonna come."

And when I didn't stop, he gathered all of my hair in one of his hands to watch me swallow his orgasm. It wasn't particularly my favorite thing to do, and he knew that, but I wanted to do this for him. Not just kneel for him, but show him how I could give, not only take. I could bend for him, too.

After I wiped the corner of my mouth, I blinked up to find him smiling adoringly down at me. "Gemma, I..." He yanked me up from the carpet by my elbow and held me against his chest so I could hear his heartbeat in his chest. "Gem, I lo—"

I interrupted him with a kiss. The first time either one of us said *those* words to the other, it wasn't going to be in his office with rug burn on my knees. "I like you too."

He snorted a chuckle and stepped away to put himself to rights. "How am I supposed to work after that?"

I lifted one innocent shoulder and backed up to the door, unlocking it. "I'm sure you'll pull it together for your meeting."

"Shit. My meeting! I'm gonna be late." He scrambled to grab his laptop and folders and stuck a pen behind his ear before shepherding me out of his office with a smack on my ass. He ran ahead of me, down the hall. "Stop laughing, Gemma. It's your fault!"

I laughed louder.

CHAPTER TWENTY-EIGHT

Jason

Friday night, I opened Gemma's apartment door with an annoyed shake of my head. I called her name over Jack Johnson blaring from somewhere, and when she didn't answer, I found her in the bedroom, dancing while she braided a few strands of her hair like a crown around the top of her head.

I propped myself against the doorframe, appreciating the entertainment her lithe body provided. When the song changed, I gave her a round of applause, and she spotted me in the mirror, not at all startled by my sudden presence. "Creep, hanging out like that, lurking in corners."

"You're lucky it's me and not some ax murderer. Your front door is unlocked."

She sashayed up to me, dragging a finger down my pectoral muscle, her fingernail scraping along my checkered blue dress shirt. "I am lucky." Then she flicked at my navy tie, purposely skewing the clip. "This color really brings out your eyes."

I fixed the clip back in place then smoothed down my tie. "Thank you, but you should lock the door." I held on to her arms, forcing her to look at me. "Seriously. Anybody could have barged in here."

"I left it open for you." She leaned up to kiss me. "There's only you."

The balloon in my chest inflated with her words, *only you*. If it weren't for her holding my hand to spin underneath my arm, I might have floated away.

There was only Gemma.

Whirling away from me so her dress floated around her, she held up her hands. "What do you think?"

The dress was somehow both loose and sexy, with long sleeves and a slit up the side of the skirt. Although the pattern reminded me of something that belonged on a kitchen tablecloth with polka dots and flowers, she could've been wearing a burlap sack and I'd still think she was the most beautiful person on earth. "I think you look like a rich woman who went to the mountains for a weekend nature retreat. She did it for the 'gram."

She cracked up. "That's exactly what I was going for."

"I figured."

When we arrived at the art museum, Gemma led the way, rattling off the name of almost every painting housed there. The party was on the second floor, in a large reception hall where the pieces to be auctioned off were exhibited. There must have been well over two hundred people in attendance, and Gemma snagged a glass of champagne from a passing server as a tall man—even taller than me—greeted her with a kiss on the cheek. With his receding hairline and wrinkled forehead, I pegged the him at about the same age as Frank.

Gemma introduced him as the curator of the museum. "Simon has been my mentor for many years."

He waved his hands in disagreement. "I've done nothing for Gemma besides give her a job. The talent this young woman possesses is far beyond anything I could have taught her." He switched his attention to me. "She is very special, as I'm sure you are aware."

"Yes. Very special." I nodded, and Simon smiled, seemingly pacified, before holding his elbow out to Gemma. "The mayor's here. She brought Congressman Carey with her this time."

She glanced back at me, gesturing with her head to follow, and we ended up with a small group of attendees. Witnessing Gemma hold court with the two government officials and fellow artists, I felt a little intimidated but mostly overwhelmingly proud. She spoke passionately about her work with the children, the importance of creative outlets available to them, and the need to keep art in schools. Simon invited the congressmen to meet the few art students who were present and volunteered Gemma to give him a tour of the museum.

She squeezed my fingers. "I'm sorry. I didn't think I'd be—"

"Do your thing. I'll be fine."

She kissed my cheek before escorting the congressman and mayor to the other end of the room, eventually lost in a sea of people. Grabbing a glass of water, I strolled around the exhibit, studying a clay bust, a few abstract paintings, and one very unusual piece of metal work. It was titled "A Mother's Gift," but it only looked like misshapen pieces of bronze metal to me. I rotated my head almost upside down. Maybe I was at the wrong angle. "Nope, still don't get it."

"What're you doing?"

I stood upright at the sound of Cole's voice. The kid from Gemma's art class stood next to me in a suit and tie, and we fist-bumped. "Hey, buddy. Nice to see you here."

"Yeah. I came over so people don't think you're weird, talking to yourself."

"Good looking out, man."

"Do you want to see my picture?"

"Of course. That's why I'm here." The little boy showed me to a wall with student work and pointed to a picture of a tree-lined street. It was no van Gogh, yet still pretty impressive for a ten-year-old. "Amazing. Did you do that with Miss Gem?"

"Yeah. It's watercolor." Cole proceeded to explain the process of painting it, and I found myself shadowing him as he spouted off about art class and Miss Gem. I saw myself in Cole, in the way he didn't bother to breathe when going off on a tangent about a subject he loved, and how he bounced on his toes to reach for a high five. Just like I used to do with my dad.

Cole's mother eventually collected him, leaving me to continue through the exhibit alone, searching for Gemma's piece. Since she'd refused to show it to me, I had to rely on the plaques to find it, having no idea what she'd created. I located her name printed below a large charcoal drawing. I stood back, marveling at it.

She had depicted a portrait of young love. A man, looking suspiciously familiar, sprawled beneath a tree with a book in hand, his long legs crossed at the ankle. His head, covered with a mop of hair, was tilted up against the trunk, his eyes above him, focused on a woman, lying on a branch jutting out from the side of the tree. Her hair cascaded down her back in long waves, and one hand rested under her cheek, while the other dangled a feather above her lover's head. Their faces expressed total adoration and contentment.

I pressed my hand to my heart, awestruck by the beauty of it. I had, of course, seen many of Gemma's scrawling designs around her apartment, and I'd sat patiently while she sketched my eyes or hands, but the scene in front of me was truly magnificent in its simplicity of romance in black-and-white.

"You like it?"

Wrenched from my thoughts, I angled myself to the man next to me who I thought I might have met before. He wore a dark suit, and I was suddenly very aware that I'd forgone the suit jacket tonight. The man held his drink aloft in greeting.

"I do," I said in reply to his question.

"Me too. I've gotten to know the artist a little, and I think this is one of her best pieces. Gemma Turney has a real interesting perspective. You know her?"

I eyed him. "I do. How do you know her?"

"I was introduced to Gemma last year. We went out on a few dates, but she ghosted me. Broke my heart." He muffled a laugh, his eyes shining in a way that told me maybe he was still interested. That idea had me grinding my molars, especially when he said, "She's quite a woman."

It was then I remembered who he was. "You're the news guy. Colin Mann."

"Yes." Colin Mann, the local news anchor, had a head full of brown hair, perfectly straight, white teeth, a Hollywood tan, and a deep voice meant for broadcasting. "Nice to meet you."

"Jason Mitchell," I said, accepting Colin's hand. "Gem's boyfriend."

We automatically sized each other up, standing a little taller, puffing out our chests. Colin was the first to break free. "You know her well then, huh?" He smirked and pointed to Gemma's art. "Are you planning on bidding?"

"Of course." I wanted nothing more than to smack Colin's smarmy grin off his face. What a douchebag this guy was.

"Well, I hope you brought your wallet because you got yourself some competition for this one."

The double meaning was not lost on me, and I excused myself to find Gemma. When I caught up with her, I latched on to her waist, kissing the skin behind her ear. The whole Bridget situation made itself perfectly clear. I'd been sympathetic to Gemma's jealousy before, but I'd never fully understood it until now.

She leaned into my touch. "What have you been up to?"

"Exploring," I said, though I couldn't hide the irritation in my voice. "Are you really going to auction off your drawing? You can't."

"Why not?"

"I don't want some asshole buying it."

She arched a questioning eyebrow.

"I met Colin Mann."

"Oh." The word contained volumes, but she only shrugged. "It's just a picture. I could always draw more."

"But that's us—"

With her index finger on my lips, she kissed the corner of my mouth, effectively ending the argument, and Simon took his place behind a small podium, announcing he would begin the auction, but first, he brought a woman to the stage. She introduced herself as Elizabeth, the president of Artist Point, and gave a short speech on the history of the charity, thanking a few important people, Gemma being one of them. I held her a little tighter.

The first piece of art auctioned off was a small oil painting, followed by a lot of uninteresting landscapes. Gemma explained the nuances of color and different mediums used in each work before, finally, her picture was put on the block. The bidding quickly escalated to a few hundred, but it was Colin who upped the ante to one thousand dollars.

"Fifteen hundred," I pronounced loudly. Gemma tugged on my hand, but I ignored her. The crowd watched with rapt attention as Colin and I warred, the tension growing higher with each rising number. A collective gasp resounded over the room when the newscaster bid three thousand dollars.

I was about to raise my hand, but Gemma grabbed it. "Enough. Stop."

Simon started counting down, and my gaze darted

between her picture, Colin, and back to Gemma. "I don't want him to have it."

She held my face between her hands, forcing my eyes to hers. "You have me, Jason. You have nothing to prove to him. You have me."

Simon awarded the prize to Colin, who was asked to come onstage so everyone could acknowledge his generous contribution to the charity. He waved to his audience, an arrogant smile plastered across his face, and I let out an angry growl. Gemma repeated her statement, pulling my arms around her waist.

Toward the end of the auction, the paintings by the students were offered up. Even though their work was only being auctioned for fun, the kids took it quite seriously, especially Cole, who whooped in delight at the front of the stage.

My animosity for Colin, my pride in Gemma, and my friendship with Cole had me raising my hand to point at Cole's landscape. "Five hundred dollars."

"Wow!" Cole shouted. "I'm rich."

The room broke out in laughter. His parents quickly tried to correct him, explaining he didn't receive the five hundred dollars; it went to the charity.

"Sorry, buddy." I patted his back. "But your painting is going to look great on my wall." Cole ran up to the podium to snatch his artwork from Simon's hands and happily handed it over to me. "I will take good care of it," I promised as Gemma eased her hand around my elbow, towing me to a quiet corner.

"You didn't have to do that." Her winding hands into my hair told a different story.

"Yes, I did. Cole's your student, and if I can't have your work because—" I stopped short, wanting to put Colin Mann out of my head. "You are in this too," I said, pointing to Cole's painting. "You're in all those kids' works. They love you and—"

"I love you."

I froze at her blurted words. "What did you say?"

She dragged her fingers down my jaw, over my shoulder, to rest in the middle of my chest. "I love you."

I enclosed her cheeks in my hands, my thumbs stroking her cheekbones, nose, and lips. I touched every part of her face, memorizing it with my fingertips. If I could, I'd sculpt her out of clay, show her how beautiful she was. Show her what she looked like through my eyes. "I love you too." My words left my lungs with a rush of air, breathing life into them. "I love you."

Then we kissed. A sweet yet timid first kiss of two people who loved each other, and when we broke apart, smiling like two idiots in love, I laughed. And then she laughed. And then we kissed again.

After a moment, Gemma backed away from me. She had that twinkle in her eyes.

"Come on." She pulled me down a flight of steps to the first floor and ducked into a deserted hall with offices. She tugged me into a small conference room with a square table and chairs, then locked the door behind us. I immediately took her in my arms, hoisting her onto the table, devouring her pleas with my mouth. My teeth bit at her neck, fingers dug into her waist. She hooked her fingers under my waistband, but I stopped her hand from moving lower. "I don't have a condom."

"I don't care. I love you. I need you. Now."

And that was it. I undid my pants, lifted her dress, and crashed into her again. She wrapped her legs around my hips as my hands clutched the table for stability, and she guided me into her, sighing with relief. There was no barrier between us. Nothing but her warm sweetness filling my senses.

She was everywhere. Her hands at my back, her breath on my skin, and I looked, smelled, tasted my fill. I wanted to remember everything about this moment and about the woman I loved.

We were both close to coming, and I bent over her, my lips grazing her collarbone as I whispered over and over how much I loved her, teasing at her swollen flesh until she panted against my ear, drowning out the echo of my heartbeat.

I love you, it drummed. *I love you. I love you.*

With one last thrust, I released hot liquid that overflowed between Gemma's thighs as I rested my forehead on her shoulder. Our ragged breathing resonated in the quiet space, and she kissed my neck over and over again until I picked up my head.

Even as my eyes were heavy, a lazy smile spread across my face. "Well, Gemma, you have every piece of me now. Don't hurt me."

"Never."

CHAPTER TWENTY-NINE

Jason

By the time the November chill rolled in, Gemma and I had fallen into an easy routine. We spent almost every night together, cooking dinners and laughing before tumbling into bed. Every once in a while, she could convince me to do something reckless, like skinny-dipping in the freezing lake or having sex on the local high school's baseball field. I always put up a fight about it, but I'd quite literally follow her into the pits of hell if she wanted me to.

Our relationship was easy and natural, when we weren't arguing. But that could be fun too, sometimes.

I heard her open and close the door downstairs before calling my name out a minute later.

"I'm upstairs!"

"Hey, you," she drawled, launching herself on the bed, disturbing my neat piles of folded laundry. She tugged on my gray sweatpants, the back of her knuckles teasing at my bare skin. "I love how you're so domesticated."

"One of us has to be. You're practically feral." I searched for a match to my sock. A lot of pairs had been going missing lately. And I already knew who the criminal was. "How was yoga?"

"Tiring."

"Tired? Really? I ran five miles and did a whole bunch of pull-ups at the gym today." I used one of her sports bras as a slingshot, the black top bouncing off her cheek. "You did breathing exercises."

She scowled. "You think you're so strong. You can't even touch your toes."

I raised an eyebrow at her before opening a drawer to put my clothes away and, without warning, took a running leap onto the bed, bowling her over. I held one of her legs up with my shoulder and nestled in the wide opening. "You're right. You are the flexible one." I pulled a tube sock off her foot. "Stealing my socks again, I see."

"They're so comfortable, I can't help—" She shrieked when I took a bite of her calf. "Hey! Play nice."

"I am." I sucked at the skin beneath her ear.

"Very nice," she hummed and angled her neck so I could kiss along the other side of her throat. "But I have to shower."

"You smell so good though." I nipped her earlobe. "Vanilla and sweat. Sweet and salty."

When she melted underneath me, I peeled off her clothes. My lips moved over hers as my hand brushed the inside of her thighs before finally settling on the soft skin between her legs. I teased her open, my fingers long since familiar with the touch and tempo she needed.

"I love you," I whispered against her breastbone before covering her nipple with a kiss.

"I love you, too." She wrapped her hand around my cock, stroking it, momentarily deterring me from what I wanted, but with a groan, I pulled away from her.

"Come on you." I rolled her on top of me, shimmying down the mattress until her knees were on either side of my shoulders. I clamped my hand around her thighs. "Show me how strong you are."

My little warrior didn't need to be told twice. She sank down, riding my face, arousal covering my lips and the skin under my nose. I loved that tangy smell of her, and I breathed deep, holding on tight to her hips when she leaned back, finding her balance with her hands on my thighs. She really was delightfully flexible.

"I need you..."

She didn't have finish that sentence. I already knew what she needed and reached one arm up to squeeze her breast, roll her nipple between my fingers.

"Yes," she moaned, circling her hips, grinding her clit down on me, and I barely had enough room to angle my jaw, but I rubbed my tongue back and forth across that tiny bud, an unsuspecting groan emanating from the back of my throat. I got off on this as much as she did.

As her cries turned sharper, I doubled down, using both of my hands to massage her breasts, leaving Gemma to take what she needed from my mouth until she was going off with a soft plea. Then I immediately flipped her over, not done yet.

"No. No more."

"Yes more," I said, sliding two fingers into her soaking wet pussy. "This is what you get for stealing all my socks and coming home in your tight pants with nothing underneath except for *my socks*."

She licked her lips, staring up at me from under drowsy lids. "I'm not sorry."

"Of course you aren't." I added a third finger, and her back arched off the bed. "Look at you, all sweaty and flushed and gorgeous."

"It's too much," she whimpered.

I nipped and licked at her throat. "You can take it. Let me feel you come on my fingers then I'll give you my cock."

She thrashed her head back and forth.

"Gemma."

"Don't use that tone with me."

I laughed. Even delirious, she could still be such a brat. I bent and bit her nipple at the same time I swirled my thumb around her clit, and she nearly shot off the bed.

Her body trembled, her inner muscles clenching around my fingers, but I didn't stop stroking her, easing her through the orgasm until she settled back against the mattress, still and obviously spent.

"That's my girl." I laid a kiss on her mouth before grabbing a condom. I swiftly returned, raising her leg over my shoulder and trailed kisses up her calf, ending at her knee, then sank into her with a low grunt, gently rocking my hips against her. "You got another one for me?"

She tangled her fingers in my hair, licking the skin of my chest, damp from effort, then pursed her lips, her energy back now. "I think the question is do you?"

"You should know by now I win this game. Should we see how many times I can make you scream my name? I have all night." I plunged hard into her, driving the point home, and she squeezed her eyes shut, her mouth open on a silent moan.

I dragged my tongue over her lower lip, calling her attention back to my face. "Don't go quiet on me now."

Dropping my hand to the base of her throat, I held her steady as reared back to my knees and gripped her leg in my other hand, pushing into her again and again, so hard the bed frame repeatedly smacked into the wall.

"Come on. Let me hear it."

She rolled her lips between her teeth. Like the tease she was.

I grunted and bit down hard into the skin above her knee.

"Jason!"

"Much better."

"Ugh." Her frustrated snarl morphed into a soft whine. "You're the worst."

"Mm-hmm. Just awful." Drawing my hand between her breasts and over her stomach, she let out a pleading, soft version of my name.

It broke my will to drag this out. My breathing quickly became uneven, the muscles in my arms and legs tightening with each thrust, straining to make sure she came one more time. I pressed my thumb down on her already overworked clit, and when she finally moaned her release, I followed immediately after, arching my neck.

My torso was covered in a sheen of sweat as I lay down next to her. "Shower?" I asked, wiping at my upper lip, and she answered by skipping off toward the bathroom. She was mid-shampoo when I took over. I rinsed her hair and finger-combed conditioner through her long tresses. "I was thinking..."

She spun around underneath the stream of water to face me.

"All right, so..."

She reached for a bar of soap, waiting patiently for me to continue. "Yeah?" When I still struggled to find my words, she washed my shoulders, chest, and stomach. "You going to tell me?"

"I was thinking. Remember the night at the museum?"

"Yes. I remember." She guided me by the shoulders, turning me away from her so she could soap up my back. "Is that all you were thinking?"

I dropped my head as she kneaded away the tight knots in my neck. "That feels great."

A few minutes passed before Gemma finished her all-over body massage. She was working on my hair when I circled back around, drops of shampoo falling from my forehead, and I rubbed at my eye when it stung.

"You know, Jason, we're in this nice warm shower, naked, soaping each other up, and somehow you look like you're not enjoying it at all. I think I might be offended."

"I was remembering how I wasn't wearing a condom." I closed my eyes to rinse my hair and face, dousing my body with handfuls of water. "I was thinking you should go on the pill. We wouldn't have to use condoms anymore."

She didn't answer me for a long time, and I wiped at my face, squinting through the bubbles still there. "What?"

"How can you ask me that?" She left the shower in a huff. "It's like you don't know me at all." She grabbed a towel, and I hurried to shut off the water, hot on her heels. I held out my hands, dripping wet, while she ignored me, dressing quickly.

"I'm sorry," I said, halting her steps.

"For what?"

"I don't know."

She rolled her eyes. "You can't apologize for something you don't know you did."

"So tell me what I did, and I'll apologize for that."

"You're such a caveman. I'm not taking a birth control pill." She marched down the hall to the laundry closet, leaving me still clad in my towel.

I traipsed right after her as she threw clothes into the washing machine. I shut the door, keeping her from escaping me again. "If I ask you another question, are you going to yell at me?" When she cocked her head at me to continue, I asked, "Why don't you like the pill?"

"Seriously? You want me to put hormones in my body?"

"You already have hormones," I told her, like I was some

kind of idiot biologist mansplaining her own body to her, but at this point I had no other argument.

"Thank you for letting me know. And, yes, my hormones are working just fine. I'm not going to alter them. If nature wanted me to have different levels of them, I would. I'm not going on the pill." She gestured to my crotch. "But feel free to get a vasectomy if you want to go bareback so badly."

This time, I folded my arms. "Don't be so dramatic. It was only a suggestion."

"Suggestion overruled." She turned back to the laundry and jammed the start button on the washer. I snapped my towel on her butt, and she let out a squeal, holding on to her backside.

"Forgot one," I taunted, holding it out to her, completely naked.

She couldn't hide her smile.

"Get over here," I said, wrapping the cotton towel around her like a robe, immobilizing her arms. I tossed her over my shoulder to haul her back to bed.

"Wait, wait, wait."

I set her feet on the floor and pushed her onto the mattress with one finger. "What?"

"I don't have class next week because of the holiday, and Laney's going to be in Chicago for some kind of conference. Her boyfriend is tagging along, and we thought we could all meet up for drinks."

"Yeah, I'd love to meet these best friends of yours." Then I opened the towel, unwinding her like a top.

———

The following week, Gemma and I planned to meet Laney and Bobby for drinks in Rockford, about midway between Galena and Chicago.

"Remind me again which one Laney is."

"She's originally from outside of Philadelphia but lives in San Francisco now. She's the prettiest one out of all of us," Gemma said, bobbing her head along to the three-piece band playing Celtic folk music.

"I highly doubt that." I placed a kiss behind her ear. "She's the one getting her doctorate?"

"No, that's Sam. She's in Michigan right now for school."

"I think I need a diagram or something." I drew an imaginary square on the table. "Okay." I tried again. "Sam is the one in school with the purple hair?"

"I think it's mermaid-colored now, actually."

"You know what? I'll figure it out eventually." Though, I didn't have to wait long. Laney and her boyfriend showed up, and the two girls squawked in excitement while I introduced myself to Bobby Magnate.

"Hey, mate," he said with an Australian accent, which had Gemma leaning back out of Laney's embrace.

"Hey, mate. I'm Gem."

"Laney's told me a lot about you. Shall we?" Bobby asked, holding his hands out so we would all take our seats.

Over our few hours together, the girls mostly chatted, while Bobby sometimes added in some colorful sayings of Aussie slang I had never heard. Laney, with blond hair, blue eyes, and a tiny mole by her nose, did have a kind of old-school Hollywood vibe about her, although she munched on peanuts, drank beer, and laughed louder than anyone in the place. She told great stories about her travels and job with the Giants, but the only thing I cared about was how happy Gemma was to be with her friend.

"So, Jason," Laney said, setting her elbows on the table and her chin in her hands, "you've managed to capture our pixie friend. You got Gem trapped in a drawer like *Peter Pan* or what?"

"Captured? I don't know about that. I think it's the other way around."

Laney smiled wide. "I'm happy to finally be able to do this. We never get to see each other." She looked to Gem. "When's the next time?"

"I don't know. Sam mentioned she was going home for New Year's for a few days, but Bronte will probably be with Hunter." She rolled her eyes, and I briefly wondered what that was about before she continued. "Maybe your birthday?"

"Oi, babe, January, right?" Bobby toyed with a few ends of Laney's hair. "I've got the restaurant opening then."

Gemma snapped her fingers. "Oh yeah. I want to hear all about that."

Bobby leaned back in his chair and gave us a short summary about how he'd made a name for himself in Sydney as a restaurateur, then moved to America to open up a place in New York City. He was apparently really popular in the food world, even had some guest judge gigs on Food Network shows. He had plans to open another restaurant in the Bay Area, which was where he met Laney. "I'm trying to convince the missus here to become the communications director for the Magnate Group, but I've yet to win her over."

Laney lifted a shoulder. "I drive a hard bargain."

"So, not January for the girls' weekend, then?" Gemma said. "Might be a while till we're all back together again."

Laney agreed with a frown, and I took that as my cue to get up. I invited Bobby to head to the bar with me, giving the girls a chance to talk alone for a bit. Bobby was a nice enough guy, although he had a wandering eye when it came to the female bartender and the woman sitting opposite us at the other end of the bar.

At the end of the night, Gemma and Laney hugged, kissed each other's cheeks, then hugged again. I shook Bobby's hand, and we parted ways.

Back at Gemma's apartment, I plopped on the sofa. George Clooney curled up in a ball next to me. "I think he's starting to like me."

"He should, you've been around long enough." Gemma took a seat on my other side and wrapped my arm around her neck. "Did you have fun tonight?"

"Of course. I always have fun with you. It was nice to see you with Laney. You guys are obviously really close, so I'm happy you got to spend time with her."

"The four of us are all really different, but they're like my sisters. I don't have anyone else in my life like them." She craned her neck back, her eyes droopy with sleep. "It was important for me that you meet Laney. I wish it could've been all of them, but thanks for coming tonight."

I kissed her forehead. "You don't need to thank me for that. I had fun, and I really like her. Jury's still out on Bobby, though."

"Really? Why? He's so hot and with that accent..." When she bit her lower lip theatrically, I jostled her.

"I guess he's hot," I said with a surly shrug, and she laughed. "But he didn't seem real interested in Laney or, like, in anything you two were saying. It was all about him—at least, that's the impression I got."

"Interesting." Her eyes went unfocused, probably thinking through that nugget, and I rested my cheek on her head, confessing the one thing I'd been contemplating for a while now. "We should move in together."

She jerked back, forcing my head up. "What?"

"Do you want to move in with me?"

She pulled her feet up onto the couch, curling in on herself, pointedly not answering, and I sat up straight, releasing my arm from around her shoulders to take her chin between my thumb and index finger. "Move in with me."

"Why?"

I huffed out a laugh. I thought it rather plain. "I'm tired of spending half the week here and half the week at my house. We should live together and stop all this back-and-forth."

Her eyes shifted somewhere beyond me, and I didn't realize she'd have such a hard time with this suggestion. We were in love with each other, spent so much time together, this seemed like the logical next step, but Gemma practically vibrated with nerves.

I could physically feel her hesitation.

"What about Mr. Clooney?"

I curved my hands around her neck, my thumbs gliding along the slope of her jaw and collarbone, and I let out an exaggerated groan. "I guess he can come too. And Leonardo and Spot, which, by the way, is a really weird name for a fish."

"It's ironic."

"So, you'll move in with me?"

"I don't know," she said after an eternity.

"What don't you know?"

She pulled out of my grasp. "It's just—"

"I love you," I told her, no longer in the mood to play.

"I love you too."

"Then what is it? I don't get it."

She shrugged, and I held back a grumble of irritation. I didn't want to push her into anything and suspected this had something to do with how self-conscious she was about her supposed failures. She didn't bring it up often, but she'd remarked about the differences in our careers and the amount of money we each made a few times.

"If this is about the mortgage or bills or whatever—"

"Jason." Her gaze fell to the couch, where she played with a fray of the material. "I love you, and I want to be with you, but this is all still very new."

"I know," I agreed, wanting to give her the space and time she needed, while also keeping her all to myself.

"It's all just...a lot." She slowly raised her gaze to meet mine. "Can we put a pin in this and talk about it after the new year?"

I breathed deeply. I could give her that. The new year was only a few weeks away. "Yeah, okay," I said, trying to mask my disappointment.

"I'm not saying no." She stood up, tugging on my hand to follow, and I unfolded from the couch, letting her wrap her arms around my waist. "Don't be mad at me."

"I'm not mad."

"Don't be upset."

"I'm not upset." When she eyed me skeptically, I gave into a smile. "I am not upset. I'll wait. As long as you want me to, I'll wait."

"Then let's not make you wait any longer to take those pants off, huh?"

I snapped awake with a knot in my throat. Stomach twisting, I threw my hand over my mouth, sprinting to the bathroom, where I fell to the floor, barely making it to the toilet before throwing up.

"Gemma? Are you okay?"

Still retching, I couldn't answer Jason.

"Gemma?" He dropped down on his knees next to me, holding my hair back. When my stomach finally settled, I rested my arms on the seat, and he stroked my head. "How do you feel?"

I breathed deeply, in my nose and out my mouth, eyes closed. "Terrible."

He handed me a cold washcloth, and I swiped it over my face and neck. "Maybe it was the beer?" he suggested.

"I only had one glass." I stood on wobbly legs to brush my teeth and swallow a few sips of water from the faucet.

He rubbed my back in soothing circles. "Do you feel better?"

"I guess. What time is it?"

"A little after four."

I slunk back to bed, and he tucked me into his side, kissing my temple, and I quickly fell back to sleep.

A few hours later, Jason shook me awake again. He sat on the edge of the bed, fully dressed for work. "I'm leaving. Are you planning on getting up anytime soon?"

I pulled the covers higher.

"Are you still feeling sick?" he asked, pressing his palm to my forehead.

"I'm so tired."

"Guess we can't go out on weeknights anymore, old lady."

I didn't even have the energy to throw a barb at him.

"I'll check in with you later." He kissed my head through the covers. "Love you."

A few minutes later, I forced myself out of bed and into the shower. Feeling much better after getting dressed and eating a little cereal, I fired off a text to Laney on my way to work.

> Do you feel okay today? I puked this morning, maybe from the food?

> LANEY
>
> I'm fine. Hope you feel better!

Being the day before Thanksgiving, customers were few and far between at Bare Necessities, but Alex kept me busy by ordering me to go through all the advertisements for Black Friday in exchange for buying lunch. I was in the middle of a vegetable burrito when Jason called.

I dabbed a napkin at the corner of my mouth. "Hey, you."

"Hey. What are you up to?"

"I'm being forced to scour every sale paper in the state. Alex wants a new toaster for his kitchen and a vacuum for his mother-in-law."

"Sounds awful. Want to trade jobs?"

I snorted. "If I had your job, I'd be making houses out of mud and tires."

Jason's deep laughter on the other end of the phone coaxed a smile out of me. "Did you eat lunch?"

I picked up a few beans that had fallen out of the burrito and popped them in my mouth. "In the middle of it. Alex bought Mexican."

"I'm starving. I've been in meetings all day. But I'm glad you're better."

Pushing the rest of my lunch away, I rested on my elbow. "I never got to say thank you for helping me this morning. You're a good nurse."

"Next time we play nurse and patient, I don't want you to be actually sick. You've got—" He stopped mid-sentence, and I heard muffled voices on the other end of the phone. "Gem, I've got to go. Let me know if you need anything, okay?"

"Okay. I love you."

"You too."

I clicked my phone off to find Alex bent over the counter, hands on either side of their face, staring at me with princess eyes. "What?"

"You and your..." They folded their hands next to their ear, lifting a leg up behind them, belting out a silly little tune.

"What about it?" I threw away my leftovers, not hungry anymore.

"You're extra swoony today. Although if I were sleeping with that Adonis, I'd be swooning too."

"He wants me to move in with him," I said, my stomach feeling a little queasy.

"What?" Alex jumped up like a jungle cat to sit on the counter. "Tell me everything. What did he say? What did you say?"

I skimmed my fingers over my throat, struggling with my

decision and this apparent food poisoning. "He said it was stupid that we're always going from his place to my place, we should just make it one place."

"And?" Alex circled his fingers.

"And I said that it was a big deal, and we should talk about it after the new year."

They laced their fingers together, placing them on their leg, one crossed over the other—lecture mode—and I groaned inwardly. "You are such a pussy when it comes to love."

"I hate that word used in that context." I tied up my hair, suddenly hot.

"Yes, I know," Alex said, waving their hand. "The vagina is the strongest organ, able to survive childbirth, blah, blah. I've sat through your TED Talk, so now you need to sit through mine."

I clunked my head on the counter, letting it cool my cheek.

"He loves you, you love him, you have to stop pretending you don't know it. That boy has shown up for you over and over, right? I know it was all hate you, fuck you in the beginning, but he's shown you how he can and will support you."

Too drained to argue, I let them continue, even as my throat grew thick. I took another deep breath.

"If you want to be with him, be with him. You can't let your past dictate your future. Not every man will walk out on you. Or, if you can't work through your fear, you'll always be stuck where you are, without that beautiful man." They sighed exaggeratedly. "And that would be the real travesty."

Alex made sense, I knew that, but still. It was hard to take that big of a leap. I required baby steps, and saying I love you to Jason already felt like walking before I'd learned to crawl.

Alex hopped to the floor, fixing their hair. "Besides, it's bound to happen anyway, right? First comes love, then comes marriage, then comes the baby in the baby carriage."

I shook my head, my thoughts and stomach churning, and opened a bottle of green tea. As I tried to take a sip, my insides lurched. The nausea came back full force, and I covered my mouth. "I'm going to be sick."

In a flash, Alex had the garbage can in front of me. In between gagging fits, I explained I was sick from last night.

"Sweetie, I don't think it's from beer or bad food."

I hung my head between my knees. "I think you're right."

"It's probably a stomach bug. Go home and rest."

"No, I'm okay," I said, shoving aside the bangs stuck to my damp forehead.

"Go home." Alex held up my bag and pressed a small bottle of ginger into my palm. "Take this. It'll help settle your stomach."

A few hours later, Jason opened my apartment door with his arms full of shopping bags. I smiled, glancing up from the television, and yawned an inaudible greeting.

"You're looking...okay" he said, and I flicked his leg on his way to the kitchen, where he unloaded the bags. He returned a few minutes later, handing me a Gatorade and settling down on the couch. He gathered the blanket around my feet and placed them in his lap. "You think you need to call the doctor?"

"It's probably a twenty-four-hour thing. I'm feeling better anyway."

"Are you sure?" When I nodded, he pointed to the blue liquid. "Drink."

I slowly sipped from the bottle. "You should sleep at home tonight, quarantine me."

"Nope. You said it yourself, I'm a good nurse."

"Go home," I ordered rather unconvincingly.

"You say the word, and my home becomes your home."

I ignored him, snuggling deeper into the blanket.

"Or we can stay up late watching cheesy pre-Christmas

Christmas movies on this broken-down sofa in your apartment, and then tomorrow, we can take a ride to my place so I can change before dinner."

"Yeah, that sounds good."

"You're lucky I like you." He pinched my little toe and hunkered down for the night with me, a comforter, and a barrage of bad holiday movies.

I don't know when exactly I fell asleep, but I didn't even feel Jason move me to my bed. In the morning, I rolled to my side to find him awake already, scrolling on his phone with one arm behind his head.

"Morning," I rasped.

He smiled. "Feeling better?"

I nodded and curled into his warm side.

His big hand landed on my ass, squeezing it. "Are you sure?"

I leaned up onto an elbow to kiss him but as soon as his mouth covered mine, my stomach swooped. He wrenched away when a very unladylike sound erupted from my throat. "All right?"

"I feel...off. Like, everything is making me feel..." I grimaced, motioning vaguely at my chest.

"Well, I have been known to take a woman's breath away a time or two," he said, and I punched weakly at his shoulder. "Here." He offered me a place in his open arm. "Lie down. Try and go back to sleep. We don't have anywhere to be for a few hours."

I did go back to sleep, but I still felt like garbage as I slumped over my mother's festive table, straight out of Martha Stewart's catalogue with two white candles, a centerpiece of acorns and colorful miniature pumpkins, and overflowing bowls of every kind of steaming hot vegetable. Mom carried in a huge dish of mashed potatoes between two oven mitts.

"You do realize there are only four of us, right?" I asked her.

"Yes, I realize that, but it's Thanksgiving." She whacked at me with the oversized gloves.

Jason snatched a green bean stalk. "Everything looks wonderful, Caroline."

"Thank you. At least someone appreciates it. Wait until you see the—"

"Turkey's here!" Frank carried in a giant, deep-fried turkey on a platter painted with miniature turkeys along the rim. He placed it in the middle of the table.

I ignored how the smell of the meat turned my stomach and pointed to the platter. "Where did you find that?"

"The turkey? I went—" Frank started but was interrupted by my mom.

"I was cleaning out a few things when I came across that art project." She looked to Jason. "Gemmie painted that plate when she was twelve."

He ruffled my hair. "My little Picasso."

"Drinks? Wine? Some pitorro, Gem?" Frank asked.

"No, no, no." I waved my hands in defeat. "I'm a little—"

"She's got a bug or something," Jason said, tracing circles on the nape of my neck.

Even though I showered, I hadn't bothered to wash my hair and had thrown it up in a bun. While Jason dressed in *real* clothes, I couldn't bear to put on anything other than a sweatshirt and leggings.

Mom stood up from the table. "Do you want me to make you soup? I can make you the kind you like with the stars."

"I'm fine. I'm fine." I was not fine. "Sit down, let's eat."

Frank clapped. "Yes, dig in!"

After everyone's bellies were full—except for mine, I mostly ate a few forkfuls of sweet potatoes—we worked together to clear the table. My mother opened a Tupperware to place the leftovers in. "I hear Jason's birthday is in a few weeks."

"Twenty-eight." I spooned the corn into a smaller bowl. "I'm dating an old man!"

He appeared next to me, sliding a gravy boat onto the counter, a lecherous grin on his pretty face. "Yeah, I'm a whole two and a half years older than you. Practically robbing the cradle."

"What are you going to do for your big day?" Mom asked, placing glasses in the dishwasher.

"I don't know." He shrugged. "It's another day."

She waved a fork in the air. "You two should do something special, maybe take a trip. A weekend getaway."

"Who's taking a trip?" Frank stepped into the kitchen, opening the refrigerator.

"Gem and Jason," Mom answered before pivoting around to see her husband with his head buried in the freezer. "And what are you doing? We just ate."

"Looking for dessert. I need vanilla ice cream with my apple pie."

As Frank and my mom bickered about when to bring out the pies, I attempted to finish cleaning up, but as I forked the turkey into a plastic container, the smell churned my insides. I dropped the greasy meat into the sink before yanking open the cabinet and vomiting my guts into the garbage bin.

"Gemma! Honey, are you okay?"

After a few moments, I steadied myself and reached for the faucet to rinse my mouth out with cold water.

"She's been sick for two days," Jason informed her, and my mother clucked her tongue behind me.

"You should make an appointment with the doctor."

Jason agreed. "That's what I told her."

"Maybe she's pregnant," Frank joked, munching on the forgotten turkey.

255

CHAPTER THIRTY-ONE

"You're pregnant. Congratulations!"

My heart skipped. "I'm what?"

The doctor pushed his glasses farther up his nose. "About six or seven weeks along, I'd say, but you'll need to make an appointment with your OB/GYN to know for sure. Get an ultrasound."

Having convinced myself it was the flu, I had suffered through one week of the daily vomiting, sometimes multiple times a day, before I'd gone to the local urgent care. It wasn't until the nurse asked me when my last period was that I officially started to freak out.

And now that I'd received the news, the walls had begun to close in. Everything got a little hazy, a little gray, and the paper cover of the cold table stuck to my sweaty palms when I tried to stand. The doctor was going on about morning sickness and vitamins when I threw up all over the linoleum floor.

The next few minutes blurred as a nurse rushed in to help. My body responded to the directions given, but my mind had totally shut down. A far-off voice told me to "Sit down. Put your head between your legs. Breathe deep. Sip this water." But it all sounded like the teacher from *Charlie Brown*.

It was the jolt of a cold, wet cloth that brought those synapses back to proper function.

"Your blood pressure is coming down."

I glanced to my left, at a middle-aged nurse wearing scrubs covered with spotted puppies. "Feeling any better?"

Better? Better than what?

My throat was thick and rough. Nothing but a croak released. I angled my head to the nurse, whose understanding smile broke through the fog in my brain.

"I'm pregnant?" The words came out flat and lifeless.

The nurse nodded. "Yes, I know."

My blank expression must have tipped her off. "Do you want to be pregnant?"

Searching the room for an escape, I remained silent as the question echoed off the stark white walls. A little too white. My eyes burned from the brightness of it all, and I pressed my fingers into my eye sockets. "I don't know."

I hoped this was all a bad dream, yet when I opened my eyes back up, the nurse was crouched in front of my chair, her hands patting my knees. "It's a surprise, huh? I was stunned when I found out I was having my first baby. It was a few days after the honeymoon, and we had barely moved in to our house. We weren't ready. I wasn't ready to be a mom at all, but you eventually figure it out, you know?" She tilted her head. "Why don't you go home, digest this new information, have a good sleep tonight, and call us back tomorrow. We will put you in touch with some excellent obstetricians, if you need it. Sound good?"

What sounded good? The information? The sleep? The obstetrician?

Somehow, I found my way home and into bed without consciously walking or driving anywhere. In fact, it seemed as if my brain had completely disappeared. There was nothing but a black hole up there. I stared at the ceiling of my bedroom, my body completely immobilized with shock.

It wasn't until Jason's voice rang out that the shock turned to sheer terror. I scrambled underneath the covers and turned my back toward the door, feigning sleep. I hoped he couldn't see me trembling when he poked his head in the door.

He crept to the bed, so heartbreakingly careful not to wake me, and placed a soft, sweet kiss against my hair before shutting the door behind him on his way out. My eyes stung as tears formed and fell down my cheeks. I was so young and still had so much life ahead of me. For all the plans I'd avoided making in my life, not getting pregnant was one I'd intended to keep. I didn't want to end up like my mom, getting knocked up and spending my life following men around.

I pressed a quaking hand to my stomach. It didn't feel any different. My eyes scanned my body. It didn't look any different. But then why was my life being turned upside down by this alien thing inside me?

Anger boiled up. I clenched my fingers together, wishing today had never happened. Wishing the night at the museum had never happened. Wishing none of this had ever happened.

And then as quickly as the anger came, it was eroded by a wave of guilt. A fresh well of tears sprang from the corners of my eyes. I was a terrible person.

I messaged the girls.

SOS SOS SOS SOS SOS SOS

Sinking down to the floor, I held my phone to my face, trying and failing to regulate my breathing. Soon, my palm vibrated with a group FaceTime call. I opened it up, and Sam's face filled the screen. "What's wrong?"

"I think we should wait for the other girls."

"Why are you whispering?"

"Because…" I hung my head. "Let's wait, okay?"

Next, Bronte came on, silent in her assessment of me, then finally Laney, whose big grin instantly dropped. "Oh Jesus. What is it?"

I lowered the volume then crawled to the corner of the room so Jason wouldn't hear from his spot in the kitchen. He was banging pots and pans around in there, probably making me dinner like the wonderful person he was, and I let myself cry in front of my friends.

"I'm pregnant."

Bronte covered her gasp with her hand.

"It's okay, it's okay, you don't need to cry. We're here," Sam said. "Are you all right?"

"No, I'm freaking the fuck out."

The girls gave me time to dry my eyes, and I stared into my phone screen, my best friends staring right back.

"When did you find out?" Bronte asked.

"A few hours ago."

Laney plopped her head in her hand. "Did you tell Jason?" When I shook my head, she moved closer to her screen. "You don't seem happy."

"Because I don't know how I feel about it."

"Do you want to keep it?" Sam asked, and I shrugged. At this point, I honestly didn't know. "You know I had an abortion," Sam reminded me. "If that's what you want, it's okay."

I nodded. We'd been with Sam as she took the pill, watched a *Twilight* movie marathon, and held her hand when she was in pain.

"We'll support whatever you want to do," Laney said, and my eyes flooded with tears again.

Bronte's mouth turned down in a frown, her eyes big and blue and glassy. Whenever anyone cried, so did she. She grabbed a tissue. "It's your decision, but I think you have to tell Jason."

"I don't know," Sam disagreed quietly. "It's not his decision. It's yours. I don't know if you have to tell him."

Bronte blew her nose. "If she wants to be with him, I think she should."

They were trying to help, but making me even more confused.

Laney cut in and smiled. It was fake but appreciated anyway. "Jason loves you. No matter what you decide to do—keep it or not—I'm sure if you talked to him, explained to him how you're feeling, you'd feel better about it all."

The problem was I couldn't explain it to him because I didn't know. Our relationship was so new, only three months old. I couldn't see how this—being pregnant—could make such a young relationship work when there was still so much unknown.

I didn't know the first thing about being in a long-term relationship, and I sure as hell didn't know anything about being a mother. How could I bring a new life into this world when I was still stumbling around in my own?

After a few more minutes with the girls, I hung up and hopped into the shower before finally facing Jason in the kitchen.

He was seated at the table, George Clooney next to help like they were old friends, an iPad in front of him with WedMD open, along with bowls of soup and plates of grilled cheese.

"Hey you," I said weakly, and he turned.

"You look like hell."

"Thanks."

He ushered me to the table with a chagrinned smile. "The vegan cheese didn't melt as well as regular cheese, and I didn't know what to use for the bread besides spray oil, so I'm not sure how the grilled cheese will taste."

"It's okay. Thanks for dinner."

I motioned to his open iPad screen with my spoon. "What are you looking up?"

He sighed and shook his head. "I fell down a rabbit hole. You know what kind of paint they used here?"

"Why?"

"Lead poisoning."

I smiled for the first time all day. "I don't have lead poisoning."

"Then what is it? Kidney failure, gallstones?"

"The flu."

He eyed me. "Are you sure? Because there's a suspicious looking patch in the corner." He tipped his chin in the direction of the living room. "Might be mold. I know you said we'd put a pin in it until after the new year, but I gotta say, the more I look at this place, the less comfortable I am that you're here."

I swallowed a spoonful of the tomato soup, trying not to gag on my lies. "I know, but it's just a bad case of the flu."

He scratched at his chin. "Really?"

I nodded, eyes down.

"Did they give you anything?"

"Uh, no." I swallowed down more soup, hoping he couldn't hear the wobble in my voice. "I guess there's really nothing to do for it. Stay hydrated and...whatever."

He combed his fingers though my wet hair, tucking a few clumps behind my ear. "I'm glad it's only the flu and not something worse."

"Mm-hmm."

"Are you feeling any better? Even a little bit? I wanted to go pick out a Christmas tree this weekend, but if you're not feeling up to it, we can do it later."

I finally met his gaze, and he encouraged me with a smile. I hated to do this to him, but I couldn't stand to be around him right now. "I think you should go home. I don't want to get you sick." He shook his head, while I plowed on. "The doctor said I am contagious, so I think it would be better if you stayed away from me for a while."

He popped a piece of grilled cheese into his mouth. "I get the flu shot every year. I'll be fine."

"It's a new strain. That's why I'm so sick."

"It's okay, Gem, really—"

"No!" I shot up from the table with a flourish, my chair grating against the floor. George scurried away, and Jason's eyes widened at my outburst.

"What's wrong? I'm sorry you aren't feeling well, but Christ, you're moody lately."

I inhaled a long breath. "I would really appreciate it if you left me alone for a little while."

He stared at me, his jaw working back and forth. He must've realized I wasn't going to give in if he glared at me long enough because he nodded. "You're sick, you want space, I get it. I don't like it, but I get it."

He cleared our plates away without another word then brushed past me, grabbing his coat and keys on the way. I stopped him at the door. "Jason."

He pivoted in the open doorway, facing me, and my shoulders slumped. I didn't want to hurt him, I just didn't know what to say or do right now, and I needed time alone to figure it out. "I'm sorry."

After a moment, he smiled and wrapped me up in his arms, kissing my temple then cheek. "Me too." He held my chin between his fingers. "I only want you to get better, okay?" His light eyes bounced between mine, and a pit formed in the bottom of my stomach.

"I love you," he said.

"I love you too."

Then he flattened his palm against my forehead one more time, seemingly satisfied I didn't have a fever. He jammed his hands into his coat pockets. "I'll talk to you later."

Then I closed the door, accepting and hating that I got what I wanted, time alone.

My phone buzzed with a text message alert. I knew it was Jason before I picked it up.

JASON

Morning, gorgeous.

I had been avoiding him, resorting to a relationship of texting.

JASON

Feeling better today?

I collapsed back in my bed, accidentally banging the back of my head against the top of the headboard, and I winced in pain.

Headache.

It had been five days since I'd unceremoniously kicked him out of my apartment on the pretext of an extreme contagion. I had gotten my physical space but felt more claustrophobic, strangled with the knowledge of what I was hiding. I'd thought I would have a clear head, be able to make some decisions, but in the past few days, I had made no progress. I didn't even know how or where to start.

I survived on a few hours of sleep each night, plagued with nightmares that involved being run over by strollers and dropping babies on their heads. although, the days were much worse. Between the morning sickness—which was really around-the-clock sickness—and the lack of sleep, I was a walking zombie. I couldn't concentrate at work, had to call off teaching yoga because I had no energy, and begged for a substitute for my art classes. I looked so haggard, no one had trouble believing I was sick, but I knew at some point I'd have to come clean.

JASON

I miss your face.

I could hear Jason's playful tone in my head and imagined the crooked smile on his lips as he typed away. I wanted to hide from the text, from the world, from everything, and was about to bury my head under the covers when the doorbell rang. With a blanket wrapped around my shoulders, I opened the door to my mother. Dressed in a long red coat and scarf, she held shopping bags at her sides.

"Gemma Rose, I didn't know if you were dead or alive. You're not answering any of my calls."

I fell to the sofa, leaving my mother to invite herself in. "I'm alive."

She pursed her lips. "You need to go back to the doctor. Whatever he put you on is not working, and we need you back to full strength for the party."

"Party?" I yawned.

"You would know if you ever picked up your phone."

I mocked her by showing I could physically pick up my cell phone.

"Honestly, Gemma," She chided, setting shopping bags on the coffee table to rummage through them. "We're planning a surprise birthday party for Jason." She held up a glittering line of letters.

H-A-P-P-Y-B-I-R-T-H-D-A-Y-!

I groaned. Great, to top off my week in self-exile, I needed to find a way to shut down this party. "Mom, I don't think that's a good idea."

She scrutinized me with narrow eyes, her hands on her hips. "Why not? It's your boyfriend's birthday. This is the first time we can celebrate something together, all four of us, and I thought it would be nice to give him this gift."

"It is." I squirmed under her gaze. "It's just that..." I picked at an imaginary pull in my blanket.

My mom sat down at my feet. "Honey, what's wrong?" When I shrugged, she curved her hands around my calves. "I've never seen you like this. I don't think this is the flu. Maybe I should take you to the hospital."

"No."

"Maybe it's mono. Let me see your glands."

I cracked when she reached for my throat, blurting out, "I'm pregnant!"

My mother's hands froze halfway between us.

"I don't have the flu. I don't have mono. I don't have meningitis or any other type of virus. I'm pregnant."

Our eyes met. Both deep brown and brimming with tears, but Mom's face lit up. "Gemmie, you're having a baby. Oh my god! This is so wonderful!" She hugged me tight. "How do you feel?"

I heaved out a breath, closing my eyes while trying to discern my exact emotions. Fear and regret, then shame for feeling the first two. But mostly, panic.

None to be admitted out loud. "Fine, I guess."

"Does Jason know?"

"No."

She glared. "It is Jason's, isn't it, Gemma?"

"Yes, of course, Mom. I love Jason. Of course it's his."

Back to smiling, she rested her hand over her heart. "Well, what's the problem? You should be so excited. You're going to be a mommy!"

"I know. I should be excited," I replied. "I should be, and I'm not."

"All new moms feel overwhelmed. Don't worry," she said, in possibly the kindest voice she'd ever used with me. "It will pass. You'll figure it out. I did."

"Yeah, after twenty-five years."

That came out harsher than I wanted it to, and my mother lost the glint in her eyes. "Being pregnant is difficult, but you aren't going to take it out on me."

She moved to stand, and I caught her wrist. "I'm sorry, Mom. I didn't..." I let out a shaky breath. "I didn't mean it. I'm just... I'm scared."

And then I cried.

She sat back down, pulling me almost into her lap as she wrapped her hands around my shoulders and head, letting me get every last tear out until I was positive I was dried up.

"I don't know what to do," I said, backing away to wipe at my cheeks.

"Do?"

I nodded, dragging the back of my sleeve under my nose.

"Do with a baby? You feed it and—"

"No. I mean, if I want it."

"Oh." She folded her hands in her lap. Whatever lecture I expected, it was certainly not, "Your grandparents wanted me to get an abortion."

I lurched back in surprise. "What?"

With a deep breath, my mom smiled sweetly, combing her hand through my hair, saying, "You need to take a shower. You smell. Worse than usual."

"Mom!"

She laughed and sat back against the cushions to get comfortable. "Okay. When I told your grandparents I was pregnant, they told me to get an abortion. They said I was ruining my life, that I wouldn't finish college, that your father was a good-for-nothing."

I snorted.

"*Most* of what they said wasn't true," she acquiesced. My mom did eventually finish college and went on to open up a very successful boutique. Although, my father...he absolutely was a "good-for-nothing."

"Why didn't you get an abortion?"

Lifting her gaze to the wall, she didn't answer for a while. "Growing up, I didn't always feel loved all the time. Sometimes it seemed as if whether I was born or not, my parents' lives wouldn't have changed. And I don't think I realized how big of a hole I had inside me until I found out I was pregnant." She turned her attention on me. "I was scared, and I was worried about your father. It wasn't like I didn't know the type of guy he was. I may be a perpetual romantic, but I'm not stupid. I had hoped he would be the man and father he had promised he was going to be, but I made the decision to have a baby, have you, because it was what I wanted. I wanted someone to love."

I swallowed past the lump in my throat, feeling slightly nauseated. "But I don't know how to be someone's mom."

"I don't either."

We both laughed. A short moment of levity after days of what felt like a dark cave I couldn't find my way out of. Finally, my mom was there, shining some light.

"No one ever knows how to be a parent. Those books they tell you to read are totally useless. But once the baby comes, you figure it out. It's kind of instinctive."

I looked to the now-empty bowl in my kitchen, where Spot used to reside. I'd found the fish floating belly up in the murky water this morning. "How am I supposed to take care of a baby? I can barely take care of my pets. I can barely take care of myself."

A few part-time jobs, a crappy apartment, a dead fish, that was what I had in this world. I didn't know how to be a mother when I was still figuring out how to be an adult, and no matter what Jason said, how often he told me he'd support me, it didn't matter.

All those men who'd dated and married my mother promised the same thing, which was why I had always focused on being completely independent. I might not have always made the best or smartest decisions, but I'd made them on my own. I'd learned not to rely on anyone else, so when they would inevitably leave, it wouldn't matter. Jason had walked out on me once after an argument. Who was to say he wouldn't do it again?

I couldn't control the flashbacks flittering through my memory. The faces of the men who had waltzed in and out of my mother's life, out of my life. Some were kind and treated me well, some weren't, though all of them vowed forever, and none of them kept their promise. None of them stayed. Married or not, they left Mom. They left me.

As if my mother could read my mind, she said, "Jason's not like your father. He is not like any of the men who have come and gone in our lives, and there were a lot. I'm sorry about that, honey. If there is one thing I would change, it would be that. You didn't deserve to live like that, and I know how it's affected you."

I felt my eyes sting with tears again. Honestly, if this was what I had in store for the next seven months, I didn't know how I'd handle it. Then again, if I was thinking about the next seven months, maybe I really did want it.

"I've never known you to be afraid, Gemma."

I huffed. That sounded suspiciously like a dare.

"Jason's a good man," she continued, tugging me closer to her. "He will be a great father, and you will be a wonderful mother. Much better than I ever was." Taking my face in her hands, she said, "Don't make your decision about your pregnancy because you're afraid you can't do it. You can. Make your decision on what you *want*. I will be here to help you no matter what you decide. Whether you want to be a mom now or in the future or never. With or without Jason."

I bit my lip to keep my tears at bay and nodded. I was scared, my nightmares were proof of that, but if I thought about my future, I knew I wanted Jason in it. And when I imagined him in this future, I pictured him singing to a baby, tossing a toddler in the air, watching some middle school math contest because whatever child we had would, without a doubt, be a nerd.

"You wrote an essay in the seventh grade."

I let out a watery laugh at whatever my mother was about to say because she'd stored up every single one of my school projects and assignments.

"It was about how you wanted to change the world." She sniffled and reached for a tissue from the box on the coffee table to dab at her eyes. Then she kissed my forehead. "You have changed the world, Gemma, because you're in it. You changed the world for the better."

It was no use. The tears started up again, and I fell into my mom's arms. Because I loved my mother more than words could express. And I was going to have a baby.

CHAPTER THIRTY-THREE

It was Saturday, the day of the big surprise birthday bash, and I was the cover story. Jason was supposed to pick me up to go Christmas shopping, then bring me back to his place, where everyone would be waiting. In the blur of the last few days, I had forgotten to get him a birthday present, but I assumed the *big news* would be present enough.

In a turn of events, I was dressed and ready long before he was set to arrive, and I wore down the floorboards pacing the living room, wringing my hands. I hadn't come up with exactly what I was going to say and hoped it would come to me in the moment.

Mr. Clooney lay on the floor, stopping me in my tracks. I'd neglected to feed him today, and he wasn't happy about it. I mumbled an apology to him as I walked to the kitchen, where I fed him before moving on to Leonardo. Spot's empty bowl still sat on the counter, untouched. I wasn't sure what to do with it. Much like I wasn't sure what the future held, but as my mother and friends had repeatedly assured me, I would figure it out with Jason.

Busy with cleaning up, I didn't hear Jason enter until he

was next to me, touching my shoulder. I swung around, pressing my hand to my heart.

"Sorry, I didn't mean to scare you," he said, easing his hands around my waist. His blue sweater matched his eyes, and when he kissed my neck, I almost swooned in his arms.

"Hi."

"You look better," he said, his gaze roaming over me from top to bottom.

"I feel better."

"Good." He brushed his knuckle down my cheek, his eyes shining brightly, staring down at me affectionately. Now was the time. I only had to be brave.

"Jason, I've been lying to you."

His eyebrows furrowed.

"I don't have the flu."

"But what about the doctor and—"

"I never had the flu."

He searched my face for understanding. "I don't get it."

"I'm sorry I made you worry, but I needed some time."

His eyebrows crimped, his voice a hard edge. "Some time?"

"To think." I raised a trembling hand to tuck my hair behind my ears, but he got to it first. His fingers barely grazed the sensitive skin of my earlobe, but it was enough to send electricity through my bones.

"You're shaking. Did you eat today?" he asked, and I nodded. I'd kept down some crackers and an orange popsicle. With his hands on me, I was having trouble finding my words, so I stepped out of his grasp.

"Are you going to tell me why you've been avoiding me?" The way his words came out like a joke should have eased me, but the rigid set of his shoulders belied his amusement. He was pissed, and I was quickly losing my nerve.

"I'm sorry, Jason. I...I've been having a hard time and didn't know how to tell you."

"What, Gem? You're freaking me out."

I rushed out an explanation. "I haven't been feeling well. I've been sick every day, that part was true. But it isn't the flu that's making me sick. I'm..." I lifted my gaze to his, hoping my growing smile would quell his anger. "I'm pregnant."

He blinked.

Took two steps back.

Blinked again.

"You're what?"

"I'm pregnant."

He shook his head like he had water in his ears. "I don't— why–why didn't you tell me? How long have you known?"

This wasn't exactly the reaction I'd been expecting, but I could understand. I was shocked too. "I really did go to the doctor. That day you made me soup and grilled cheese. I found out then."

"And you didn't tell me." He lifted a finger first at me then at himself, his voice growing not in warmth but in a quiet fury that had my smile dropping. "Why didn't you tell me?"

"I was afraid. I—"

"Afraid of me? So, you lied to me instead. Jesus." He dragged his hands through his hair and down his face. "Gem, I don't get it."

"I felt like I was being suffocated. Like I was being forced to do things I wasn't ready for."

"I'm forcing you?" His voice rose another octave. "I'm forcing you? To do what? Because as it stands now, I'm not forcing you to do anything. You're the one forcing *me*."

I blanched, my arms dropping to my sides, and for a split second, something that looked like regret crossed Jason's features. But it was gone before I could be sure.

We stared at each other for a moment, and when I didn't say anything else, he spun away from me, his fists clenching and unclenching at his sides. His shoulders rose and fell with deep breaths I could see even through his coat. "You lied to me. You knew for two weeks and didn't tell me. How could you not tell me?"

I shook my head, even though he couldn't see with his back to me. "I'm sorry. I didn't know how and—"

"I'm sorry too," he snapped. "I need to go."

"What? No. Jason."

He shook me off as he headed to the door.

"Please, listen to me. I had stuff to deal with. It had nothing to do with you."

He whipped his face around to frown down at me. "It's not you, it's me... That's what you're going with? I didn't think you were such a cliché."

I gasped, pressing one hand to my chest, where my heart broke underneath my ribs, and one to my stomach, where my baby—our baby—was growing. And then he walked out the door.

I stared at it for a few minutes, too stunned to move, too dazed to cry.

Jason had changed, bent so far from his straight and narrow, and maybe this was too much, too far. I had asked him to bend so much, he finally broke.

And all my worst fears were about to come true. I was pregnant, unprepared and ill-equipped to become a parent, and the perfect world Jason and I had built together ended with the slam of the door.

Like mother, like daughter, history was repeating itself.

CHAPTER THIRTY-FOUR

Jason

Outside, I jumped into my car, peeling out of the parking lot, much like the first night Gemma and I met. Although, unlike that day, I didn't have to wonder what it was like to be with her. I knew. A goddamn roller coaster, that's what it was.

And it was all getting to be too much. The ups and downs, the push and pull. The secrets and lies.

I'd been living my life thinking if I could do everything right, be perfect, the people around me would never wound me. I was an idiot because, of course, that wasn't true. The one person I loved most in the world had hidden this huge, life-changing thing from me. The one person I loved most in the world had cut me in two.

And then to throw out that line about it being her and not me? Of course it was me. Otherwise, she wouldn't have avoided me. She wouldn't have been lying all these days. She didn't trust me, didn't respect me enough to give me the truth. And... "Fuck!"

I opened all the windows in the car and blared some screaming emo music, trying desperately to drown out the thoughts racing through my mind as I sped onto the highway. I didn't know how to process any of this, my anger, my hurt, my surprise, my utter confusion. Just a few weeks ago, she had told me she didn't want to move in with me, and suddenly, we were going to have a baby.

A baby.

What the actual fuck?

After a few hours of aimless driving, I pulled into my garage, thoroughly windswept and heartbroken. I jostled my keys into the back door and was immediately blown away.

"Surprise!"

A crowd of friends and coworkers huddled in the kitchen, smiling and laughing. I stood stock-still, eyes closed, hoping I'd dreamed this whole disaster of a day.

Although what happened with Gemma was a nightmare.

I opened one eye at a time—fuck, they were still here—to find the group had descended on me. They handed me off, down the line, well-wishes from all. They thrust cards and presents into my hands. When I made my way to the edge of the crowd, Frank encircled me in a bear hug.

"Happy birthday, kid."

"Thanks."

"Gotcha good, huh?"

"You got me," I deadpanned.

He chuckled, smacking my shoulder before moving on to entertain a few of the guests, and Caroline bounded over, hugging and kissing me. "Happy birthday, sweetheart!" She took my coat. "Where's Gem?"

"Not here."

"Yes, I can see that." She playfully pinched my arm. "Where is she?" When I didn't answer, she narrowed her eyes, smile long gone. "Jason, where is my daughter?"

I met her gaze, unsure of what to say or do. "At her apartment."

"Why?"

I didn't know how much Caroline knew about our *situation*, and I sure as shit didn't know how much I was supposed to say. If anything at all. I shrugged.

"Jason."

Luke and Kevin appeared at my side, luring my attention away. They spoke animatedly about the great tickets they had scored for a Bulls game, but Caroline clenched my arm, holding me in place. "What about the baby?"

I could only meet her gaze with a hardened jaw. I couldn't answer her question because I didn't have one.

Caroline rushed away, her hand on her temple, muttering curse words I'd never thought I'd hear come out of her mouth. I didn't know what a heart attack felt like, but I had a pretty good guess from the shooting pain in my chest. My skin went cold, my knees literally shook underneath me.

"You okay, man?" Kevin asked.

I staggered into the living room, and my two friends followed me to a couch, where I plopped down, body numb.

"You look like you're going to puke," Luke said. Kevin nodded in agreement.

Words became harder and harder to form as my tongue stuck to the roof of my mouth. I couldn't seem to focus, my eyes blurry, my brain like a train charging down a track without brakes.

"What's going on?" Kevin urged.

"Gem's pregnant."

Like a sitcom, they snapped their faces toward each other than at me. If I wasn't about to die, I'd laugh.

"Pregnant?" they repeated.

I nodded.

"It's okay, man. It'll be fine," Luke said, patting my shoulder, although he didn't sound very assured.

Kevin rubbed at his forehead. "I need a drink for this."

I licked my parched lips. "Shit, me too."

"Hold on," Luke said, standing up. "I saw somebody brought you whiskey. You really want a drink?"

I nodded even as my best friends gazed at me with weary eyes, but Luke retrieved the bottle anyway. He unscrewed the top and swallowed a gulp straight from the bottle before passing it to me. With a sigh, I put the cool glass to my lips and took a long pull. The last time I'd tasted alcohol was over ten years ago, but tonight seemed like the night to break the dry spell. I winced at the burn in my throat and handed it to Kevin.

As the party raged on, the three of us sat together, passing the whiskey back and forth, slowly getting drunk.

CHAPTER THIRTY-FIVE

Thump.

Thump.

Thump.

I tried to ignore the low, constant sound. I assumed it was the person in the apartment next to mine stomping around, but eventually, it grew too loud to ignore. Getting up to investigate, I realized it was coming from outside my apartment. I opened the front door to find Jason sprawled on the floor, his leg bent up as if he'd been hitting the wall with his foot. He toppled inside the apartment like a sack of potatoes.

"Jason?"

He regarded me with glassy-eyes. "You rang?"

"What are you doing?" When he eventually scrambled to his feet, I got a whiff of him. "You've been drinking."

He stood up to his full height, hanging on to the doorframe for balance as he leaned inside, pronouncing each word deliberately. "Very astute observation, Gemmie."

"How did you get here?"

"I rode my bike."

"Don't be a jerk."

He smirked, wobbly and derisively. "Can I come in? This jerk wants to talk to you."

I stood in the door, blocking him. "I don't think we should have this conversation right now. Especially when you're like this."

"We have to have this conversation." He loomed over me, his hands above my head on the doorframe. "Now."

Our bodies were so close that my chest met his torso with the rise and fall of each breath, and he stared down at me with red eyes. His mouth slanted down in something which looked an awful lot like loathing, and I slumped against the doorframe. "Jason, please…"

I wanted a life with him, one full of laughter and kids and vegan pizza, and had cried about him walking out on me with my mom, who had arrived earlier to talk. She'd told me about how he had walked into the party, looking wrecked. Not that I could blame him.

I had looked and felt that way for a while, and when I finally had my ducks in a row, my life figured out, I had turned his inside out. By hiding away from him, I was able to do some soul-searching, but I'd obviously shattered his heart in the process. I did need to talk to him but feared this time I had really fucked it up.

"I'm mad as hell," he said. "Of all the things you are, I never thought you to be a liar."

I narrowed my eyes on his lips, wanting to be sure of every syllable he spoke.

"But you're full of surprises, aren't you?" he said. He was drunk and angry, and I tried not to take any of his words to heart, though it was almost impossible with the way he scowled at me. As if he hated me.

Really hated me.

"I'm driving you home," I said, leaving the door open to walk back inside.

"Not until you tell me why you lied."

"I didn't lie." I grabbed my keys from the coffee table.

"Lie of omission."

I stalked to the kitchen, where my coat hung on a chair. He closed the door and halted me from putting my arms inside. "Why didn't you tell me you're pregnant?"

The answer was too long to explain now, and I shook my head.

"If you were hiding this, what else have you been hiding?"

I held up my hand, attempting to stop this. He wasn't in the right frame of mind for this particular chat, nor did I want to have it at three in the morning.

He plunked down on a chair and slammed his fist on the table. "Tell me!"

My eyebrows shot up at his outburst, but my alarm only served my own temper. "I'm not going to talk about this when you're drunk, and it's the middle of the night. Stop screaming." I wound my hair up on the top of my head as sweat beaded on my neck. "You're acting like a dickhead."

He let out an irritated breath through his nose, leaning back in his chair so its front legs hovered above the floor. "These raging hormones have certainly brought out your mean side, haven't they?"

"No. You did."

The chair slapped back down. "You don't get to be angry right now, Gemma. I got that market cornered. I was totally blindsided by you today—for not one, but two reasons. You tell me you're pregnant and that you've been afraid to tell me for two weeks. Two weeks!" He pulled at his hair as he hung his head, his elbows propped up on his knees. "I don't understand," he began but stopped when his voice quaked.

"I'm sorry."

"You've been sick, and I was so worried, and you didn't care that I thought..." He sniffled and wiped at his face. "The internet told me it could have been anything. Lead poisoning, cancer, a tapeworm."

I dared to brush my hand over his hair. "You're an engineer. How could you believe everything WebMD says?"

"Because I'm an engineer, Gemma!" He threw his arms up, forcing my hand off of him. "That's what I do. I research and read and make Excel spreadsheets. How could you think I wouldn't worry? I love you! I fucking love you with everything inside of me, Gem, and you..." He dropped his eyes toward the floor, not bothering to wipe his tears anymore. "You have this thing inside you now, and you kept it from me. How can you love me like I love you, with everything inside of you, if you keep it from me?"

I had trouble following all of his thoughts but got the gist of it. He felt betrayed. I had broken him, broken him so much he had resorted to drinking, which he had a personal aversion to. And here he was, drunk as a skunk, confessing his heartbreak in fits and starts.

"After everything I've been through with my parents...after everything we've been through, how could you not tell me? We don't keep secrets from each other. We argue and fight, but we don't keep secrets," he said, his words slow and quiet, his head in his hands.

I took the same pose, my elbows on the table, guilty sobs racking my body, and yet there was still a small part of me that knew I had to have that time away from him to get to this point of self-assurance. That was what I needed to process, and this was what he needed to process.

After many silent minutes, I dried my eyes and ventured an uneasy touch to Jason's shoulder. He was still. "I'm sorry."

Nothing.

I slipped off the chair and knelt in front of him, taking in his placid face. I poked him. "Jason?"

He breathed slow and even, asleep.

I huffed, half annoyed and half relieved he had passed out with his head in his hands. He may have walked out on me before, but he was here now. And that was a good thing, no matter what happened next.

I slunk back to bed, replaying the last few weeks in my mind until the early morning hours when my brain finally gave up the fight. My eyes drooped closed as the sun rose, streaking through my window shade.

CHAPTER THIRTY-SIX

Jason

I cracked one eye open, my body sputtering to life, and I immediately clapped my lid shut, a headache building behind my temples. I gradually picked my head up off the table, disoriented for a moment as the room spun. I grunted, blinking, trying to remember how I ended up asleep in Gemma's kitchen.

Bits and pieces of last night broke through the fog, my chest heavy with the memories. I smacked my lips, mouth stale with whiskey and in need of water. I stood up, my joints cracking in response, and swayed on shaky legs to the sink, where I dipped my lips to the stream.

"He lives."

I whirled around a little too fast, clinging to the counter to get my bearings. After rolling my neck to get the kink out and waiting until my brain had a chance to catch up, I studied Gemma—wet-haired and fresh-faced—before bending over the countertop, heartbroken and hungover.

Quietly making her way around the cabinets, she dropped two pieces of bread in the toaster and brewed a pot of coffee. When the toast was ready, she put it on a plate then placed it and two ibuprofen next to me with a tall glass of water. I gulped down the red capsules and sagged back to the counter.

"What was your drink of choice last night?"

"Jack Daniel's," I said around a bit of toast that was like sand in my mouth.

"Lightweight." Her lips tipped up in a slight smile as she handed me a cup of black coffee. "Did it make you feel any better?"

I sipped the coffee, waiting as the caffeine push the blood to my brain a little faster, and picked at the counter with my index finger. "I didn't want to feel anything. I wanted to forget. But that's stupid, right? How do you forget that the love of your life is hiding the fact that she's pregnant?"

I set the coffee down and cupped the back of his neck with both hands, staring at the floor, the crack running alongside the bottom cabinets. "Why, Gem? What did I do?"

"You didn't do anything. It was me."

I dragged my eyes to hers, tired of the excuses.

"It's true. That's why I couldn't tell you."

I dropped my hands, confusion and anger clouding my reason so I could only say, "I didn't know I could be so fucking mad at you."

She nodded, as if it was a forgone conclusion. As if we were a forgone conclusion, and I felt that heart attack pain again.

"My head is so..." She spun her hands by her temples. "I didn't know what I wanted to do."

"To do?" I repeated, the fog beginning to clear. "Like, if you wanted to keep the pregnancy or not?"

She nodded.

"Okay. Why couldn't you talk to me about it? You hiding it makes me feel like you don't trust me." I swiped my hand across my pounding forehead. But I needed an answer. "Do you trust me?"

"How could I tell you? You're always so wonderful and good at everything, and I'm a screw-up. I'm barely making it through my daily life as it is." She threw her hands up at a sudden thought. "And I killed my goldfish! How can I raise a baby when I can't even keep a goldfish alive?"

I couldn't help it. A pitiful chuckle escaped from the back of my throat, and Gemma threw her hands over her face.

"Let me get this straight," I said, moving away from the counter to tug at her wrists. "I'm awesome at life, and you suck at it?"

She nodded.

"And you were afraid to tell me you're pregnant because you killed a goldfish?"

"In essence, yeah." She nodded again.

"You are out of your mind." I didn't know whether to laugh or leave. "No one can keep a goldfish alive."

"But I'm just figuring out how to be an adult—and your girlfriend, for that matter. I have no idea how to be a mother." Her eyes misted over. "I'm scared I'm going to mess this up. I'm scared I'll mess it up, and you'll leave me. Like you did yesterday."

The puzzle pieces fit together in my head, despite my brain still functioning below capacity. It all made sense. I didn't like it. In fact, I hated it. But I got it.

"First of all, I swear, I will *never* leave you," I said, the pain of not being with Gemma worse than any hangover or heart attack. "I know I haven't had a lot of time to earn your trust, but please hear me when I say, there is nothing I would love more than to be with you for the rest of my life. Okay? I'm sorry I walked out on you yesterday. I needed time to think and process it."

When she nodded, I continued, "You think, because of your experiences, that you have to do everything on your own, but you don't. I want you to do what you want, live your dreams, and I will be here to support you. I don't want you to be afraid I'll sneak out one night after a fight or something. I am not going anywhere."

Giving in a little, she slanted closer to me as one tear fell over her cheek. I wiped it away.

"Second of all, you are not a screw-up or a mess or any stupid idea you have of yourself." I held her face between my hands, forcing her to look me in the eyes. "You are brilliant, creative, kind, and so fucking stubborn. When you put your mind to something, you do it. You jump in headfirst, you're brave and wild, and you think I'm this, like, robot who never makes mistakes, but I only ever do things I know I can be good at. I don't like to color outside the lines, and you, Gemma, you are an artist. You showed me how life is better when you take chances."

When she chewed on her bottom lip, I tugged it free of her teeth, and she nestled into my touch. "I...I never expected to fall in love with you so fast. I never expected—" Her hands cupped her flat belly. "I never expected us to have a baby so soon."

"So..." My heart pulsed in a funny rhythm, my stomach flopping around. "That means you actually want to have this baby?"

Her gaze skirted around behind me for a few moments before landing back on my face. "Yes. But do you?"

Frantic now, desperate for her to understand my feelings, I couldn't stop my words from tumbling out. "I know this isn't what you expected. It's not what I expected either, but we can do this. I want to do this with you. I will make mistakes. You will make mistakes. Let's make mistakes together."

A corner of her lips rose, her brown eyes finding life again. And that gave me life.

"With your good heart and my good looks, this baby is going to turn out amazing, no matter how bad we screw up."

"Get out of here." She laughed, a balm to my weary soul, although when I tried to pull her to me, she strong-armed me. "With everything going on, I didn't get you a birthday present."

"You really think I care about a birthday present? I don't. I only want you."

I tangled my hands in her hair and lowered my lips to hers. It was our first real kiss in over two weeks. I dipped my tongue into her mouth, a man tasting his first drink of water after a long drought, and she wrapped her arms around my neck, allowing me better access.

One of my hands slipped over her spine to her backside, and a startled squeak leaped from her parted mouth when I gave her ass a good squeeze. She smiled, her hands roaming over the planes of my chest before her fingers clawed at my shirt, yanking me closer to trail kisses down my jaw, before settling next to my Adam's apple, where her teeth nipped at the tender flesh.

"God, I missed you," I bit out, wrapping my arms around her waist, taking much of her weight against me in a snug embrace. I crushed my lips to hers, my patience wearing thin with the need to get her underneath me, and I started off toward the bedroom. The toe of my shoe caught on a broken piece of linoleum, and I stumbled, clunking our heads together.

"Ow."

"Shit. Sorry."

We separated a few inches, laughing. I kissed the reddening circle on Gemma's forehead, changing my mind. "You want to go for a drive?"

"You don't want to take a nap first?"

I grabbed her coat. "No, I have to show you something. Come on."

A light snow covered the hard ground as Gemma and I stepped out of her car, our breaths forming puffs of smoke. I led her by the hand to the middle of an open field, and she spun in a tight circle, examining the sparse, flat land dotted with evergreen trees and a low-lying mountain range in the distance. "This is what you had to show me?"

"We're breaking ground in the spring."

She pointed to the dead grass. "Oh? This is it? This is going to be your famous environmentally green development?"

I held my arms open. "What do you think?"

"I think it's a tremendous waste of resources," she said, her dark eyes twinkling at the line she'd tossed at me a few months ago.

I took both of her hands in mine then brought them to my chest. "How much would you hate it if I wasted some of those resources on a house for us?"

"Huh?"

"I want to make you the house of your dreams. Mud, tires, Coke bottles, whatever."

She stuttered, and I bent my knees so we were eye to eye. "I want to take care of you, and I think having a house you love is a good start."

"But you already have one," she pointed out as if I'd forgotten.

"Yes, I do. But *we* need a house. You, me, and this—" I placed a hand on her belly "—thing we made need a house."

"Why don't—"

"There is no way you're talking me out of this. Your sarcasm and name-calling will not change my mind."

"You can't—"

I silenced her with a finger on her lips. "You said you're

afraid, but so am I. As long as we take care of each other, we can do anything. So, let's agree to take care of each other and worry about the details later."

I ran my hands over her hair, my eyes memorizing every line of her face, her freckles, her lips. I could stare at her forever and never tire of it.

Finally, she smiled. "I can't believe you dragged me out to the middle of nowhere in this freezing weather when I'm pregnant. You want this baby of yours to catch a cold?"

"So, say yes already."

She rolled her eyes. "Yes. Yes, I want a house with solar panels and overhead lighting and ceiling fans and a vegetable garden. Yes, of course, that's what I want."

"So, we're doing this? We're having a baby?"

"I guess."

I hooted and twirled her in a circle before putting her down with a kiss on the tip of her frozen nose. "Let's get you back into the heat." I guided her to the car, where I opened the passenger side door and helped her in.

"I'm only two months along and completely capable of getting in and out of cars myself."

I shut the door on her argument and got behind the wheel. "Hey, I said I'd take care of you, and I will. Now, are you hungry? Is the baby hungry? Is it craving anything? You want ice cream? No, it's too cold for ice cream. Unless you want some. Do you want some? How about breakfast? You want waffles or something?"

She leaned over the console, sealing her lips over mine, heightening the pressure of the kiss by forcing my head back against the headrest. She paid extra attention to my bottom lip, drawing it between her teeth.

When she finally shifted away, I unhurriedly opened my

eyes to her. Who needed whiskey? I was already addicted to her. "What was that for?"

"You were rambling." She strapped on her seat belt. "Now take me home and take me to bed."

I gunned the engine. "Yes, ma'am."

Epilogue

JASON

"You're doing so good."

"Shut up."

"No, really, you're the strongest person I know."

"Shut. Up."

"Just keep breathing, like we practiced. Focus on—"

"Jason. I swear to everything unholy, I will rip off your balls and shove them down your throat. I don't want to hear your platitudes. Shut up and get me the epidural!"

I reared back as Gemma fumed in the hospital bed, her hands in a stranglehold on the rails. Sweat beaded on her upper lip and brow, her hair wrapped up in a messy bun that hung limply on the side of her head.

"You said you wanted to do it natural."

"I know what I fucking said, Jason, and I changed my mind. Stop trying to convince me otherwise. Get a nurse in here. Now!" Her shout cut off with a hiss of pain, and her complexion turned beet red once again as another contraction blipped on the monitor next to the bed. She exhaled and shifted onto her side toward me, her face racked with pain. "Jason."

"I'm here, I'm here," I said, not knowing what to do first, completely helpless.

After nine rough months of Gemma struggling with severe morning sickness for the first half and then being so exhausted and swollen at the end, it was apparent this baby did not want to leave its home. The OB/GYN waited a week and a half at Gemma's insistence to see if the baby would make their way into the world on their own, but eventually, the doctor said Gemma needed to be induced.

She wasn't happy about it but agreed, and she'd spent the first few hours of the day stoically taking each contraction in stride as the nurse pumped up the Pitocin little by little. She had taken a walk, tried to bounce on a ball, and even spent some time on all fours—anything to ease her discomfort. But once the shaking set in, my anxiety skyrocketed. The nurse assured me it was totally normal, simply Gemma's body's reaction to the adrenaline, but I couldn't stand it anymore. Between her increasing temper and pain, I wanted to avoid being murdered so I could actually meet my baby.

"Uh, excuse me," I said, jogging out to the nurses station. "My girlfriend's in a lot of pain, and she'd like the epidural now. Please. As quickly as you could get it to her."

The nurse—a pleasant-enough woman who surely had a name, though I'd long forgotten it—smiled congenially and said, "I'll let the doctor know."

"Okay, great. Thanks."

"Gem, they're coming," I said, back at her side. "Pretty soon, you won't feel anything."

"Great, because right now, it feels—" She gritted her teeth, holding back half a scream as another contraction hit, and I yanked at my hair.

After witnessing this, I had no idea why people had babies at all. I didn't know whether to get down on my knees in appreciation for Gemma or to apologize for putting her through this.

"Fuck!" she yelled at the end of the contraction, breathing slightly easier. "It feels like a watermelon is trying to come out of my ass. Stop laughing, you asshole, and get over here."

I dropped to the bed. "What do you need?"

"I'm so hot. Take my socks off."

I did. "What else?"

She frowned, looking wholly spent. "Have this baby for me."

I took her hand in mine, finding it warm and clammy, and kissed the back of it. "I wish I could. I really, really, really wish I could."

"Is my mom here?"

I nodded, but another contraction took hold—they were coming so fast now—and this time, she let out a primal bellow to get through it.

"Do you want me to go get her?" I asked when it was over, but she could only shake her head. I ran back out to the nurses station. "Is the doctor coming soon?"

The nurse pointed to the female doctor rounding the corner. "Right now."

"Great. Good. Perfect." I led the way for the doctor like a flower girl at a wedding. "She wants an epidural now, please."

The doctor smiled. "How are you feeling, Dad?"

"Terrible."

She laughed. "Not uncommon."

Gemma moaned, so did I, and the doctor slid on gloves. "Let's see if you've progressed any further, and then we'll assess if you're able to get the epidural or not."

"*If?*" I repeated, and the doctor nodded, positioning herself at the foot of the bed, her face changing almost immediately when her hand disappeared under the hospital gown, between Gemma's legs. "What? What is it?"

"That's ten centimeters. Plus one station."

"What does—" My question was cut short by Gemma's guttural wail, and the doctor said something to the nurse, setting a flurry of activity into motion. More nurses and medical students entered the room, introducing themselves, but Gemma didn't pay attention and I plumb didn't give a shit.

"Gemma, there is no time for an epidural anymore. Your baby is ready, so we're going to start pushing, okay?"

"No." She shook her head. "No."

"Right now?" I asked, my stomach in knots. "She has to do it without anything for the pain?"

The doctor nodded. "Yes. The baby is ready now."

I sank down next to Gemma, trying to sound more confident than I felt. "Okay. You can do this."

"No, I can't. It hurts." She squeezed her eyes shut, and I couldn't tell if it was sweat or tears that formed in the corners.

"I know it does, but you can get through it." I smoothed her hair back from her face. "You're almost done."

The nurse instructed Gemma to lean forward and hold the backs of her legs. I took hold of one for support as the doctor suited up with a mask and gown, a light shining down on her when she sat at the foot of the bed.

"Gemma, when you feel your next contraction, take a deep breath and bear down," the doctor said. "Nice, deep breaths, you can do this."

Mere seconds later, a contraction hit, and Gemma bore down, whatever that meant.

"Nice, Gemma. Great job," the doctor said. "The head is right there. Give this next one a big push."

"I can't. I can't. It hurts." Gemma inhaled deeply with a

wince, and then her breath caught. "I—ah!" She screamed and pushed and cried. "It's burning!"

"Push, push, push, push, push," the doctor chanted.

She screamed again, and I thought I might pass out.

"The head is out. You feel that?"

She shook her head, her whole body trembling. "I don't feel anything but burning. I'm being ripped in two," she whimpered, slanting her bloodshot eyes up to me, and I had never been so in love with her. "I can't do it anymore."

"Yes, you can," I told her then leaned over, getting a glimpse of the wrinkly, circular thing poking out from between her legs. That was *our baby*. "You *are* doing this. I can see him."

"How do you know it's a him?" she said, her mouth curling up in momentary jest before twisting in pain.

"Push, Gemma," the doctor ordered. "One more push."

She breathed out a garbled cry, her face covered in a mixture of sweat and tears, and she had never been as beautiful than in this moment.

The doctor chanted again. "Good, good, good, good. Here it comes."

"Holy shit," I said, watching as the good doctor pulled out the rest of my baby's body while Gemma sagged into the pillow. "That's our baby."

The doctor held up the bloody, mucus-covered, little alien. "Congratulations on your baby girl."

I wheezed out a breath, overwhelmed with so much love I thought I might burst. A nurse took the baby to clean her off, and I cut the umbilical cord, a little dizzy, a lot in love.

My eyes glazed over with tears, and I knelt down next to Gemma, who smiled and cried, her hands still shaking as she held our baby in her arms. With the help of the nurse, they positioned her on Gemma's chest, swaddled in a blanket and cap, still a little goopy and gross and utterly perfect.

The doctor started talking about placentas and stitches and other horrible things, but I could only focus on the two women in my life now.

"It's a girl," Gemma whispered, a content smile curving her lips, her hands gently patting the baby's back. How she could have ever thought she'd mess this up was beyond me. "What do we call her?"

I propped my head next to Gemma's shoulder, exactly in line with my daughter's scrunched-up face, her tiny mouth wriggling up and down a bit. "You don't like the name we had picked out?"

She flinched, and I glanced down to where the doctor worked on her, a medical student by her side. I spied a needle and thread and flinched too.

"I don't know," she whispered. "Seems a little plain now that I've seen her."

"Okay, whatever you think. I'd call her Wednesday if you wanted," I said, referring to the day of the week, but when Gemma's eyes parked with interest, I backtracked. "I'm joking."

"I'm not. Like Wednesday Addams. I kind of love it."

I lightly drew my fingertip along the baby's cheek and then Gemma's. "I'll make you a deal. You agree to marry me, and you can name the her whatever you want."

She huffed out an exhausted laugh. "That's a terrible deal. I would've agreed to marry you without any conditions."

I grinned. "I love you so much. I'm not letting you or this little girl go. Ever."

She lifted her chin, seeking a kiss, but the baby let out a tiny wail.

"I think it's time we try nursing," one of the nurses said, and I scooted away, letting them do their thing, ducking out to deliver the news to Frank and Caroline.

I didn't believe I could contain any more joy inside my body, but when I walked back into the hospital room to see the love of my life gazing down at the other love of my life while she fed her, my heart proved how flexible it was, expanding by the second. More and more love. More and more joy. I checked my chest, sure I would see the outline of my heart shoving through my skin like a cartoon.

After the room had cleared, and Gemma had a chance to clean up, and Frank and Caroline met their first grandchild, I crawled into bed next to my fiancée. She glowed. I was sure if I could somehow engineer a way to capture her smile, I'd be able to power our house with it. "When I texted the girls earlier to update them, I told them you'd call. Do you want to do that now or later?"

She lifted a serene shoulder, seemingly unbothered by anything, even after twelve hours of labor. "We can do it now."

I opened up a new FaceTime call and held out the phone so the screen could capture all three of us in it. In seconds, Bronte, Sam, and Laney showed up, alternating between peals of delight and sweet coos.

"I'd like to introduce you," Gemma started, catching my eye before continuing, "to Willow Jane Mitchell."

"Willow Jane!" Laney crowed.

"She's beautiful," Bronte said, crying. "You did such a good job."

"How do you feel?" Sam asked.

"Terrible." Gemma laughed. "But also, really happy."

My eyes teared up for what felt like the thirty-eighth time in the last two hours. "Jane? For my mom?"

"For your mom," she said, a little wobble to her lip. "Is that all right?"

"Yes, of course." I kissed her. "I love the name. I love you. I love Willow. I love everybody," I said with a drunken chuckle and tipped my head to the girls on the screen. "I love you guys."

They all laughed.

Gemma gazed down at Willow, who closed her eyes, her eyelashes settled on heavenly pink cheeks. "I think she fell asleep." Gemma pushed her lips out in an attempt to shush everyone, then said to the girls in a whisper, "I'd also like to introduce you to my fiancé too."

The girls all screamed, Willow woke up crying, Gemma rolled her eyes, and I smiled.

True perfection.

Acknowledgments

Indie publishing is a wild ride. Thank you, reader, for coming along with me.

I wouldn't be able to put out these books if not for the encouragement of my friends, especially Ellis Leigh and Brighton Walsh, and the help of my editors, Libby and Lisa. I'd especially like to thank my street team for helping me spread the work about my books. I'm forever grateful.

If you'd like more information about me, you can find it at: https://sophieandrewsauthor.com.

About the Author

Sophie Andrews is a contemporary romance author who writes steamy books that will leave you smiling. As a millennial, she's obsessed with boybands, late 90s rom-coms, and will always be team Pacey. When she's not writing, she's most likely trying to wrangle her children or drinking red wine. Or both at the same time.